Masquerade
FALL

Masquerade FALL

Estelle Tudor

★ ★ ★ ★ ★ ★
Inlustris

First published in the UK in 2023 by Inlustris Publishing, Wales
Text © Estelle Tudor 2023

Proofread by Jessica Netzke ©
Cover Design by Inlustris Publishing ©
Interior formatting and designs Inlustris Publishing ©

A CIP catalogue record for this book is available from the British Library.

Paperback ISBN 9781915950284

To those who fall... and find their wings.

With curses cast them down upon the dust,
And gnash'd their teeth and howl'd: the
wild birds shriek'd
And, terrified, did flutter on the ground,
And flap their useless wings;

~ Darkness. Lord Byron

One

April 1836
London

"Elodie, my dear, whatever has captured your interest so ardently. Are you well?"

Elodie Di Silva turned from her pensive gazing out of the drawing room window. The torrential April rain and grey skies exactly matched her mood. She settled her gaze on her guardian and smiled. "Quite," she said, knowing Lady Lucille Beaumont would only worry.

"Then do come away from the window, you will catch your death. I can feel a draught." Lady Beaumont gave a delicate shudder and pulled her black lace shawl tighter around her thin shoulders.

With a quiet sigh, Elodie directed one last longing look out of the window. She wanted nothing more than to cast off her boots and go dancing in the rain. There was something freeing about it, and she knew it would perversely lift her dark mood. She settled onto the chaise, furthest from the stifling fire, and accepted the dainty teacup Lady Beaumont offered.

"There, isn't that better?" Lady Beaumont said with a contented smile. After taking a sip of her tea, she set the cup down and dabbed her thin lips with a snow-white handkerchief. Elodie gave the expected nod, but Lady Beaumont's next words had the gloom settling once again. "Lord Beaumont shall be here shortly. Oh, I cannot wait to see him. The beginning of the Season has been positively dreary without him." Lady Beaumont stared across the room at the window, thinking of her only son. Blessed with three daughters – only one of which still unmarried – Lord Lucan Beaumont was his mother's favourite and she doted on him.

Elodie flinched behind her teacup. She had only met Lord Beaumont a handful of times since being placed with Lady Beaumont last year after her parents' untimely death in a carriage accident. With no other family, Elodie had been sent to her mother's best friend, Lady Lucinda Fitzherbert's family home. Lady Beaumont's eldest daughter mostly resided in Scotland with her husband and children, therefore Elodie had been welcomed into the Beaumonts' London home. She had resigned herself to becoming a companion to the widowed Lady Beaumont... that was until Lord Beaumont had decided it was time Elodie made her debut in Society and secured a husband.

Elodie had been grateful for a place to call home, but something about Lord Beaumont unsettled her. The way his eerie pale blue eyes captured her. For those few seconds, she felt as if she had been plunged into an ice-cold bath and the breath stolen from her lungs. The way he had smiled knowingly, as though he knew a secret she should know but did not, caused a sliver of unease to work its way up her spine. As the lord of the house, he had a power over her, one that filled her with a sense of impending doom.

A flash of lightning filled the room, causing Lady Beaumont to shriek and drop the teacup she had just picked up again. A dark stain mottled the pink chintz rug as thunder rumbled ominously overhead.

Elodie immediately sank to her knees to mop up the tea, but a hiss of outraged breath had her straightening. A prickle of unease hooked the place between her shoulder blades, and she slowly turned, meeting the pale disapproving gaze of Lord Beaumont.

Without breaking eye contact, he reached back and pulled the bell cord for the maid.

"Lucan, darling!" Lady Beaumont, her fright and spilled tea forgotten, nimbly leapt up from her chair to rush over to Lord Beaumont, hands outstretched.

Lord Beaumont finally released Elodie from his blue prison, and she sucked in a breath, putting a hand dizzily to her head, while he greeted his mother.

"Mama, please sit, no need to exert yourself." Lord Beaumont tucked his mother's hand into the crook of his arm and walked her back to her seat, just as the maid hurried in. "Clean that up," Lord Beaumont ordered in his haughty clipped tones, and Elodie cast a sympathetic look at the trembling Hannah, as she bobbed a curtsey.

Another flash illuminated Lord Beaumont's distaste as he watched Hannah dab at the rug. The thunder – quieter this time – punctuated the click of porcelain as Hannah collected up the cup and saucer and removed herself from the drawing room. Elodie wished she could do the same.

"There, now that is dealt with, come and warm yourself by the fire, you appear a trifle damp." Lady Beaumont gave a titter, as she looked over her son.

Elodie wondered, not for the first time, how the kind Lady Beaumont could have birthed such a cold, serious man as Lord Beaumont.

Lord Beaumont gave a tight smile and leant against the fireplace, his eyes on the flames. Elodie's eyes wandered warily from the top of his burnished gold hair, past his perfectly fitting black jacket to his fawn breeches and shiny black hessian boots. He seemed the epitome of the perfect society gentleman, but he left her feeling hollow... and somehow a little afraid. Her Society debut was mere days away, but the thought of Lord Beaumont escorting her, of holding her close to his side as she was presented, caused her stomach to turn over.

His eyes abruptly flicked up as though he had heard her thoughts. "Is everything ready for your debut, Miss Di Silva?"

Elodie moistened her lips, but she was saved from speaking as Lady Beaumont jumped in. "Oh yes, Lucan, we have the most beautiful white dress being delivered from the modiste tomorrow. It is div-"

"No."

"No?" Lady Beaumont faltered as Lord Beaumont took a seat next to his mother and languidly sat back.

"No, her dress will be silver." His eyes once again captured Elodie's. "A nod to her eyes, and her name of course," he added.

Elodie's already dry mouth caused her tongue to cement itself to the roof of her mouth. She took a hurried sip of her tea, in part to moisten her mouth, but mainly to break the uncomfortable eye contact.

"Then silver it shall be. We will visit the modiste tomorrow and have a new dress made." Lady Beaumont clapped her hands together in delight.

Elodie barely hid her surprise before she remembered how much sway Lord Beaumont held among the ton. No doubt the mere mention of his name would have her dress put above all the other debutantes'.

Lord Beaumont stood. "I am off to my club." He bowed over his mother's hand before turning to Elodie and inclining his head.

"Oh, but you have just arrived." Lady Beaumont pouted. "Will you at least be back for dinner?"

With a shake of his head and an unreadable expression in his eyes, Lord Beaumont said, "I am afraid not, but I shall escort you both to the modiste tomorrow."

Elodie's heart, which had lifted at the thought of Lord Beaumont's presence missing from the dinner table, dropped like a stone.

When the door had closed after his departure the warmth returned to the room and Elodie felt beads of sweat spring up along her brow. Perhaps she was running a fever, she hoped. That would excuse her from having to be closed up in a carriage with Lord Beaumont the next day. A suffocating feeling came over her and she stood.

"I – I am going to rest," she said abruptly.

"What a splendid idea, we will need all our energy for tomorrow. What an exciting day we have planned now."

Leaving Lady Beaumont to her excited mutterings about dresses and balls, Elodie escaped into the coolness of the hall and leant against the closed door for a moment. With surprise, she noticed her hands shook as she smoothed down her pink gown.

Pushing off from the door, Elodie took a deep breath before making her way along the hallway. Perhaps writing a letter to her old friend, Caroline, would calm her tumultuous thoughts. For one fleeting moment she debated veering off to the garden and indulging in her desire to allow the rain to wash away her doubts and dread. But with Lord Beaumont back home, no doubt he would have brought his valet with him. The thought of her being spied upon and tales of her seemingly unbecoming behaviour reaching Lord Beaumont's ears had her doubling her steps to her room.

Elodie opened the door, and pressed it tightly shut behind her. Suddenly she felt at ease, the bands constricting her chest had fallen away and her hands remained steady as she plucked a piece of thick white writing paper from her desk drawer.

She settled herself to her task and poured out a steady stream of correspondence to Caroline. Her friend's parents, with seven children in the household, did not have the means for a debut for each of their daughters, so Caroline's had been put off to the following year when her younger sister, Charlotte, would be coming out, and the girls would be presented together by a generous relative. Caroline devoured every piece of news Elodie sent her, and Elodie in turn was sad that she and her friend would not be experiencing the excitement of their first entrée into Society together.

Signing her letter with a flourish, Elodie felt a weariness come over her, and decided that a short nap before dinner would be just the thing.

She slipped off her boots and laid down, thinking Hannah would wake her to dress for dinner.

Her eyes fluttered closed.

Something stalked her. She could hear the rustling of something large brushing against the dense hedge walls of the labyrinthine maze she ran through. Her heart beating a furious staccato in her chest, she whipped her head left to right as she paused at a divergence in the paths.

"Elodriel... Elodriel of the Silver Wings," a voice floated down the passage behind her, and the tone and inflection had her running again, not caring which way she went only that she knew she mustn't let whomever the voice belonged to catch her.

She had made a grave error. The foliage tunnel ended abruptly, and she found herself on a cliffside, overgrown with impenetrable greenery to either side and open to the heavy black sky above. No moon lit the way, just a mere scattering of stars.

A scratch at the spot between her shoulder blades had her turning but no-one stood behind her, just an ice-cold whisper, *Elodriel...*

She tried to brush away the sensation but it persisted, so she forged on and felt her way with her bare feet. The long silver gown flapped around her legs as a sudden wind erupted from nowhere, and mist swirled in to snake around her body. She held up a hand to shield her face as a black shadow swooped down from the sky. Before she could look to see who, or what, stood before her, a sharp jolt between her shoulder blades had her tumbling from the cliffside. A scream ripped from her throat as a bellow of rage... or was it grief, followed her down.

Inky black water tumbling over sharp grey rocks rose up to meet her, and a sigh escaped her throat as she accepted her fate. Again.

Elodie's eyes shot open, and she sucked in a

shuddering breath. She gazed unseeing at the canopy above her bed, trying to capture the remnants of the dream, but the tendrils stubbornly floated away like misty wisps on the Cornish moors where she had grown up. She could never remember her dreams in their entirety, just flashes, but that was the first time she had heard a voice calling a name. But *what* was the name? A strange name, of that she was certain, but also somehow curiously familiar.

Shaking her head, she flipped over to her side and her breath stuttered in her chest. A dark rose lay on her pillow, its petals so faded, they appeared silvery-grey. But what disconcerted Elodie the most was the white feathers it lay upon.

She shivered. The temperature dropped suddenly inside the room, and an icy sigh stole her breath away.

Two

The carriage rumbled along the street and Elodie once again found herself staring out of a window at the sheeting rain.

Lord Beaumont leant forward and though his knee barely brushed Elodie's skirts, tremors rippled along her legs. "Is something troubling you, Miss Di Silva, you appear, ah, out of sorts."

Elodie forced herself to breathe. She had almost forgotten where she was, her thoughts were filled with the troubling dream and the phantom rose. "Oh, I was just lost in the rain," Elodie replied, and Lady Beaumont patted her arm.

"It is most vexing, is it not, we shall get drenched simply alighting from the carriage."

"Fear not, Mama, I will ensure not a drop of rain sullies your bonnets." Lord Beaumont smiled at them and Elodie raised an eyebrow. He appeared to be in high spirits that morning; perhaps he enjoyed a visit to the modiste. If he did, he was certainly alone on that matter. Elodie thoroughly disliked being prodded and poked with pins.

"You are a dear boy." Lady Beaumont's frown turned into a sunny smile, and no sooner had she spoken, the carriage rumbled to a stop and Lord Beaumont was jumping down from the plush interior.

"There, you see, the rain has stopped just for you." He helped Lady Beaumont from the carriage as if he had indeed caused the cessation of the downpour.

Elodie steeled herself as Lord Beaumont offered her his hand. A visceral pull deep inside made her hesitate, but the challenging look in his eyes had her gripping his hand lightly and allowing him to help her down. He towered over her for a moment, and she felt herself shrinking, desperate to distance herself from him. Despite her kid gloves, a tingle shot through her fingers, so sharp it was almost painful. She tried to withdraw her hand, but his fingers tightened on hers and he pulled her inexplicably closer. The amiable manner had vanished, and his icy mask was back on.

Elodie shivered.

"Come along, my dears, we haven't got all day. I am meeting Lady Withers for tea this afternoon." Lady Beaumont turned in the doorway of the modiste to see what was keeping them.

Finally, Lord Beaumont let go of Elodie's hand and she placed it into the pocket of her pelisse, flexing the fingers to get the blood flowing once more.

"Of course, Mama. I was simply struck by Miss Di

Silva's beauty. I wanted to get a better look at the colour of her eyes, all the better to assist in choosing the exact colour of fabric." Lord Beaumont spoke in genial tones, but there was something underneath the words, something that clawed at the back of Elodie's neck, clamouring for her to get away, to get far away.

Elodie's stomach roiled as Lady Beaumont turned speculative eyes upon them. She could see the wheels of a matchmaking mama turning in the older lady's blue depths. She had to put a stop to that line of thought, promptly.

Turning to Lord Beaumont, she swallowed down her aversion and tried her sweetest smile. "You are so kind to assist me, my lord. I feel as if I were one of your sisters." She added a silvery laugh.

Lady Beaumont's eyes cleared as she gave an approving nod. "Quite right, my dear. You are indeed family now."

As Lady Beaumont turned to enter the modiste, Lord Beaumont edged passed Elodie with a harsh whisper, "I will *never* see you as one of my sisters."

The smile dropped from Elodie's face. What had he meant by that? Did he think her beneath him, or — she tremored — did he have other plans for her?

A shadow fell over Elodie and instinctively she looked up. A black feather fluttered from the sky and, without thinking, she reached out to catch it. A tantalising scent, like the moors after the rain, floated up her nose, and she took a deep breath, letting the aroma fill her. *More feathers,* she thought, suddenly light-headed. She remembered the rose and white feathers that were now hidden away in her desk drawer. What could it all mean?

"Elodie!" an excited voice called and Elodie hastily tucked the feather into the pocket of her pelisse.

Lady Luisa Darlington skipped out of the modiste to pull Elodie into a hug. "Mama said you would be here today. Isn't this divine? And with Lucan here too. It is like a family get together."

Elodie gave Lady Beaumont's youngest daughter a genuine smile. Luisa was closest in age to Elodie; at twenty, Luisa was only a year older. She had recently married and Elodie sorely missed her company, especially as Luella, the unmarried Beaumont sister, was in Scotland with Lucinda presently. Feeling more settled that she would at least have Luisa as a buffer between her and Lord Beaumont, she allowed the older girl to draw her into the dressmakers' shop.

Various members of the ton awaited service, no doubt stocking up on last minute fripperies or alterations.

"Miss Di Silva." A tall lady with eyes so brown they seemed black appeared at her elbow.

"Lady Murrow," Elodie acknowledged, looking around for Luisa but she had deserted her. And for good reason. Lady Murrow and Luisa were not on good terms. Luisa had fallen in love with a young lord, one who Lady Murrow determined should marry her own daughter, Mariska. But it had been love at first sight for Luisa and Thomas. There had been no understanding between Thomas and

Mariska, but Lady Murrow still held a grudge.

"Collecting your debutante gown?" Lady Murrow sniffed, casting an eye over Lady and Lord Beaumont, who were in deep discussion over a bolt of silver fabric. It sheened with an almost ethereal glow, and Elodie prickled uncomfortably. She would never get away with wearing a dress made from that fabric. She would cause a scandal.

"Will you excuse me a moment, Lady Murrow?" Elodie didn't wait for her reply and hastily joined her guardians.

"There you are, my dear." Lady Beaumont stroked a hand over the fabric. "We have chosen this one for you."

"But..." Elodie trailed off. How to word it delicately? She did not want to appear ungrateful.

"Does it not please you?" Madame Le Coeur, the modiste, asked, one elegant blonde eyebrow raised.

"Well, yes, it is lovely, but is it acceptable?" Elodie couldn't help but touch the fabric. She itched to remove her glove and run her hand across it, instinctively knowing it would have a soothing coolness to it.

Madame Le Coeur unravelled the bolt and Elodie immediately saw the silver dulled somewhat to an opalescent shimmer as it was pulled out. "It will appear almost white in some lights, so *oui*, it is acceptable." She smiled.

Elodie swallowed. "Very well," she acquiesced.

Lord Beaumont moved behind her and she trembled. "Perfect. No expense spared please, madame." He rose his voice slightly, so everyone within the shop could hear him. "Miss Di Silva will be this year's incomparable."

A flush of embarrassment worked its way across Elodie's cheeks, and she heard the murmurs start.

"This way, mademoiselle." Madame La Coeur ushered her into the back room. "Deidre, see to our other customers please." She spoke to the girl sorting pins. Deidre shot a look at Elodie, perhaps wondering why Elodie warranted special treatment, before disappearing out into the main shop.

Madame pulled the privacy curtain across the archway and Elodie gave her a grateful smile.

"We do not want the incomparable missing her own debut." Madame La Coeur gave a wink and Elodie felt her smile slipping. What game was Lord Beaumont playing? He was placing her directly in the glare of the matchmaking mamas and the ire of the other debutantes. They would not take kindly to his completely unfounded prediction, however well-respected he was.

The next half-hour passed by in a blur of measuring tapes and pins. Elodie found herself daydreaming as Madame hummed to herself. The off-key tune sent Elodie tumbling back into dissecting her dream. Why did she keep having the same dreams and why had they only started after her parents' accident? Perhaps, it was some latent anxiety. Elodie had been thrown from the carriage, the mossy moor cushioning her fall, while her parents had tumbled over the cliffside in the carriage. Their screams cutting off abruptly.

Elodie pushed away the memory, the familiar suffocating sensation beginning to overwhelm her. *No*, she wouldn't think of it, not now. What good would it do? They were gone, and she was all alone in this world. No one would save her if Lord Beaumont decided he would amuse himself by toying with her debut.

A misplaced pin jolted her back to awareness.

"Oh, mademoiselle, please forgive me," Madame La Coeur implored as she removed the offending pin from her side.

Elodie murmured out a response, her mind still fuzzy from memories and dreams.

"Are you well? You appeared to have gone somewhere else." Madame watched her closely, as she toyed with the pin between her thumb and forefinger.

"Quite well. Are we finished?" Elodie ignored the last part of Madame's question.

Madame continued to watch her for a moment, her light brown eyes speculative. Finally, she tossed her blonde-ringleted head in assent. "*Oui*, I have what I need." She placed the pin into a small dish.

Elodie stepped down from the podium in relief. As she turned away, a shadow moved across the window, and this time Elodie thought she saw the shadow take shape. Ignoring Madame's startled look, she rushed over to the window and peered out. *There.* A tall, broad man stood on the opposite side of the road; his face obscured by a large hat pulled low on his forehead. Long black hair waved to the shoulders of his dark greatcoat. Elodie knew he stared at her as she did him. Her heart pumped furiously in her chest and a knowing warmth worked its way through her stomach. A carriage passed between them, and when it moved on the man was gone.

With a gasp, she took a step back, and collided with something immovable. A pair of cold hands steadied her, and with an inner tremor of understanding, she turned to face Lord Beaumont.

He searched her face before striding to the window. Elodie watched him curiously. He seemed almost angry as he scoured up and down the street. He turned back to her. "Who did you see?" he asked, darting forward to grip her wrist.

"I do not know." She hissed out a breath of pain as he gripped tighter. "A man... a man with black hair."

Behind her, Madame La Coeur let out a small squeak and Lord Beaumont's whole demeanour changed. With slow deliberate movements, he released Elodie's wrist and straightened his cravat.

"Forgive me." He gave a stiff bow and moved through the opening.

Elodie collapsed onto a small chair, her whole body shuddering. She fought to keep tears from springing into her eyes. She had never felt so terrified by another person before. Lord Beaumont's eyes had lit with an almost inhuman glow. She shook her head. Her nightmares had obviously affected her more than she realised.

A small glass was pressed into her hand. "Drink this, mademoiselle."

The brandy sloshed in the glass as Elodie lifted it to her lips. She savoured the warmth as it worked its way down her throat. Feeling steadier, she handed the glass back to Madame La Coeur. "Thank you."

"Be wary of that one," the words came out in a rush and Elodie locked eyes with Madame who lowered her head. "I am sorry, it is not my place."

"No, I appreciate your words of caution, but they are unnecessary, I am already... wary," Elodie said, feeling like a bird that had had her wings clipped before being thrust into a cage - a gilded cage, but a cage, nonetheless.

Madame nodded her head in understanding before stepping back and allowing Elodie to rise. "Your gown will be ready in two days – I will personally see it is finished."

Elodie's heart gave one sudden thump. She couldn't bear to contemplate spending the evening on Lord Beaumont's arm. Not trusting her voice not to quaver, Elodie gave the modiste a small smile and made her way out into the throng of the shop.

Madame La Coeur opened the back door and cast a furtive look up and down the alley way. A shadow passed over her and she looked up in alarm; her hand, holding a small glass jar, fluttered to her chest. "Oh, it is you," she said in relief.

"Do you have it?" The dark-haired man, his face

26

shielded by a top hat, enquired.

"*Oui.*" Madame held out the jar, before pulling it back towards her slightly. "I am in your debt, Your Grace, and honoured you entrusted me with this, but she is such a sweet girl."

"I assure you; I wish her no harm. I simply need to know..." his husky voice trailed off as he inspected the glass jar. The pearl-headed pin inside glimmered with a drop of blood. Did it have a shimmer to it? He couldn't be sure, he needed to get it home. "Thank you, Madame." He was gone with a flap of his coat, like a pair of giant wings.

The man exited the alley way and crossed the street, so he stood across from the modiste's shop.

"Raphael – cousin, have you lost your mind?" A tall, elegantly dressed blonde lady stepped into the man's path. "What if she saw you?"

"Angelina," Raphael acknowledged. He stared across the street. "I think, perhaps, she already has. This journey-" he waved a hand between them and across the road, "-has already begun. Things were set in motion before we even realised. Now, we must see it through." He held up the jar.

Angelina narrowed her bright blue eyes. "While I would love to return home and inspect the specimen. Hunt and I have promised to call on Darlington. We do have pretences to keep up. We can't all fall back on the convenient excuse of being a recluse." With that pointed barb, she lifted her head and carried on down the street to a creamy-coloured carriage.

Raphael stood frozen on the street, looking

across at the modiste's. His very being knew it *was* her that was inside the shop right now. But it didn't matter how close they were, it might as well be the deepest darkest chasm separating them.

He felt himself spiralling into it even now.

"There you are, Lo, thank heavens that dreadful woman has gone." Luisa clutched Elodie's arm and pulled her over to a tray of ribbons. By 'dreadful woman' Elodie assumed Luisa meant Lady Murrow. A smile tugged at her lips as she allowed Luisa to hold up various shades of silver and pearl-white ribbons to her hair.

"Oh, this will look simply divine against your black locks." Luisa lowered the ribbon; it was a shimmering opalescent white shot through with silver thread. "You are a bit peaked though, nervous about your debut?"

Elodie latched on to that excuse with a nod. She couldn't very well explain the reason that she appeared ghost-like was because she was deathly afraid of Luisa's beloved only brother.

Luisa patted her gently on the arm. "You are coming with me. We will have tea and it shall be just like old times." She wafted away, calling for her mama, and Elodie breathed a sigh of relief, grateful she would not have to endure a carriage ride home with Lord Beaumont.

"There, that is all settled," Luisa said as she returned to link arms with Elodie. With her lady's maid trotting after them, the two ladies exited the stifling dressmakers. Elodie's neck prickled as the door swung closed behind her. She hadn't seen Lord Beaumont as she left, but she knew he was there... somewhere.

"Oh, Penny," Luisa said to her maid, "I left my reticule... never mind... I'll get it. I won't be a moment, Elodie." She gave an exasperated shake of her head and disappeared back into the shop.

The Darlington carriage moved along the street towards her and for one moment, Elodie thought she saw the mystery man from earlier stood opposite her. The carriage pulled up in front of her and, without waiting for the footman, she hopped aboard and hurried over to the far window to pull back the red velvet curtain.

The man still stood in the same spot and for one moment his hand reached out as if to claim her. Her heart stuttered as the strange name shot into her mind.

Elodriel.

Three

"Elodie, whatever are you doing?"

With an inelegant bounce, Elodie lowered herself onto the seat, as Luisa and Penny entered the coach. "I thought I saw someone," she said awkwardly.

"Oh, who? Has someone caught your eye? Oh, I long for a bit of ton gossip. I can hardly wait until your coming-out ball, Lo. It will far surpass all others. Lucan has such exquisite taste." Luisa chattered happily as the carriage set off, and Elodie made sure to nod and smile at intervals so her friend would think she was listening to her, but in reality her mind was awhirl with thoughts of the dark stranger, and the curious name that had exploded into her mind. It was the name from her dream, she was now certain of it. But why had it come to her, and *who* was Elodriel?

Such a strange name.

"Elodie, are you even listening to me?"

Dash, Elodie thought, she had missed her cue. "Of course, Lu, I was simply caught up in your excitement."

Luisa smiled indulgently. "Quite right, you have so much joy ahead of you. Sometimes I wish I could have my debut again – not that I would be without my Thomas you understand, but just so I could meet him all over again." Her blue eyes sparkled reminiscently, and Elodie couldn't help the smile that broke across her face.

The carriage stopped and Luisa gave a titter. "Speaking of dear Thomas, let's go and see if he is at home."

Elodie was fond of Thomas Darlington, an amiable man, he doted on his young wife, and was friends with everyone.

"Penny, call for tea please, and ask Lord Darlington to join us if he is free," Luisa set about giving her maid the order no sooner than they had set foot inside the large entrance hall of the townhouse.

"Yes, my lady." Penny gave a curtsey and disappeared down the hall.

Elodie and Luisa dispensed of their pelisses, gloves, reticules and bonnets before entering the drawing room.

Luisa reclined upon a love seat near the window, and let out a puff of breath. "Shopping really is quite wearying, is it not?"

Elodie sat demurely on a seat opposite and nodded. She didn't want to appear too agreeable on the subject and come across as ungrateful. After all, the Beaumonts had been most generous with her pin money. She had her dowry of course, left to her by her parents, but the beautiful gothic mansion she had

31

grown up in on the rolling Cornish moors had passed to an obscure beneficiary. Apparently, it had been willed away as part of some agreement. One Elodie had been told nothing about. So not only had she lost her beloved parents, but she had also lost her adored home too.

With a sigh, she found her gaze trailing over to the window. It was still overcast, but the rain held off. Perhaps it would return in time to lull her to sleep that night.

"Miss Di Silva! What a pleasant surprise," a warm voice said from the doorway.

"Thomas, darling! Will you join us for tea?" Luisa jumped up from the sofa to flit over to her husband, hands outstretched.

Thomas Darlington, a slender man with a mop of chestnut curls and dancing brown eyes, smiled down on his new wife and clasped her hands. "I will indeed, and I brought guests."

Elodie sat up straighter, and watched as two of the most striking people she had ever seen walked into the room. The statuesque lady had pale blonde hair caught up into a twist, leaving a few ringlets down to frame an oval face and bright blue eyes. The gentleman, possibly her brother, had the same blonde hair, but swept back from his forehead, and curled over the nape of his high-necked shirt. His blue eyes zeroed in on Elodie and fancifully she thought he could see into her soul. Did the newcomers perhaps exchange a startled look, or did Elodie imagine it?

She rose as Thomas brought the pair over. "Miss Di Silva, this is Countess Angelina Godwin and her brother Lord Nicolas Huntingford. They are newly into town, but Hunt and I were in school together."

Elodie curtsied to them both, before Luisa gave a huff of exasperation. "Do not vex yourself, we are all friends here." She pulled Elodie and the countess over to the sofa as a maid wheeled in the tea trolley.

Thomas and Lord Huntingford took seats opposite as Luisa poured the tea. She handed a cup to the countess. "Angelina, Elodie has her coming out ball in three days. I am sure my brother would love to extend an invitation to you and Hunt. It will be the ball of the season!"

Elodie blushed as Angelina zeroed in on her. "Is that so?" her voice was a soothing low tone. She looked over at her brother, who lounged back on his seat. His eyes were fixed on Elodie as he spoke.

"We have a cousin staying with us, do you think your brother would mind three extra guests?" His voice, a deep timbre, somehow quieted Elodie's frazzled nerves. She couldn't fathom whether the pair thought her beneath them, or whether she intrigued them. Their curious gazes and inspection of her made her think she was being tested. But to what end?

"Oh, I am sure it will be fine, Lucan does not care about the guest list as long as it contains the cream of the ton." Luisa offered Elodie a cup of tea.

Elodie accepted the tea and asked politely, "From where do you hail?"

The countess and her brother exchanged a small

smile, and Elodie watched them curiously.

"Our country estate is in Cornwall, we were raised in our cousin's family home; Mistbourne, but he has recently inherited another Cornish estate, so we split our time between them – we much prefer the quiet moors to the hustle and bustle of the ton," Lord Huntingford said with an arch to his perfect blonde eyebrow.

Elodie almost bobbled her teacup, so she carefully set it down on the lacquered side table. She had heard of Mistbourne Manor.

"Oh, but this is just too diverting! I had forgotten your estate was in Cornwall, Lina. Elodie was raised there too... until her parents' unfortunate accident." Luisa's eyes dimmed as she leaned over to take Elodie's hand. "But she has us now." Tears sprang into Elodie's eyes at the seriousness in her lively friend's voice.

As Luisa released Elodie's hand, and Elodie sat back, she just caught the look that passed between the siblings. Abruptly, she needed to get away from their speculative glances, even if it meant fleeing back to Beaumont House.

"I am so sorry, but I have a sudden headache, Luisa. I should go and rest." She stood, and immediately both gentlemen stood too.

"Oh, then do let us escort you home," Countess Godwin said, throwing her brother a pointed look.

"No!" Elodie said. She flushed at her outburst as all eyes turned to her; some concerned, some curious. "I mean to say, please stay and enjoy your tea. The walk in the fresh air will help."

Luisa frowned. "You cannot walk alone. My brother would have a fit of apoplexy. Penny will walk with you," she said decidedly, before ringing the bell.

"I agree with Luisa, not the thing to be walking alone, not at all," Thomas said, concern marring his agreeable features.

Thankful at not having to be sequestered in a carriage with the disconcerting brother and sister, she nodded politely at them and said, "It really was lovely to meet you."

"We shall look forward to seeing you at the ball," Angelina said, and took a sip of her tea. Lord Huntingford gave a slow smile, revealing straight, white teeth.

Elodie inclined her head. Her skin suddenly felt too tight, and she was thankful when Penny arrived.

"Escort Miss Di Silva home, Penny, she has the headache." Luisa pressed a kiss to Elodie's cheek and linked arms with her, walking her to the door. "I shall call on you tomorrow. We have much to plan for your debut. But go and rest, dearest."

"Thank you, Luisa," Elodie murmured and followed Penny out into the hallway to collect her things. Eager to be gone, she stuffed her gloves into her pocket instead of putting them on.

The Darlingtons lived a mere street away from the Beaumonts. Elodie walked ahead of Penny as they traversed the steps and down the path, keen to retreat to the haven of her chamber. She glanced back at the Darlingtons' house and noticed the countess and her brother stood at the window watching her go. Her feeling of unease doubled as Lord Huntingford's attention was caught by something beyond Elodie. With a shiver of foreboding, she followed his look. Her heart thumped a double beat as she saw the dark-haired stranger stepping out of an all-black carriage. His face, while still obscured, turned in her direction and she knew he saw her.

"Come, Penny," she urged, and picking up the pace, trotted off down the pavement, the maid hurrying to keep up.

Elodie sensed his presence and hoped they were not being followed. She debated whether or not to not go directly home, worried about leading him to where she lived, but if he had questionable intentions the longer she stayed on the street the stronger the possibility of him catching up to them increased. As they reached the gate to the Beaumonts' town house, the feeling intensified. Elodie threw a glance over her shoulder, certain that a hand would be reaching out to grab her, but all she saw was Penny's flushed face.

"Th-thank you, Penny. I shall be fine now," she told the girl, who looked most relieved at being able to return back to the Darlingtons – more than likely anticipating a slower and more seemly walking pace.

"As you wish, Miss," Penny said, and bobbed a curtsey before turning on her heel and starting back the way they had come from.

Elodie gripped the gate, noticing her already pale knuckles whitening. Deliberately, she took five deep breaths and relaxed her hand. She wanted to appear composed when she entered the Beaumonts' house. One look at her, and Lord Beaumont would be questioning her again.

"Rafe, what are you doing here?" Hunt gripped his cousin's shoulder, and pulled him back towards the carriage, away from the escaping Elodie, and maid. "You are scaring the girl."

Raphael shrugged the hand off. "It is *her*. I checked it; it really is her." He thrust the jar at Hunt, who inspected the glimmering pin. Raphael started off along the street after Elodie. "I cannot let her go back there."

Hunt once again gripped him. "*Think*, cousin. He will not harm her. There is no need to *hurt* her. As far as he is concerned he has the upper hand. Why do you think he is making such a spectacle of her debut; he is arrogantly thumbing his nose at us. But, he doesn't know we have a plan. You risk all by going after her now; she hasn't looked into both your eyes, and if our plan works, she won't be able to. It will give us time to see how things will play out."

"But this time he has her in his grasp. She could go this whole existence shackled to him. I would see it started over before I let that happen," Raphael uttered in low tones. He removed his hat and ran a weary hand through his thick black hair.

"Then you are no better than him, wishing ill on her when it doesn't go the way you want it to," Hunt said quietly.

The words had Raphael backing up, horror rippling across his face. "You are right," he said and returned to his carriage.

A final glance at the street confirmed Elodie was alone, except for a maid walking a small dog across the street. But she had nothing to fear from them. She didn't even know if she had anything to fear from the mysterious man. Perhaps, her mind was playing tricks on her. Perhaps, she was overcome from the nightmares and the exertion of her coming-out preparations. Because... was it even *fear* she felt, or was it anticipation? She knew she feared Lord Beaumont with his ice-cold manner and suffocating demeanour. But she did not feel like that when she saw the stranger, instead it was as though her whole soul had been laid bare, that if she stepped towards him instead of fleeing, then her very existence would change. It was a knowing and a question all at once. And she was too small, too insignificant, to untangle it.

With a sigh, she pushed open the gate and made her way up the steps. No sooner had she reached the checkerboard tiled entrance-way, than the glossy black door was yanked open, and she was impaled by a pair of livid frost-blue eyes.

Four

Lord Beaumont reached out a hand and unceremoniously yanked Elodie over the threshold and into the entrance hall – strangely absent of footmen.

Elodie's head swam as she whirled around, almost dropping her reticule. The black feather, the one she had placed into her pocket outside the modiste's, fluttered from her pocket to land at Lord Beaumont's feet.

His face froze. His mouth set in a stony line, as he bent and picked up the feather as if it were a disgusting insect. "Where did you get this?" he ground out.

Elodie took a step back. His face had gone almost feral and she could imagine him snarling and snapping if she didn't answer. "I found it. On the street. I thought it would be the perfect hair adornment," she said in a rush, trying to think of a plausible excuse as to *why* she had kept it, when she herself didn't even know. She had just felt compelled to do so.

He pinned her with his icy gaze for what felt like an eternity, before his mouth released into a smile. "Oh no, my dear. This will not suit you *at all*." He gave her a tight bow, before turning and disappearing down the hall, the feather clutched firmly in his grip.

Elodie drooped, not even realising how rigidly she had been holding herself. A real headache now clamouring behind her eyes, she rushed up the stairs and entered the sanctuary of her room.

She threw off her pelisse, and went over to the dresser to pour some water from the jug into the basin and splash it onto her flushed face. Slowly, Elodie rose her head, meeting her wary silver-grey eyes in the mirror. Tiny wisps of black hair framed her heart-shaped face. With a cry of anguish, she pulled out the pins tightly holding her long hair and the thick black waves tumbled down to settle around her waist. Immediately, some of the tension in her head released and with a sigh, she turned away from the mirror.

Something out of the corner of Elodie's eyes had her turning back to the mirror with a whirl. Ghostly shapes formed behind her shoulders, and she narrowed her eyes with a gasp. She turned, trying to catch a glimpse of what they could be, but no large spectral silhouettes floated behind her. She waved her hand through the dust motes dancing in the weak sunbeam filtering in through the window. With confusion, she faced the mirror once again, but whatever she had seen – or thought she had seen –

was gone.

A knock at her door startled her from the unnerving vision and had Elodie cursing her impulsiveness at removing her hair pins. She hoped she wasn't about to be summoned to amuse an afternoon caller.

"Come in," she said.

Hannah entered the room. "Lady Beaumont is asking for you."

Elodie considered taking to her bed pleading the headache, but Lady Beaumont had been so kind to her. She owed the older lady her company at the very least. She gave a nod. "Tell her I will be down momentarily."

Hannah gave a small bob and left.

Elodie hastily twisted up her hair and secured it loosely with pins; she didn't want the headache to return. She smoothed down her dress, before leaving the room, hoping with a fervent desire that she would not encounter Lord Beaumont. With any luck, he had gone to his club and wouldn't be back until after she was abed.

She pushed open the drawing room door, and winced at the heat blasting from the fireplace.

"Ah, Elodie! How was your visit with Luisa? I just spent a pleasant hour with Lady Withers." Lady Beaumont sat alone, as close to the fire as she could, embroidery in hand.

Elodie gave her a smile and sat on the small sofa nearest the door. "It was... pleasant," she said, trying her best to come up with a word that would adequately describe *how* she had felt in the company of Countess Angelina Godwin and her brother. Pleasant wasn't precisely it, but she did not want to arouse Lady Beaumont's worrying nature.

Lady Beaumont leant forward. "I am extremely pleased you are settling in so well here. I do believe Lucan is right; you will be the toast of the season."

Elodie couldn't even force the expected smile. She didn't *want* to be the toast of the season, she wanted to go back home. She wanted to walk across the moors until her hem dripped with dew, and her hair smelled of heather. She wanted to curl up on her window seat, while the moonlight illuminated the pages of her favourite book. She *wanted* her parents back. Feeling tears threaten, she stood to make a cup of tea, and distract herself. There was no good to be found in wants and wishes. She had to simply hope that she would somehow find somewhere she belonged with someone who she could be herself with.

As if summoned by her desperate thoughts, a gust of wind burst open the drawing room window, blowing in blossoms from the tree outside... and one lone black feather. Barely registering Lady Beaumont's startled shriek, Elodie crouched, feeling everything around her move as if in slow motion, to retrieve the feather from where it had landed at her feet.

It was just her and the feather. A talisman against everything that threatened to consume who she truly was. Her mind swam at the thought, *who she truly was*. What did that even mean. She did not know, but she was certain of one thing - she refused to let Lord Beaumont take this feather. She slid it down the bodice of her gown, and it nestled against her heart. Immediately, a calmness overcame her, and she returned to the here and now to see a flustered Lady Beaumont, surrounded by blossoms, staring at her.

"Are you leaving calling cards now, Rafe?" Angelina said snippily from her seat opposite him in his carriage. He had waited to escort Angelina home as Hunt had an errand to run and had commandeered Angelina's carriage.

"Hmm?" Raphael asked. He looked down and saw the black feather he had been absentmindedly twirling in his fingers had gone. He stuck his head out of the window and watched as it floated over the Beaumonts' wall. *Serendipity*, he thought, and closed his eyes.

"I have too much to do to be watching over you, Rafe."

"But it is what you are good at," Raphael said with a reminiscent smile, not opening his eyes, hoping the feather would make it way to *her*; a talisman against evil intent.

Angelina paused. With a shake of her head, she settled back against the plush cushions, and did what her cousin said she did best. Watch over him.

With a contrite smile, Elodie moved across to the window to latch it firmly. She took a deep breath, before turning to meet Lady Beaumont's curious gaze.

Before the older lady could ask her what she had picked up, Elodie spoke first. "I do believe you have your dinner with the Braithwaites this evening?"

"Oh, heavens, yes, I do!" Lady Beaumont jumped up, scattering blossoms. "Excuse me, Elodie, I must dress for dinner. Lady Braithwaite is most particular about punctuality."

Elodie knew this, and was thankful she could divert Lady Beaumont so easily.

Lady Beaumont hurried from the room, and Elodie sat and enjoyed a quiet cup of tea. Not yet out in wider Society, she had not been invited that evening. Perhaps she would take a tray in her room.

A sudden staccato at the window had her smiling. Better yet, a rainy walk in the gardens would be just the thing.

Feeling more at ease than she had of late, Elodie collected the fragrant blossoms and deposited them into a silver bowl on the sideboard.

Humming to herself, she left the drawing room and wandered down to the dining room, and taking advantage of the scarcity of servants, let herself out of the double doors that led into the gardens.

The first droplets of rain on her face, added another layer to her newly-found serene feeling. For a few blessed moments, she allowed the rain to wash over her. With it, it took the trepidation and somehow *unclean* feeling that smothered her every time Lord Beaumont's eyes covered her.

Elodie crossed the terrace and quickly took the steps down into the hedged garden. Here, she would be shielded from view and could indulge in her cleansing rain walk.

Her hem dragged, and her gown plastered to her slender frame, but she knew from previous experience that the rain was somehow healing to her. She did not fear a fever claiming her because of it.

She came to the centre of the garden and tilted her face up to study the winged statue that dominated the circular stone walkway. Its face tipped up to the heavens, while its wings and arms stretched out as if preparing for flight. She had always felt safe here. She breathed in deeply and closed her eyes, as the rain around her softened to a soothing mist.

The sound of a twig breaking behind her had Elodie's eyes flying open. She turned, her heart suddenly hammering in her chest.

"Who's there?" she called out, expecting a footman to reveal himself and usher her inside, but nobody came into view.

The feather, nestled against her breast, fluttered and Elodie stumbled backwards into the statue. Her sodden gown caught on the foot of the angel statue, and in her haste to get away, she tore the dress. It ripped along the length exposing one slim, white stockinged leg.

Her heart now beating out of her chest, she flew along one of the secluded paths, the dress sticking to her legs and hampering her escape. Throwing a glance over her shoulder, she didn't see a gnarled root sticking up across the path. Her foot became entangled, and she pitched forwards. She threw out her hands to protect herself and instead of meeting the cold, wet floor, she met cold, unyielding flesh instead.

Her forearms gripped tightly, Elodie found herself being righted. But she didn't feel as though she had been saved. In fact, as she rose her gaze to meet a pair of enraged pale eyes, she realised she had run headlong into danger.

A frisson of terror nestled between her shoulder blades. "I – I..." she trailed off.

"Yes?" Lord Beaumont drew out the word.

"I took a walk in the gardens and-" she broke off with a nervous laugh "-as you can see, I got caught in the rain."

Lord Beaumont slowly released her arms, but didn't back away. Instead, he roved his eyes up and down her dress, narrowing on the long tear. A flush of shame stained her cheeks, as something flared in his eyes. He quickly dampened it down, and Elodie questioned if she had imagined the flicker of heat that had bloomed there.

"Do you realise how this would look, if we were to be caught in this manner? Unchaperoned, with you in disarray?" A sly smile played around Lord Beaumont's mouth, a disturbing contrast to the stern words, and Elodie stepped back in horror. He was right. If they were to be caught... she would have no choice but to either marry him or be cast out.

"I must go and change into a dry dress," Elodie said, turning back towards the house. She had, it seemed, a more ominous threat to deal with than simply wet clothing.

A hand at her elbow stayed her. "Not so fast, my dear. Perhaps providence has smiled on us today. Perhaps, we should tarry just a moment longer."

Elodie turned to face him. She tried to compose her features into a neutral expression, lest forbid the disgust she felt curdling deep in her stomach, be displayed. What game was he playing now... surely he did not want to *marry* her?

Five

As if mesmerised, Elodie couldn't move. Lord Beaumont shifted closer, one hand skimming her face in a ghostly caress. *I have to get away*, her mind screamed, all while her feet betrayed her.

Her breath clogged in her throat, as he hovered over her.

Abruptly, he dropped his hand and stepped back. "No, I have languished far too much money on your debutante ball and your gowns for your first foray into Society. I must first show you off, allow you a *taste* of the ton, before you are wedded."

Elodie blinked in confusion.

With a knowing smile once again on his lips, Lord Beaumont waved a hand, dismissing her. As if released from his spell, Elodie found she could move her feet. She didn't question what had just happened, she simply accepted the reprieve. Turning, she ran as fast as her deluged gown would allow her. What had spooked her initially – the broken twig behind her? If that hadn't been Lord Beaumont, then she had to entertain the thought that there was not one, but two predators in the garden that afternoon. But no, that wasn't right – she only felt preyed upon by Lord Beaumont, the other man was still very much a mystery to her and how he made he feel, and she was certain he would not dare to breach the protection of the Beaumonts' home.

"Oh, Miss Di Silva. I had no idea you were caught out in the rain. I will get a bath drawn for you, right away." Hannah looked askance at her, as they met in the hall.

Elodie hadn't realised she was shivering until the maid mentioned the word bath. The suggestion was much welcomed. "Thank you, Hannah. May I request a tray in my room as well?"

"Yes, Miss. I will see to it myself."

Elodie gave Hannah a grateful smile before making her way up to her room.

Stripping off her damp dress, she wrapped herself in her robe and sat on the bed, pulling her legs up to her chest. She realised she wasn't shivering from the rain, but from the near miss with Lord Beaumont. She was starting to grasp she was nothing but a pawn in his twisted charades. Her very existence dangled on his every whim. *He* would determine who would be permitted to court her, *he* would decide who she would be betrothed too. Even if, by some miraculous chance, she fell in love, she knew he would not allow her to be happy. No, for some reason, Lord Beaumont had decided Elodie was his to do with as he pleased. He might even, in the end, demand she marry *him*. She shuddered at the very thought.

A sob burst out of her mouth, surprising her. Tears racked her body as her fears and emotions collided. What could she *do*? She should have pleaded to stay with Caroline and found a position as a governess, or written to her father's old friend, Dominic, who lived in France, and asked to live with him and his family. She should never have agreed to come to the Beaumonts – and now she was trapped.

A tap at the door had her hastily wiping away her tears. She crossed to the door and admitted Hannah holding a food tray, and two footmen carrying steaming jugs of water. Hannah set the tray down on the side table, while the footmen entered the dressing room and proceeded to fill the screened-off copper claw-foot bath.

Elodie ate sparely, her appetite gone, and as soon as the bath was filled, she finally put down her knife and fork, leaving most of her roast venison and vegetables uneaten.

The door closed after the footmen one last time and Elodie gratefully slipped into the bath, allowing her long hair to fan out around her like wings. She let the heat wash over her, and dreamily wafted her hand through the steamy tendrils rising from the rose-scented water.

Her drowsy thoughts took a swift dark turn as the steamy tendrils became thick fog in her mind. She blinked and she was back in the carriage with her parents on that fateful night...

"Oh, Mama, did you hear? Caroline's cousin is coming to visit from Bath." Elodie leant forward to press her hand to her mother's. She gave a squeal of surprised laughter as the carriage jolted over a rock on the deeply rutted moorland road.

"I did hear," her mother replied with a smile. Her silver-grey eyes – a match to Elodie's – crinkled at the corners. "Perhaps, we could take a visit to Bath ourselves soon. I hear the waters are most soothing."

The thrill of visiting Bath and all its diversions flew from Elodie's mind as another lurching thud came, stronger this time, and the carriage veered wildly.

Elodie's father tapped the roof. "Steady on there, Clark," he shouted, then clutched his wife when she spilled into him as the carriage tilted.

"Have we lost a wheel?" Elodie asked, no longer finding the wild ride amusing. She peered out of the window.

"Elodie, sit back!" her father ordered as the carriage gave another jolt, but it was too late. It threw Elodie's weight against the door, and it swung open, with Elodie barely hanging onto it.

"Elodie! Bastion, save her!"

Elodie heard her mother's screams as she implored Elodie's father to save her, but the door took her away from the carriage, her legs dangling a mere fraction from the quickly-moving ground. The door swung against the carriage, and the resulting bump caused Elodie to lose her grip.

With a scream of her own, Elodie tumbled to the ground, barely missing being swept beneath the carriage. With her father's shouts ringing in her ears over the sound of the terrified neighs of the carriage horses, she rolled away, to land breathlessly on the mossy ground of the cliffside moor.

Her head ringing, and her arm throbbing, Elodie scrabbled up and watched, as if in slow motion, the horses buck and paw at the air. The fog swirled and danced, causing the scene to take on an eerie quality. The horses' momentum broke their tethers, and they ran away from the cliff edge.

"Mama! Papa!" Elodie screamed as the carriage, now rolling free, disappeared over the cliffside, a flash of sudden lightning following it, taking its occupants with it. "No, no, no..." she moaned in disbelief, falling to her knees.

Elodie tried to fight her way out of the memory, but it wasn't done with her yet. Previously unremembered pieces came back to her in fragments. Two large shadows crashing together with a roar in the sky above her, and feathers floating down to land in her fog-drenched hair. Elodie put a hand up to her hair now, as if she could pluck the ghostly feathers out. Her hand came away empty, but still, in her mind's eye, she could see them... one white feather... and one long, glossy black feather, one that assailed her senses and enticed her with its intoxicating scent.

Immediately, she jolted up, splashing the now tepid water over the sides of the tub. She gave a whimper. Was she losing her mind?

After the accident, Elodie had staggered back to the manor, in shock, and a rescue party had been sent out, but they returned, confirming what Elodie had refused to believe – that her beloved parents were truly gone, taken by the merciless sea. The shock of it sent her into a spiral, and her mind, in order to protect itself, shut out the memory of that tragic night.

But it appeared something stronger was forcing her to remember her most darkest memories. But now, she had to question, had it really been an accident? Because – and she was terrified to confront the possibilities – *what* had been battling in the skies above her?

A metallic tang in her mouth, Elodie wrapped her arms around herself. No, she refused to contemplate the thought that there were things she could not even begin to fathom in the world. Things that were not *of* this world. No, it was simply the residual trauma causing her to doubt her sanity, and birds often flew above the moors, even on foggy nights.

Convincing herself – comforting herself – with these reassuring explanations, she pulled herself up and out of the bath, wrapping herself in the robe. On unsteady legs, she dripped onto the rug, shivering, not only from the chill, but also from the thought that she was so out of her depth. She longed to seek her mother's counsel, longed to walk with her father, or sail on his ship with him, and truly breathe.

On a long sigh, she released those longings. She could not dwell on the past, she must centre herself in the here and now, and do what she ought to secure a marriage as happy as her parents had shared. She knew in order to do so she needed to place a shield around herself, because – despite what Lord Beaumont declared – he would not launch her into Society with his protection, not when she wasn't even protected from *him*. Her mind whirring, she realised it was up to her to find a way to be free of Lord Beaumont. She needed to find someone to *offer* her protection... someone even Lord Beaumont would not be able to refuse.

She would need Luisa's help – her friend had made it her business to know every eligible bachelor in the ton. But first she would become the biddable debutante Lord Beaumont expected her to be, so he would not suspect a thing, while she put her plan into action.

It was time she spread her wings.

Feeling more settled now she had a future to focus on, rather than dwelling in the past, Elodie dried off before the fire. She donned a long, lace-necked silvery-grey nightgown with low back. Her nightgowns were cut in such a way to allay the discomfort of itchy fabric against the two marks, near her shoulder blades, she had been born with. She braided her thick swathe of hair, securing it with a silver ribbon.

Hannah had picked up her earlier discarded gown and draped it over a rack near the fire. Now dry, Elodie, moved it back to stop it from catching alight. As she did so, the feather she had hidden inside it, floated out. Without hesitation, she plucked it from the air, and the same alluring awareness swam over her as she inhaled its scent.

She dropped to the bed. Who was she deceiving? She would never be free from the past, not when it was doing its very best to anchor her there. It haunted her nights and dogged her every waking step.

She whirled away from the bed impulsively, and thrust the feather into the drawer with the other feathers and the rose, slamming it shut, as if hiding it from view, would block out its very existence. Erase everything it could possibly represent. To solidify her intent, she turned the key in the drawer's lock, removed the key and hid it beneath the cushion of the window seat. She didn't want to be tempted to take out the feather and inhale its heady aroma. The scent released something inside her, like the final piece of a puzzle slotting into place, or a riddle finally being unravelled to make sense, but she determined to not use it as a crutch, she *had* to find her own way. Only then, could she truly be free.

With a satisfied nod, she pulled back her covers and settled into bed, hoping the bath would work its magic and now soothe her into dreamless slumber.

Six

"Oh, Miss, you were sleeping so soundly last night, you didn't even hear me come in to remove your dinner tray." Hannah gave a bright smile, while pulling open the drapes to let in the pale sunshine.

Elodie sat up to collect the cup of fragrant chocolate Hannah had set upon the bedside table. Taking a sip, Elodie noted that she did, indeed, feel refreshed.

"Will you be coming down for breakfast?" Hannah asked from by the door.

Elodie set the cup down, and nodded. If she was to become the epitome of a perfect young lady of the ton, she must act as one. Lady Beaumont would expect her, and if Lord Beaumont was there, then all the better, for she must learn to temper her fear of him. Perhaps familiarity would breed complacency. And perhaps he would tire of her, and move on. Thinking of him terrorising another young lady did not sit well with her, but she could not afford to think of faceless misses.

Dressed in a sprigged muslin gown with lavender flowers dotted over it, Elodie entered the breakfast room, and noted with dismay it lay empty. "Where is Lord and Lady Beaumont?" she enquired a passing footman.

"My Lord has already breakfasted, and Lady Beaumont is still abed with the headache, Miss," the footman told her.

Elodie felt the carefully constructed mask slipping. "Thank you," she murmured, and resolved to breakfast alone.

Helping herself to some eggs and toast from the sideboard, she had just settled herself at her seat, when a commotion out in the hall, had her dropping her napkin. Luisa barrelled in, one hand clutching her bonnet, the other brandishing a thick cream-coloured square of card.

"Luisa!" Elodie exclaimed, more in amusement, than surprise. Her friend was often known for her high-spirited entrances.

"Good morning, Elodie. Is my brother here? Oh, I have the most wonderful news. I did not want to say anything before, not until I knew for certain." Not waiting for Elodie's response, she slapped the card down in front of Elodie. Elodie felt her eyes widen as she picked up the card to inspect it. She whipped her gaze from the card to meet Luisa's dancing blue eyes.

"*Almack's*?" Elodie uttered.

"Yes! I have secured you a place at Almack's annual coming-out ball. A debut there will set you up for the Season." She sat across from Elodie.

"Absolutely not, Luisa." The icy tones had the card dropping from Elodie's suddenly stiff fingers. Steeling herself, she looked across to the door to see Lord Beaumont framed there. Though he spoke to Luisa, his eyes were firmly on Elodie.

"Oh, Lucan, whyever not?" Luisa pouted. "I worked so hard to impress the patronages of Almack's. If we turn them down, it may ruin Elodie."

"Because, sister dear, I have Miss Di Silva's coming-out ball planned down to the minute detail. I will speak to the ladies myself. She will not share her ball with any other chits. No, no, no, she will have the ball to end all balls." Lord Beaumont plucked the card up from the table, and in one swift move tossed it into the fire.

Luisa gave a squeak of dismay, her fingers reaching out as if to will it back from the flames now currently devouring the edges of the lavish invite.

Elodie, frozen, could do nothing but watch the invitation crumble into ash. Had Lord Beaumont just sentenced her to the cut direct before she had even entered Society? Remembering her plan, her stomach curdled like the eggs on her plate as she realised Lord Beaumont may indeed be manoeuvring her demise, so she would *have* no other offers.

She rose her eyes to his. Something lurked behind their cold depths. It vanished as she tilted her chin up slightly. Yes, she would play her part, but she couldn't resist a hint of defiance. He smiled tightly. "The modiste will be here with your gown today. Ensure you are free to receive her."

"Today?" Elodie, startled into speaking, couldn't keep the surprise from her tone.

"Yes, I can be most ah – *persuasive* – when I want something."

Luisa looked from her brother to Elodie, a frown marring her forehead. "Would you like me to stay, Elodie?"

"That won't be necessary, Luisa. I am sure you have calls to make." Lord Beaumont smoothly intercepted Elodie before she could even voice her own answer. "You will have a most pleasant surprise when you see Miss Di Silva at her ball."

Luisa brightened. "How divine! We shall all be struck by your beauty, Elodie dearest." Luisa clapped her hands together in delight, before rising. She waggled a hand in farewell at her brother and Elodie, before hurrying from the room.

A silence fell, punctuated only by the crackling of the fire. Her appetite gone, Elodie pushed her plate away, and rose. She wanted – no, she *needed* – to be away from him.

She made to move past Lord Beaumont, but his low words had her pausing. "Luisa is right-" Elodie raised a questioning eyebrow "-we shall *all* be struck by your beauty."

A shiver skated down Elodie's spine, its origins beginning from the point between her shoulder blades where the unusual-shaped marks branded her skin. *Remember your plan*, she reminded herself. She allowed a small smile to curve along her lips. Dropping her eyes demurely, she murmured, "You are too kind."

"Hmm," Lord Beaumont intoned, and Elodie took the opportunity at disconcerting him to give a hasty curtsey and move away from him to the door.

"I shall await the modiste," she said and left the breakfast room at an acceptable pace, before, once out in the hallway, hastening her steps – and her distance – away from the room containing the most dangerous man of her acquaintance.

Elodie settled herself in the drawing room with a book, but the words kept swimming in front of her eyes. Thinking only to distract herself, it was having the opposite effect; trying to track the dancing words only caused her uneasiness to mount. With a huff, she tossed the book onto the sofa and rose to pace in front of the window.

The weak April sunshine tried futilely to filter through the grey clouds, instead only succeeding in painting the front garden a muted shade of murky yellow. Elodie grimaced, she couldn't even bring out her watercolours and try to capture the view. Nobody would want to gaze upon such a sickly piece of art.

A carriage pulled up to the curb, and roused Elodie's interest. Madame Le Coeur alighted from the conveyance with her assistant, Deidre. Together they removed a large, long box, and proceeded to carry it between them up the Beaumonts' path.

Elodie moved away from the window to sit on the chair facing the door. For some sudden unknown reason, she felt decidedly nervous. Butterflies clamoured in her throat, and her hands trembled in her lap. Perhaps she knew that once the dress was out of the box, once it was settled over her skin, nothing would ever be the same again. The future barrelled towards her, while the past tried to hold her back. Once they collided, would she still be the same? Or would she be someone new entirely. A someone Elodie would not even recognise.

Only time would tell.

The Beaumonts' butler appeared in the doorway. "Madame La Coeur, Miss."

"Show her in, please, Wells."

Wells gave a small bow and moved out of sight. A few moments later he ushered Madame La Coeur and Deidre into the room. The atmosphere changed immediately, it was if an airy lightness filled the room, and Elodie felt her uneasy feeling simply float away in the face of Madame's obvious delight.

"Mademoiselle Di Silva. Are you ready?" The modiste rested her hands on the pearly-white box.

Elodie moistened her lips, before giving a nod.

Madame La Coeur shared a wide smile with her assistant before, as one, they removed the lid and spread the gossamer thin paper aside to reveal a confection of a gown. It was in the silvery fabric Lord Beaumont had picked, but in the low light filtering in through the windows, it looked pale as moonbeams shot through with a sprinkling of the stars themselves.

Elodie ran her fingers over the dress. It felt cool to the touch, as she had previously predicted. She longed to put it on; the very thought thrilled and terrified her in equal measure.

As if hearing her thoughts, Madame said, "Shall we take it up to your chamber, I am most desirous to see it on you."

"Very well," Elodie found herself consenting.

She led Madame and Deidre as they carefully carried the box up the wide staircase, along the landing and finally, into Elodie's room.

Elodie, at Madame's urging, rounded the dressing screen, and allowed the modistes to help her out of her day gown. A whisper of silk behind her, then over her head, had her closing her eyes. She kept them closed while the laces were tightened at her back. She didn't want to look yet. She wanted to stay in this suspended moment. Being neither Elodie of the past nor Elodie of the future, just the Elodie who stood on the precipice of possibility.

"Turn around, Mademoiselle Di Silva," Madame La Coeur said in awed tones. Elodie paused. A gentle hand guided her around. "Open your eyes, you will not be disappointed."

The sound rushed away as Elodie opened her eyes. She stared at the vision in the floor length mirror. She did not recognise herself. Her eyes were too wide, her skin too pale, and the dress? The dress was everything. It fitted her perfectly. Just on the right side of modesty, it scooped low at the front, while its puff sleeves were like wisps of ethereal mist. The skirt itself draped from the high waist in a silvery waterfall to the floor. But the modiste's talents did not end there. Two delicate pieces of sheer fabric floated from the back of the gown. The ends were attached to two silver ribbons delicately tied around Elodie's wrists, and when she raised her arms they were like two otherworldly, silver...

"Wings."

Elodie jolted at the word.

"My Lord, I do not think this is appropri-" The modiste's words were cut of as Lord Beaumont waved one hand at her in a dismissive gesture.

He stalked up to Elodie, his eyes predatory and assessing. "Turn," he commanded, and exchanging a nervous look with Madame La Coeur, Elodie did as he bid.

"Don't you think this-" he gestured a hand at the gossamer wings "-is a bit much?"

Madame La Coeur flushed, but her eyes were determined. "I thought you wanted your mother's charge to stand out from the others. This will ensure she does. But if you do not like it, I can remove them..." she trailed off as Lord Beaumont gave Elodie another assessing look.

"I did not say I disliked it. I do, however, wonder whatever gave you the idea?"

This time Elodie detected a trace of *fear* in the modiste's brown eyes. Whyever would Madame be afraid to say where she had gotten her inspiration?

Madame gave a nervous-sounding laugh. "Oh, my dear Lord Beaumont, you cannot expect me to reveal all of my ideas. I must keep some secrets." The teasing tone did not appear to have the result Madame expected. Lord Beaumont's mouth flattened into a thin line, spoiling his handsome yet austere features.

"Quite," he ground out. "Very well, I approve of the gown. Miss Di Silva will look most *angelic* in it." He drew the word out, rolling out the 'l'.

Madame's eyes widened. Hastily, she turned, collected the box, and snapped her fingers at her curious assistant. Without meeting Elodie's eyes, she curtsied to them, and muttering a quick, "Good day to you both," ushered Deidre ahead of her to exit Elodie's room.

Elodie stared into space for one confused moment. *What on earth could have unnerved the modiste so much?* Caught up in her thoughts, it took a cough from Lord Beaumont for her to come to the sickening realisation that she stood behind a screen in close quarters, to the very man she wanted to distance herself from.

Again, completely unchaperoned.

Seven

"I must call Hannah to help me undress." Elodie moved away from Lord Beaumont towards the call bell.

"If it wouldn't be vastly improper, I would offer to help you."

Elodie's breath hitched in her throat as he came up close behind her. His breath stirred the gauzy wings, and she had the sudden impulse to yank them from the dress so he would not dare sully them again. She gasped, not understanding where that violent thought had emerged from.

"What is it?" Lord Beaumont asked urgently, turning Elodie to face him. She flinched away from him, and his eyes darkened. He dropped her arm instantly and stepped back. He gave a stiff bow. "Forgive me. I will have Hannah sent up."

He was gone before Elodie could make sense of any of it – Madame La Coeur's strange behaviour, her own disturbing thoughts, or Lord Beaumont's contrary conduct. Usually, he seemed to relish in causing her discomfort. Why had he backed off so quickly? She glanced down at the gown. Was it not a mere dress, but something *more*. Perhaps seeing her like this had allowed her to wield some kind of power.

With a derisive laugh, Elodie shook her head at the fanciful nonsense. No, Lord Beaumont was simply using mind tricks to keep her off-balance.

Hannah entered the room, and stopped short. "Oh, Miss," she breathed out. "You look beautiful. You will be this Season's diamond, I bet my bonnet - if you don't mind me being so bold."

Elodie thought that was a bold assumption indeed, but simply murmured, "thank you," before turning to allow Hannah to un-tie the ribbons criss-crossing the back of the delicate gown.

Once Elodie was dressed in her day clothes, she felt returned to her normal self. Being in the gown had somehow made it all so real. Her current status allowed her some anonymity, shielded from the bright lights of the ton, she existed on the fringe, but soon, she would be stepping into the spotlight with all eyes upon her. Judging her. Testing her. Weighing her up. Would she be found wanting, and discarded. Or like so many had prophesised, would she be this Season's incomparable?

Elodie did not know which outcome she feared most.

"Shall I have tea sent up, Miss?" Hannah asked, once the gown had been hung up in the dressing room.

"That would be most welcome," Elodie replied,

from her position on the window seat. The rain had moved in once again, and Elodie wanted nothing more than to spend the remainder of the morning listening to the fat drops dance against the glass pressed to her cheek. For two more days she would be allowed that indulgence. After that, her days would be filled with afternoon tea, calls, soirees, promenades, and balls.

She felt the tears threaten before one errant tear escaped to skim down her cheek, mirroring the raindrop Elodie traced along the glass. Her mother should be here. Her mother should be sharing this with her.

Before the accident, they had planned Elodie's coming out. She would be launched into Society at eighteen – her father teased it was so he would have more time with her. Elodie had been only too keen to concur; she had been in no rush to leave her beloved home, but had hoped to find someone who would love her moors as much as she did.

But, instead of a coming-out ball, she had attended a double-funeral, followed by a year of mourning. Now, at nineteen, it would be Lady Beaumont guiding her out into the world of the ton. And she and Lord Beaumont would have vastly different ideas of who would make a suitable partner for Elodie. Her parents would have allowed her to choose, but she suspected – no, she *knew* – that her preferences would not be tolerated, let alone entertained by the Beaumonts.

Dashing away the tears, Elodie sat up to receive

the tea tray. Hannah gave her a worried look, before bobbing a curtsey and leaving Elodie to her melancholy.

Elodie poured herself a cup of sweet tea, and sat back to resume her perusal of the rain. If she thought she saw a dark figure stood opposite gazing back at her, she determined to ignore it.

She had more pressing concerns to worry about.

"Today's the day, Miss! Oh, how exciting." Hannah hovered over Elodie, as she fought her way from her bedcovers. Another night had found her tossing and turning. Sleep had eluded her, but when she had managed to catch a few moments of slumber, they had been fraught with nightmares.

One had seen her floating from the chandelier, while gazing down upon a ballroom scene. But instead of bright and joyous colours, everyone had been dressed in dark and muted hues. Mourning hues. Perhaps, in her dreamy state, she mourned her old life.

Elodie smiled her thanks as Hannah passed her a breakfast tray. "Lady Beaumont wants you as rested as possible for your grand debut." Hannah beamed, before leaving.

Elodie let out a shuddering breath. Grateful, she would not have to compose herself that morning, she took her time eating her egg and toast, and sipping her chocolate. Not really wanting it, she knew she must fortify herself for the long day and night ahead.

The day itself passed in a whirl of visits from Luisa along with her older sisters, Lucinda and Luella. Lucinda had returned to London briefly to support Elodie, and escort Luella home.

"Elodie, dear. You are the image of Grace." Lucinda smiled a watery smile as she held Elodie's hands in greeting.

"I am blessed indeed to favour my mother." Blessed and also cursed. For every time Elodie gazed upon her countenance in the mirror it was like a stab to the heart.

"You will be the toast, just as your beautiful mother was. Although, the poor eligible bachelors did not stand a chance when she locked eyes with Lord Sebastion Di Silva. Now *that* was a love match." She let go of Elodie's hands to sigh reminiscently and dab at her blue eyes with a lace handkerchief.

Luisa patted the sofa next to her, and Elodie joined her. "I just know you will find a love match too, Lo. Just like Thomas and I."

Luella rolled her eyes. Of the three sisters, she was most like Lord Beaumont, both in looks and manner. "Please, Luisa. Stop harping on about love. Elodie need only make a match to secure her future. Love has nothing to do with it."

Lucinda pursed her lips while Luisa frowned. "But it is definitely a bonus," Lucinda said, laying a placating hand over Luisa's.

She settled herself the other side of Luisa, accepting the teacup Lady Beaumont offered.

"Perhaps if you stopped looking at marriage as nothing but a business deal and opened your heart, you might secure a husband yourself," Luisa said and popped a biscuit into her mouth and chewed angrily.

Luella flushed, while Lady Beaumont said, "Luisa, really! Luella has had plenty of offers."

Luisa snorted. "Ones our brother did not approve of." She selected another biscuit.

"If you keep eating that way, your dear Thomas may take a disgust of you." Luella's eyes flashed as she saw her barb hit her mark. Luisa dropped the biscuit, a flush staining her cheeks.

"Stop it, both of you! This is Elodie's special day. I will not have it tarnished." Lady Beaumont shot a look from one daughter to the other.

"Now, who is spoiling Miss Di Silva's day?" The smooth tone cut though the tension in the room.

Elodie wondered if she was the only one who noticed the temperature drop. Lord Beaumont had been notably absent for the past two days, an absence Elodie had welcomed. But, she had no hope he would continue to be missing. Of course he would appear for this day. He had planned everything and would want to see it unfold.

"Lucan!" Luella jumped up, an amiable smile on her pretty, haughty face. "It has been an age. I have missed you."

Lord Beaumont held her at a distance, put clasped her hands in greeting. "Luella, you are looking well. The Scottish air must be good for you."

Luella pouted. "I would rather have been in town,

but Lucinda needed me during her confinement. But I am so excited to be back."

An indiscernible look crossed Lucinda's face and Elodie wondered if she was glad to be leaving her sister in London, once she returned to her husband and children. Elodie did not relish the thought of being under the same roof as both Lord Beaumont and Luella. It would be most suffocating.

"Lucinda, I trust you leave your brood well." A fleeting, distasteful look crossed Lord Beaumont's face. Perhaps, he disapproved of her continuing to bear children well into her thirties.

"Thank you, brother, they are most well. In fact, I will be returning to them shortly. I only came to return Luella, and support Elodie tonight."

Lord Beaumont inclined his head at his older sister. "We are grateful for your support." He settled his gaze on Elodie. The first time he had done so in two days, and it felt like the first time he had ever done so. Almost painful.

Elodie broke the gaze and smiled at Lucinda. "Indeed. It means so much to have you here. Things will feel less... daunting."

"We will all be there, my dear. You have nothing to fear." Lucinda leant across a misty-eyed Luisa to clasp Elodie's hand.

Elodie squeezed back gratefully, feeling like a piece of her mother was with her in the form of her best friend.

"Now, I think you should go and rest, Elodie." Lady Beaumont set down her teacup and stood to draw Elodie to her feet. "You have a busy evening ahead. We will all partake of a light supper before the ball. I will have Hannah awaken you to dress."

Elodie nodded, latching onto the window of escape. She enjoyed having afternoon tea with the ladies, but Lord Beaumont's brooding presence was making the spot between her shoulder blades tingle uncomfortably.

"I cannot wait to see your dress, Lo." Luisa's eyes sparkled. "Lucan says it will be unique."

Oh, it was certainly unique, Elodie thought. She couldn't bring herself to look at Lord Beaumont as he said, "She looks enchanting in it."

A silence fell in the room, before Lady Beaumont let out a confused titter. "You – you have seen her in her dress?"

Elodie paled at his faux pas.

Lord Beaumont lifted one shoulder in an unconcerned shrug. "So I heard from Hannah."

"Of course," Lady Beaumont said, understanding replacing the confusion marring her face.

Luella leant back, a calculating look in her eyes, while Luisa and Lucinda seemed content with the explanation.

"I will see you at supper," Elodie said and made good her escape. Was Lord Beaumont out to *ruin* her? She decided the question did not warrant an answer. Only he knew what games he continued to play.

Too distracted to nap, she wrote another letter to Caroline, knowing it had been but days since she had sent the last one, still it felt cathartic to dash off her feelings and thoughts in a multi-page missive. It all came out in a torrent of ink, and tears. The quill a mere conduit to her heart.

Finally, chest heaving, Elodie stared down at her ink-stained fingertips. A sudden pain shot through her. She couldn't send this. Caroline wouldn't understand. Yes, she would be sympathetic to Elodie's homesickness, but she would tell Elodie that she should be grateful – *flattered* even – that Lord Beaumont continued to pay her so much attention.

In one sudden move, Elodie crumpled up the pages and stood to march over to the fire and heave them into the flickering hearth. She watched them burn. Could she destroy her fears so easily. Could she rise from the flames like the mythical phoenix, and endure?

She lifted her head and gazed at her reflection in the mantel mirror. Her vision wavered, and for one moment she thought her mother gazed back at her. Pride and love in her silver-grey eyes. Her parents would want her to endure. Not only endure, but soar.

And soar she would. Her gown had the illusion of wings, perhaps Lord Beaumont sensed how dangerous they could be, and that was why he had questioned Madame La Coeur. Perhaps, he sensed in imbuing Elodie with the sense of freedom, she would embrace it and he would be powerless to do nothing but watch her fly.

When Hannah came to help her dress, Elodie was ready. Her mood sober, she stepped into her dress and donned the silvery slippers to match. In her dressing room mirror, she watched impassively as her hair was tumbled on top of her head in an elaborate mass of curls, and pearls and tiny gypsophila flowers.

She took a deep breath, accepted her long pearl-white gloves, and followed Hannah out into the hallway.

Raphael looked into the mirror and adjusted his silver cravat. "Do I really have to wear this?" He held up the brocade eye patch.

"We have been over this, Rafe. I think Hunt's idea is inspired - it is the only way we can ensure she will not look directly into both your eyes. If she does..." Angelina trailed off, meeting Raphael's eyes in the mirror.

"Yes, yes, we all know what happens. She runs and so on and on and on," Hunt said with a long-suffering sigh.

"Hunt, really!" Angelina snapped. She smacked his feet off from the arm of the sofa. He had the good grace to look ashamed.

"Sorry, cous, I am tired of all of this. I would love nothing more than to go home." Hunt stood and poured himself a glass of brandy.

"*You're* tired of it?" Raphael said. "How do you think I feel? No, do not answer that, we have to leave." He tossed back his own brandy. With a resigned sneer in the mirror, he placed the eyepatch over his left eye.

He led the others from the room. They had a debutante ball to attend.

Eight

A shadow melted from an alcove. "I will escort Miss Di Silva." Lord Beaumont did not even spare Hannah a glance. Out of the corner of her frozen eyes, Elodie saw Hannah curtsey and head down the staircase.

Lord Beaumont's intense gaze pinned Elodie, and the armour she had erected around herself cracked. She was only deceiving herself. Lord Beaumont would never allow her to soar... not when he held the key to her cage.

He was dressed in a black jacket, with a cravat to match Elodie's dress. Her breath hitched. What signal would that send? Dispassionately, she accepted how handsome he was, with his golden hair swept back off his brow, and his unusual pale-blue eyes, but he left her cold. So cold.

He held out an arm to her. "Let us practice for your entrance tonight."

As if compelled, Elodie put on her gloves and rested a hand on his arm, and together they walked down the stairs, and along the tiled hallway. Her gauzy 'wings', not yet tied to her wrists, floated behind her. Footmen and maids paused to watch their progress. Tension radiated from Lord Beaumont, and Elodie did her best not to falter. Being on his arm felt *wrong*.

The chatter in the dining room ceased as Elodie stood framed in the doorway on Lord Beaumont's arm.

"Oh, Elodie," Luisa said in hushed tones, before hurrying forward to draw her into the room. Lord Beaumont's hand flexed, as if he wanted to draw Elodie back to his side, but Elodie accepted Luisa's fingers and followed her over to the table where a light supper awaited.

"Why does she get to wear that? I had to wear a simple pure white gown." Luella waved her glass in Elodie's direction.

"Because, Luella, it suited your colouring. Miss Di Silva has a – ah – *unique* look." Lord Beaumont poured himself a glass of brandy and leant against the fireplace, watching Elodie with hooded eyes.

"Luella, you looked beautiful, as you are well aware." Lady Beaumont said with a censorious frown. "As does Elodie."

"She does indeed." Lucinda toasted her with her wineglass.

The ladies were dressed in their ballgowns, ranging from Lady Beaumont's lavender silk, to Lucinda's soft blue taffeta and Luisa's powder pink organza. Luella favoured brighter colours; her tulle was a golden-yellow, designed to stand out. Perhaps, she hoped to eclipse Elodie and secure a husband herself that night.

Elodie hoped she would. Anything to take the focus off herself. She thought she was prepared to begin her search for a soulmate, but now the time had come, she felt terrified.

She nibbled pastries and cold meats, shaking her head at an offer of more wine. One glass dulled her senses enough to soften the edges, but she still wanted to be in charge of her actions. Especially with Lord Beaumont stalking her every movement with his eyes. Soon, she would be thrust into a situation where her every action, word and step would be watched, not only by him, but through the lens of the ton elite.

"My lord, carriages are beginning to arrive." Wells bowed at the door.

Lord Beaumont took his time rising. "Shall we, ladies?"

Elodie's heart thrummed in her chest as Lady Beaumont, Lucinda, Luisa and Luella also rose with various looks on their faces. Most were of excitement, one of bored derision.

"See you in the ballroom, Lo. I must see if Thomas has arrived yet. He would have been here for supper, but he had some urgent business to attend to." Luisa pressed a kiss to Elodie's cheek before leaving with the others, leaving a footman by the door.

"Miss Di Silva." Lord Beaumont offered her his hand and helped her rise from her seat. She would make her entrance once the ballroom had filled.

Knowing Lord Beaumont, he would ensure it was filled to crushing. All the better to ensure talk of Elodie's debut would be on everyone's lips the following day.

The air between Elodie and Lord Beaumont became charged, and it did nothing to settle Elodie's heart. As if he could hear its furtive rhythm, Lord Beaumont smiled his arrogant, knowing smile. Did he think it beat for him? Oh, how she longed to allay him of his mistaken notion. No, it beat with understanding, the understanding that once he led her from this room, and presented her, she would, however much he disabused himself of the idea, belong to the ton, a part of the wheel that turned as precisely as the couples who took to the ballroom floor.

The dizzying thought whirling through her mind, she allowed Lord Beaumont to walk her to the open terrace doors to await the moment when she would be called. The early April breeze wafted over her heated cheeks, and she closed her eyes, inhaling the promise of rain.

Sounds filtered through from the open ballroom doors further along the terrace, like the sound of sand pouring through the narrow waist of an hourglass.

"It all changes tonight," Lord Beaumont observed.

Elodie jolted, she had almost forgotten he stood near her, so caught up in her own mind. Did he mean for the better? The sounds grew louder; the hourglass growing bottom heavy.

"Allow me to tie your ribbons. We would not want you to become inadvertently entangled." Elodie tried to decipher his words, noting the emphasis he put on the last two. There would be no inadvertent anything – Elodie determined to approach the evening's events with clarity and resolve.

Lord Beaumont moved behind her to catch one of the filmy pieces. With slow and deliberate movements, he tied it to her gloved wrist, followed by the second piece. Elodie watched his long fingers, thankful her gloves muted some of the icy sensations. Caught up in the breeze from the open doors, the wings billowed up, and his eyes widened as he looked at her fully.

"My lord, it is time." Wells' voice brought Lord Beaumont out of his fixating stare. He stepped away from Elodie and took a composing breath. He turned, his icy mask once again on his face; the disconcerting hint of vulnerable longing completely obliterated from his features.

Without a word, he held out his arm. Elodie lifted her foot, but found herself frozen in mid-step. She lowered her foot, unable to take that first step. With a huff of exasperation, the mask slipped for a moment, as Lord Beaumont took her hand, and none-to-gently pulled her forward. Mobilised into action, Elodie took one footstep, then another and before she knew it they were at the doors of the ballroom.

Panic clawed up Elodie's throat. Once the doors were thrown open, everything would indeed change.

I am not ready!

"Ready yourself, my dear," Lord Beaumont said icily. Was he reading her thoughts now? Elodie stifled a hysterical giggle.

She threw him a questioning look, one he caught and held as the double-doors were opened. His eyes still on her, he walked her forward, presenting her to the throng below.

"Lord Lucan Beaumont presenting Miss Elodie Di Silva." The shout from the footman had silence falling in the room.

Applause had Elodie turning and pasting a smile on her face to acknowledge the crowd congregated at the bottom of the curved staircase.

"Careful not to fall, my dear," Lord Beaumont leaned in close to whisper in her ear, as he guided her down the steps. She shivered at the intonation and at his cold breath.

Luisa and Thomas met her at the bottom. "Here is your dance card, Lo. I bet it will be filled in moments."

"Save one for me, Miss Di Silva," Thomas said with a friendly smile. He turned to survey the crowd as Lord Beaumont plucked the dance card from Luisa's offering fingers. With a quick scrawl, he filled in one of the spaces before handing it to Elodie.

"I have the rounds to make, but I will be back for our dance." He bowed over her hand, before walking away.

Elodie didn't even have to question which dance. She was certain which one it would be. Her suspicions were confirmed as she sneaked a look. *The waltz*. She was surprised the patronesses of Almack's would allow it after their snub, but Lord Beaumont had obviously smoothed a few ruffled feathers as she saw the ladies grouped together with Lady Beaumont, cups of lemonade in hand.

They talked, heads bent close together, and Elodie knew she would have to get used to being the topic of conversation for weeks to come.

Elodie scanned the rest of the crowd, faces blurred as she passed over them, before she focused on two familiar faces; Lord Huntingford and his sister, Countess Godwin. The lord raised his glass, while Angelina inclined her head.

"Oh, there's Hunt. Put me down for a quadrille, Miss Di Silva," Lord Darlington said before he slipped into the crush.

Luisa rolled her eyes affectionately. "Come along, let me introduce you to a few people."

Elodie followed her along the edge of the dance floor as the first strains of a jaunty tune filled the air.

The first hour of the ball passed in a blur of new faces and names, of dancing, and navigating social niceties, while avoiding those Luisa and Luella deemed unacceptable company.

"Miss Di Silva, I have brought you a cold cup of lemonade." Lord Worthing, a young man in his early twenties with a tidy cut of copper-coloured hair, emerged from the crowd, brandishing a half-filled cup. He looked at it downcast. "My apologies, I got jostled."

Elodie took it gratefully. "It is most welcome,"

she assured him and was just putting the cup to her lips, when a cold chill had her pausing.

"My dance, I believe, Miss Di Silva." Lord Beaumont rounded her from behind. He took the cup from her and handed it back to the other man. "Worthing," he said shortly.

"B-Beaumont," Lord Worthing replied, clearly in awed respect of the other gentleman, but Elodie felt affronted on the affable young man's behalf.

"Did you have to be so sharp with him, he is perfectly harmless," Elodie snapped without thinking, as Lord Beaumont guided her into position.

Her breath sucked between her teeth as he stepped up close, his hand at her waist. He speared her with daggers made from blue ice. "Know this, my dear Miss Di Silva, no man is perfectly harmless. All men have their limits, mortal or otherwise." He swung her around as the music started, and Elodie caught Worthing's face in the crowd as he lifted the cup in salute.

Elodie shook off Lord Beaumont's words. Perhaps *he* himself had limits, but there *were* good men, her father had been one of them. She intended to find another. She stumbled as she pondered the rest of his sentence. Whatever did he mean by mortal or otherwise? Now who was being fanciful.

The thought fled from her mind as Lord Beaumont manoeuvred them around another couple and they spun close to the edge of the dancefloor. An elbow, or perhaps a hand, brushed the back of Elodie's arm just above her glove and with a dizzying swoop of her head, a scent washed over. A heady, *familiar*, scent. She whipped her head around. A man was walking away from her, a broad-shouldered man, dressed in a black suit, with his long black hair brushing the collar of his high silvery shirt.

She had to get to him, she had to see his face.

Elodie struggled in Lord Beaumont's arms, not even caring that she would cause a scandal if she left him standing alone on the dance floor, at her own debutante ball.

"What are you doing?" Lord Beaumont hissed, holding her so tightly, his fingers dug through the fabric of her gown and into her skin.

"I must go, I must see," she said, not even registering the pain or what she was saying.

Lord Beaumont followed her gaze. His unexpected oath shocked Elodie out of whatever spell she had been under. She looked at him and recoiled. He looked almost inhuman. A savage light glowed behind his eyes and his face had twisted into something monstrous.

He dropped his gaze to hers and, with a roaring in her ears, Elodie slumped in his arms to be claimed by the creeping darkness.

Nine

"Did you have to *touch* her? She fainted." Hunt rounded on Raphael; his bright blue eyes hard.

"I did not mean to, but it was just the merest of touches. How was I supposed to know she would react in such a way."

Hunt exchanged an incredulous look with Angelina. "How was he supposed to know?" he repeated, shaking his head. "Oh, I don't know, maybe it's because she reacts like that *every damn time*."

"Hunt," Angelina warned, casting her eyes skyward.

Hunt let out a bark of derisive laughter. "Stay here," he said to Raphael. "I am going to get us some drinks."

Raphael watched his cousins make their way back along the terrace, before turning and heading into the gardens, his heart thundering.

"Elodie... Elodie, wake up, dearest." A bitter smell

beneath her nose had Elodie jerking up from where she reclined on the sofa in the drawing room.

"What happened?" she asked weakly. She scanned the concerned faces around her. Luisa stoppered the bottle of smelling salts and set them onto the side table. Lucinda held her hand, while Lord Beaumont and Luella stood framing the fireplace, both wearing unreadable, haughty expressions.

"Well done, Elodie. That little scene will ensure your ball is all anyone can talk about. Imagine, fainting in the middle of a waltz and in *the* Lord Beaumont's arms, no less." Luella moved away from the fireplace, a sneer on her face. "And when he carried you from the room, well..." she trailed off, leaving her implication perfectly clear.

Elodie couldn't bring herself to think about Lord Beaumont carrying her anywhere, especially in an unconscious state. "I *fainted*?" But she hadn't felt faint, she had actually been enjoying herself at the ball. Luisa and Thomas' friends were a welcoming bunch. She shook her head, trying to slot the memories into place. Yes, she had been enjoying herself... up until the waltz, that is. Her eyes flew to Lord Beaumont's face. He watched her, as if he could see the images in her head displayed upon her face. *His face.* She sat up abruptly and her head swam.

"Careful," Lucinda said, helping Elodie to swing her legs around, while Luisa placed cushions behind her back to prop her up.

Why had Lord Beaumont's face changed like

that? He had been livid. Something – no, *someone* – had caused the transformation.

"The man!" Elodie exclaimed, before putting a hand hastily up to her mouth as if she could stuff the words back in.

"What man?" Luisa asked, curiosity colouring her tone. She sat beside Elodie and looked at her.

"Yes, Miss Di Silva, what man?" Lord Beaumont's voice could have cut glass. He pushed away from the fireplace and prowled towards the sofa.

"Did I say m-man? I meant the *fan*, of course. That is what I meant. I tripped on someone's dropped fan – on the dancefloor, I mean." She babbled, and even to her own ears it sounded implausible. "The pain in my ankle caused my dizziness."

Luisa's face cleared, while Lucinda bit her lip in concern. "Well, that explains it. How is your ankle now, dearest?" Luisa asked.

Elodie pushed her foot to the floor. "Surprisingly better," she said, wincing slightly at the lies she was telling. She had no idea why she was hiding the fact that there was a mysterious man in the ballroom that had caused such a reaction in her – and apparently in Lord Beaumont too – that she felt the need to conceal it.

"Hmm surprising," Luella said in disbelieving tones.

"Indeed." Lord Beaumont said. "You ladies return to the ball; I will escort Miss Di Silva back. Unless you would care to retire?"

Elodie grasped the unexpected lifeline he had just

offered her. On one hand she longed to go back and scour the dance floor, but knew Lord Beaumont would now not let her out of his sight. The dark-haired man was of interest to them both. But who knew if it was for the same or differing reasons. Elodie had no way of knowing, she could only hope an opportunity to find out would present itself. "I would like to retire, please."

"Oh yes, that will just add to your mysterious allure." Luella sneered. "Come along, sisters. Some of us have a husband to procure."

"I will call on you tomorrow before I leave," Lucinda promised, while Luisa bobbed a head behind her.

"Sleep well," Luisa added.

Luella waved a mocking hand and followed her sisters out.

Elodie, once again, found herself alone with Lord Beaumont, but she had no desire to remain so. She stood, and was pleased to note she managed it without her head swimming.

"I knew you had many accomplishments; I did not believe lying was one of them." Lord Beaumont stepped into Elodie's path, blocking her escape. His face in half shadow, she licked her lips nervously.

"Lying, my lord?" she stalled.

"Do not play the innocent miss with me," he snapped, moving into the candlelight. "It appears I must be more discerning of the guest list in future. You are to stay away from him. Far away. Do I make myself clear?"

Elodie was tempted to keep the pretence going, but thought his wrath would only intensify. She gave one jerky nod.

A satisfied smile crept across Lord Beaumont's face. "Excellent. Then I will bid you good night." He gave an elaborate bow, before striding from the room.

The urge to drop where she stood warred within Elodie. But she couldn't afford to be found thus. She needed to get to her room. She hurried out of the drawing room and along the hall. But a breeze snaked along behind her, coming from the dining room, carrying with it a scent. A scent she knew.

She paused, then turned to walk back in the direction of the dining room. She stood, a hand on the doorframe, torn between investigating or finding refuge in her room. Without realising it, she was moving through the room and stepping through the open terrace doors.

Lord Beaumont would unleash a storm the like of which she had never known if he caught her, but the wheels had been set in motion and she was powerless to stop them. Something far bigger than the games he favoured was at play. And she needed to discover who the players were. She just had to roll the dice.

Out on the terrace, she lifted her chin to better locate the scent. *Elodriel...* the whispered voice came out of nowhere, and beckoned her on. Moving along the terrace, away from the ballroom doors, Elodie moved as if summoned. She stopped at the far end of the terrace and looked below into the gardens.

A shadow detached itself from one of the trees

and moved closer. It was *him*; she knew it. Caught in shadows herself, she did not know if he had yet seen her. She stepped back hastily as Lord Huntingford sauntered along the grass, two glasses in hand. He met the shadowed man and held out a glass to him.

Elodie couldn't stop the gasp that left her lips. Lord Huntingford was friends with the mysterious man? Perhaps she shouldn't really be surprised. Caught in her thoughts, she missed both men turning to look in her direction. As if one, they made a step towards where she stood.

Move! She knew it was too late to stop being seen by them both now, so she peeled herself away from her hiding place and hurried down the terrace. At the dining room doors, she threw one glance over her shoulder. Lord Huntingford stood watching her, but of the mysterious man, there was no sign. Perhaps she had imagined him.

Hurrying up to her room, she argued with herself. Of course, she hadn't imagined him. Her imagination was not so skilled as to create a man so visceral...so *real*. She *had* seen him, well, a shadowy version of him, she conceded. She still did not know what his face looked like, and with a sudden clarity, she realised how important it was that she found out. Her very future depended on it.

Sat on her bed, her stomach churning and her mind whirling, she couldn't understand why that particular thought fought for dominance. Why did seeing one man's face have to determine her future?

The long day took its toll, and Elodie lay back on

the pillows. Sleep would be a welcome reprieve from her scattered thoughts and tattered emotions.

"Hold him down! I have never seen nightmares take him so fully before," Angelina fought to grip Raphael's right arm, while Hunt battled with the other.

Raphael's eyes shot open. "I cannot stop it!" he roared. With inhuman strength he easily shook them off. He launched himself from the bed and flung himself onto his balcony.

Angelina and Hunt could do nothing but helplessly watch him go.

"Elodriel, find me. Remember me." The words penetrated the fog of Elodie's sleep, but didn't awaken her fully.

In her state of sleep, she sat, and swung her legs over the side of the bed and walked away from her bed and into her dressing room. Set on the corner of the house, the balcony there overlooked the back garden. In her dreams she saw a man, shrouded in shadows. Saw him beckon to her, while black and silver feathers rained down from the cloudy sky.

"Show me your face," she pleaded. "I need to see you. I need to know you."

"You do know me, your heart knows me, but more than that... your *soul* knows me." His voice was deep and smoky, but so gentle and loving, that she no longer felt afraid. She knew he spoke the truth. It was like the click of a key in her cage, allowing the door to swing open. Now she had to fly free.

Sleep-walking, she unlocked the balcony doors and pushed them open. She walked straight through, not even to stop as the wall of the balcony butted up against her waist. Still in her debutante gown, she clambered on top of the wall. She must fly free.

She must fall.

She rose her arms, her 'wings' billowing, and put one foot out, even as the loving voice in her head took an indrawn breath. The heavens itself held its breath.

Arms with a steel-like grip surrounded her from behind and pulled her back. Elodie awoke with a gasp, as she tumbled onto the stone floor. She opened her eyes to see Lord Beaumont's face mere centimetres from her own.

She gave a squeak of shock, but he barely spared her a glance, instead he pushed up and flung himself at the balcony wall, gripping the edge so tightly his knuckles whitened in the moonlight.

He shouted into the night, "You will not win this way. She must remember freely. You will not have her this time, or ever!" The words echoed into the night, before they were sucked away by a sudden wind created by what implausibly seemed to Elodie like giant wings. Lightning zigzagged across the sky, lighting up a shape above. "Leave!" Lord Beaumont roared before it was drowned out by clap of thunder. Rain cascaded down from the clouds, and Elodie scuttled back as Lord Beaumont turned to her, his wrath not yet sated.

He leaned over her and yanked her up, dragging her into the dressing room. He slammed the doors shut and locked them, pocketing the key.

"You have ruined my dress," Elodie said in a small voice, seeing the remnants of the fabric fluttering in rips around her arms. Shocked as she was, she needed to focus on the tiny things, the scope of everything else that had just happened was vast. Too vast.

"I would tear the very wings from your flesh to keep you from him." Lord Beaumont strode up and down in front of her, raking a hand through his tousled golden hair.

Thinking he was speaking in metaphors, Elodie turned away, seeking a way of escape while he rambled. A hand snaked out to clasp her to him.

"But, this time, this time, he will not even get a chance."

"I do not understand," Elodie whimpered, seeing madness behind his eyes. "It was just a *dream...* wasn't it?"

Lord Beaumont released her abruptly. "Of course, my dear, just a nasty nightmare. One that will never be repeated. I will get Hannah to bring you a sleeping draught. I will keep this key; we don't want any more night time near misses now do we?"

The about-turn in his manner had Elodie faltering. If it was simply a dream, why had he been shouting into the wind? And to whom? Or perhaps she had but dreamt that too.

"Settle yourself into bed now, my dear. I have business to attend to tomorrow, I must seek counsel from my associates. I will be gone a few days – a week at most." Lord Beaumont smoothed back his hair and adjusted his cravat. But suddenly the piercing look was back in his eyes. "You are not to leave this house unchaperoned. And any gentleman callers will be vetted by my sister. I will leave strict instructions with her."

Elodie stared at him for a moment, before giving him her assurances for the second time that night.

He left her, standing in the centre of the room, in a tattered gown, and the remnants of a scattered dream.

This time she did drop where she stood; she folded to the floor and wept.

Raphael paced up and down in front of the fire, drenched to the bone, but he refused to change his clothes. "I almost killed her. What would have happened? I could have condemned her."

"It wasn't your fault; you were pulled into the nightmare as much as she was. From what I understand she had no control over it any more than you did. And you *know* you would have caught her, Rafe." Angelina inserted a piece of blotting paper and slammed the book, she had been writing in, closed. The teardrop-shaped opal stone on the cover shifted and gleamed in the firelight.

"Must you really document every teeny tiny part

of this?" Hunt asked, gesturing with his brandy glass at the book.

Angelina scowled at him. "Yes. I must. One of us must try to make sense of it all. We are denied help from exalted quarters; our old friends and kin are forbidden to assist us, as you well know, so it is down to us. Something about this time feels different somehow. I need to find out why."

Raphael tore his gaze from the opal on the book's cover; his heart twisting painfully at the myriad of memories assaulting him, and sank into the chair nearest the fire. With a shaking hand he accepted the glass Hunt passed him. He rose his intense gaze to Angelina. "You are right, this time is different."

Hunt winced at the hope he heard in his cousin's voice. He wondered if he had done the right thing in planning his own ball, and inviting *her*. A few days ago, It had seemed a perfectly harmless way to spend their time here, but now he was not so sure.

Ten

The sleeping draught did the trick. Elodie awoke the next morning thinking all that had happened had just been the result of a sleepwalking episode twinned with a nightmare. She refused to believe it had been real, she had simply been overwrought and overtired. She pushed Lord Beaumont's erratic behaviour away, locking it in the same box as the nightmarish events, convinced her heightened imagination had deceived her into thinking he had been raging at someone outside her balcony. To believe that was insanity. But one part did ring true; he had gone, hopefully for the full week, and she would be able to breathe again.

True to her word, Lucinda arrived late morning with Luisa. Luella and Lady Beaumont were still abed, so Elodie took tea with Lucinda and Luisa alone.

"Well, Elodie, I can safely say your debut was a success. Leaving early only piqued the interest of the gentlemen. I would not be surprised if you were not inundated with callers today." Lucinda toasted Elodie with her teacup.

Elodie fought to hide her grimace. While she wanted nothing more than to escape Lord Beaumont, she did not relish the idea of being simpered over. She wanted what her parents had had – real, true, eternal love. Sadly, she took a sip of her tea.

"Oh, I almost forgot! Hunt is having a masquerade ball in two days. He has extended you an invitation, Elodie. Thomas and I will chaperone you." Luisa bounced in her seat, her blonde ringlets dancing.

"Really, Luisa. Masquerade balls are most scandalous. Lucan will not approve," Lucinda said, setting down her teacup.

"Well, he is not here, is he?" Luisa replied, a mischievous twinkle in her eye. "And besides, no will recognise Elodie, because her face will be hidden."

"*I* do not approve, Luisa, but I have to trust you will take care of Elodie, for I must depart back to Scotland today." Lucinda leant forward to clasp Elodie's hands. "I am truly sorry my visit has been so fleeting, but my children need their mother, and I miss my husband." A becoming blush stained the older lady's cheeks.

Another love match, Elodie thought with affection, and only the merest hint of longing. She was surrounded by so many love matches, surely she could find one too?

"I understand," she told Lucinda. "Luisa will keep me busy, I'm sure."

"Oh, I have no doubt of that," Luella said, coming

through the door. She put a dainty hand up to stifle a yawn.

Luisa and Lucinda exchanged a telling look. Would Luella approve of a masquerade ball? Elodie wondered. Had Lord Beaumont issued strict instructions to her before his departure? She did not have to wonder for long.

Luella took a seat opposite Luisa and Elodie. "Our dear brother pulled me aside last night. I am to – boringly – stay close to Elodie. Apparently he is concerned some rake will take advantage of her while he is gone. So-" she narrowed her eyes at Luisa, then, Elodie "-where you go, I apparently, must go."

Luisa slumped, then her eyes narrowed slyly. "You danced with Lord Huntingford last night, did you not, Luella?"

Luella put a hand up to her face and fanned it slightly. "I did – oh, and also the Duke of Mistbourne too – with his long black hair and eye patch, he looked like a dashing pirate. Did you not see?" All remnants of tiredness gone, she sat up straighter and looked around at them all.

Long black hair... a memory washed over Elodie in dizzying waves. She tuned out the chatter of the sisters as the events of the previous night, fought their way passed the barrier the sleep draught had provided. Was the duke the mysterious dark-haired man she had seen in the ballroom and again in the garden? If so, why had Lord Beaumont demanded she stay away from him?

"Elodie?" Luisa pressed a hand to her arm, jolting

her out of her thoughts.

"Oh, I am sorry. You were saying?"

"Luella has agreed to attend the ball with us." Luisa's eyes flashed merrily. "Apparently, she is much taken with Hunt and the duke, even if our dear brother is not. The duke is Hunt's cousin, though enigmatic, I am sure he will attend. I do not know him well; he is pretty reclusive, so what has brought him to town, I know not. But, everyone is speculating that perhaps he is looking to take a wife."

"Did you not just tell us Lucan has forbid the Duke of Mistbourne or his friends from calling on Elodie," Lucinda said, and Elodie realised she must have missed that part in the sisters' conversation while she had been musing.

"Yes – from calling on her – but they won't be *calling* on her. If we all happen to meet at a ball, than I have no control over that." Luella shrugged delicately, and Elodie was both impressed and astounded by her cool deducement.

As the sisters continued to squabble, a full-body flush worked its way up and down Elodie. She felt torn; both excited to attend her first masquerade ball, but also nervous to discover if the duke was indeed the man who had been haunting her. The dark-haired stranger evoked a reaction in her. One she couldn't discern if it was a longing to be welcomed into his world, or one of fleeing so far away from him. But now, with Lord Beaumont's violent reaction the night before, she knew she must find out who the Duke of Mistbourne was, and if he was indeed the dark-haired stranger who acted as if he pursued her. This would be her only chance. With Lord Beaumont gone, she was free to find out, and thankfully Luella's desire to secure herself a husband outweighed her concern at disobeying her brother.

"Then it is settled," Luisa said triumphantly, while Lucinda let out a groan.

"Thankfully, I will not be around to see our brother's ire. On your heads be it," she said, then stood. "I will go and say my goodbyes to Mama. Write me, dearest ones." She pressed kisses to each of her sister's cheeks, before drawing Elodie up and into her arms, to whisper into her ear. "Your mother would be so proud of the composed young lady you are turning into, but please have a care. Do not be dragged blindly into my sisters' schemes."

Elodie hugged her back, taking comfort from the motherly embrace. "I will keep my wits about me," she whispered back.

Lucinda gave her a smile as she pulled back. "I will visit again as soon as I am able."

With a final wave, Lucinda walked from the room, and Elodie sat back down, wondering if she was really ready for Society life. She did not feel composed, she felt like a tempest, one which simmered beneath her debutante surface, one that threatened to consume her, if she did not figure out how to control it. The marks between her shoulder blades itched, and she wanted nothing more than to soothe it with a cooling poultice.

Wells appeared at the door. "Callers for Miss Di

Silva."

Luella pouted, and waved an imperious hand, beckoning the butler over. She scanned through the cards on the tray. "Send them in."

Elodie's heart shot into her mouth. Did she not even get a say?

"Very good, Miss," Wells said. Apparently not.

Luisa smoothed Elodie's hair and adjusted her pale blue gown. "There. You are ready."

Was she?

She did not have time to find out, before three gentlemen were shown in, one of whom, Elodie was relieved to see, was Worthing. He, at least, was a friendly face.

"Miss Di Silva! A pleasure to see you are looking well this morning." Worthing wasted no time in making his way over, while the other two gentleman exchanged frustrated looks. Luella gave a delicate but pointed cough, so he added, "Oh, and Miss Beaumont, Lady Darlington, a pleasure to see you both this morning too."

Luisa threw Elodie an amused look, while Luella accepted Worthing's hand, a haughty look on her face.

The other two gentlemen – Elodie recalled them as Lord Bamford and Lord Chester, who she had briefly met at her ball – ranged themselves near the fireplace. No doubt waiting for a moment to swoop in and claim her attention.

Elodie's head swam as the rest of the morning was filled with small talk and copious amounts of tea.

Longing to visit the retiring room, Elodie murmured a distracted 'Mmm-hmm," at Lord Bamford who had finally succeeded in ousting Worthing from his seat.

"Wonderful, then I shall call on you at noon tomorrow," Lord Bamford said in satisfied tones.

"I – pardon?" Elodie focused in on the conversation.

"Tomorrow – a ride in my new barouche." Lord Bamford said slowly, his face a work of confusion.

"Oh, capital! Worthing and I were just discussing going for a carriage ride. Shall we make it a four?" Luella leant forward in excitement, although her eyes danced slyly. Elodie hoped she wasn't planning on a spot of matchmaking.

Lord Chester set his cup down in disgust.

Elodie gave a slow nod. She did not want to encourage Lord Bamford. She knew instantly he was not for her, but surely a carriage ride would do no harm. It would give her a chance to see how Society worked in the daytime hours.

"I shall look forward to it," Lord Bamford said, bending over Elodie's hand. She lowered her eyes.

"As will I," Worthing said amiably.

As the gentlemen took their leave, Lord Chester tried one final time to claim Elodie's attention. "I hope I will see you at the Huntingford ball?"

"Oh, of course, Elodie is most excited to attend." Luella smiled around at all three gentlemen.

With satisfied exclamations, the gentlemen left, and Elodie slumped back upon the pillows.

"I would not get too comfortable," Luisa observed

from her position by the window. "Two more gentlemen are walking up the path."

Elodie goggled before leaping up. "Oh, please say I am indisposed," she said flustered by all the sudden interest. Yes, she wanted to secure a love match, but at the same time she wanted to have a moment to catch her breath.

"Fine," Luella said. "I will entertain them on your behalf. Make sure they are worthy of your attention."

"Or suitable for yourself, you mean," Luisa said with a titter.

Luella's face darkened. "Really Luisa, sometimes I dislike you very much."

Elodie left the sisters to their bickering and hurried up the stairs to her bedroom before Wells opened the front door. She ran to her window seat and carefully peered out. She gave a groan as another two carriages pulled up outside. Was this really what Society was all about? Endless mornings of inane chatter, and afternoons parading oneself for all to see? She wished she could skip this part. It wasn't anything like she'd hoped it would be, but then if things had been different she would have been sharing it with her parents, and everything would be painted in bright colours, instead of overlaid with a dull lacquer.

She decided to write about her ball – omitting the fainting and night-time terror – to Caroline, who would want to hear all about it, and it would help distract herself.

She hunted on her desk for a clean piece of paper,

but none was to be found, so without thinking she grabbed the key to her drawer from underneath the window seat cushion and unlocked it to grab a sheaf more, forgetting that was where she had hidden the feathers – the unnerving white ones, and the enthralling black one.

The potent scent of the black feather rose from the drawer, and Elodie closed her eyes as a vicious vision swamped her.

Huge black wings flapped behind a shining torso, arms reaching out to enfold her as she stumbled; her shoulder blades burning. On a cry, she pitched forward and knew only endless darkness.

Eleven

"Isn't this refreshing?" Luella said turning her face up to the gentle April sunshine. Lord Bamford watched her from his seat beside Elodie, and Elodie hid a smile as his throat bobbed up and down. Had he developed a tendre for the haughty blonde lady?

Selfishly, she hoped he had. It would save Elodie from having to rebut his advances. Not that he hadn't been anything other than gentlemanly, but he had mentioned numerous times since they had left the Beaumonts' town house, how he was only in town to find a wife, so perhaps he wasn't being as selective in his choosing as Elodie wanted to be. Love was a complicated affair, she thought, but it shouldn't be discarded entirely, even if one was in a hurry. *Especially*, if one was in a hurry – that was when mistakes were made, and being stuck in a loveless marriage for a lifetime, was not something easily rectified. No, she determined to forge a true connection.

She tilted her head as she observed Worthing

pointing something out to Luella, a wide smile on his face. Harmless, amiable and kind, he would make a wonderful husband... but not for Elodie. She wanted something fierce and all-consuming, something that had its roots in the dawn of time, winding through all of eternity.

She put a hand up to her brow at the ferocity of the resolute thought. She had always believed she wanted the kind of love her parents experienced, but what yearned within her heart was something far more powerful. If only she were brave enough to embrace it. Perhaps it had come from her vision-like daydream the day before. Yes, it had unsettled her, but the intensity she had felt as she was enfolded in those powerful arms had almost undone her. She had come out of the vison with tears streaming down her face grieving at the absence of that potent love. She needed to find it again.

"Shall we take a turn about the park, Miss Di Silva?" Lord Bamford asked, and Elodie gave a nod of assent. She needed to walk and dissipate some of this residual energy.

The barouche turned to pull in at the park. Another carriage coming the other way made a sharp turn in front of them cutting them up, so Bamford's driver had to pull sharply on the reins.

"Oh!" Luella exclaimed, as she was nearly jolted from her seat. Lord Bamford righted her, and Luella gave a pretty smile, blushing at the brown-haired lord. Elodie looked carefully from one to the other. Yes, there was a definite spark brewing there.

"I do apologise for that cur, Miss Beaumont." Lord Bamford looked at the pure black carriage, now in front of them, in disgust.

"That was Mistbourne wasn't it?" Worthing mused.

Mistbourne? Elodie craned her neck to better see the carriage. It stopped, but no one exited.

The barouche pulled up behind, and Worthing and Lord Bamford helped Luella and Elodie alight. Elodie couldn't help but cast furtive looks at the black carriage. It had tightly drawn black velvet curtains, with four black stallions at the front. The crest on the side of the coach was of two wings with the Latin phrase *Amor Alas Dat*. How curious, Elodie thought, translating it to, *Love Bestows Wings*.

Her breath hitched, as the curtain gave a twitch. Someone was observing them from within.

"Is this really the best idea?" Raphael asked, pulling the curtain back to watch Elodie and her group. His mind called to her, while his heart yearned for her.

Angelina gave a sigh. "You need to meet at some point, this should ease you both into it. Surrounded by lots of people, in the daylight. I do not foresee any problems. Just... don't look directly at her, this is all just speculation on our part." She waved a hand at his eye patch.

Hunt gave a laugh before turning it into a cough. Angelina shot him a narrowed-eyed look. He held up his hands in surrender. "Let the experiment begin," he said.

"Come along, Miss Di Silva. We shall remove ourselves from this unmannered company." Lord Bamford scowled at the carriage, before drawing her away.

The back of Elodie's neck tingled. *Elodriel*. There was that strange name again. Had it come from her mind or... she turned her head, while Bamford was distracted by Luella struggling to open her parasol. The door to the carriage opened and she saw Countess Angelina Godwin emerge, followed by a tall, broad-shouldered man. Mistbourne. The mysterious man. Elodie was now certain they were one and the same.

"I knew it was Mistbourne... oh, and Huntingford," Worthing said enthusiastically. "Excuse me, I will just go and say hello."

Elodie noted Lord Huntingford had also emerged from the carriage and stood watching the promenading melee disdainfully.

"Worthing would do well to disassociate himself from certain company," Lord Bamford observed with a frown.

"Oh, but I think he is very dashing," Luella said with a sigh, looking at the duke. "Especially with his eye patch. Although, he would do well to add some colour to his attire." She narrowed her eyes critically, completely missing Bamford's shocked expression.

"Miss Beaumont. You of all people should not entertain such notions. Especially with your brother and Mistbourne being at odds."

Elodie was torn between frustrated amusement at Luella sabotaging her own chances at a match with Bamford by her declaration about 'dashing' Mistbourne, and intrigue at what the dispute between Beaumont and the duke could possibly be.

Luella flushed, dropping her eyes.

Elodie turned back to watching an animated Worthing conversing with Lord Huntingford. Countess Godwin leaned in close to Mistbourne and spoke. As one, they turned to look in Elodie's party's direction. Now it was Elodie's turn to drop her eyes, as her stomach did a somersault.

"Oh, how positively diverting!" Elodie looked up as Luisa and Thomas stepped in front of them. "We simply must all join our groups and promenade together." Before Elodie could even utter a squeak of protest, Luisa had linked arms with her and was propelling her towards the duke's group.

She threw a helpless look over her shoulder, but Luella looked delighted and followed with alacrity. Lord Bamford scowled but followed more sedately with Thomas.

"Angelina! Hunt! Look who I have found, our dear Miss Di Silva, and this is the Duke of Mistbourne," she added to Elodie.

Luisa positioned Elodie mere feet from the duke, and she trembled as the sun slipped behind a ragged cloud. "Your Grace," she murmured. She could not bring herself to look at him, it was as if something physically stopped her from doing so. She wanted to, oh, how she wanted to. She yearned for that first full look at him, but instead she inclined her head in greeting before focusing on Countess Godwin.

"A pleasure to see you again. We missed talking with you at your ball, did you not have an attack of the vapours?" Countess Godwin spoke in measured tones, ones that had Elodie frowning.

"I *was* taken unwell," Elodie conceded, "but I am much improved, and I am looking forward to your ball tomorrow, Lord Huntingford."

She sensed the Duke of Mistbourne looking at her, but still, she could not turn her to neck to look back. A weakness was working its way down her back; she hoped she would not embarrass herself again and faint.

"And we will be delighted to have you there," Lord Huntingford replied gallantly.

"Shall we walk?" Luisa asked.

The group fell into step, Luisa with Thomas, Countess Godwin with her brother, and Lord Bamford had apparently taken it upon himself to protect Luella from the duke. He took her arm, leaving Elodie alone. Worthing noticed and caught up with her. Elodie could barely concentrate on his chatter; she could sense Mistbourne mere steps behind her. If she turned, she would be in his arms.

She stumbled.

What was going on with her thoughts lately? What a scandalous thing to think.

"Careful," a deep voice said huskily behind her, and Elodie quivered. She *knew* that voice. Knew it like she knew her own. She turned, fully ready to look at him, but Worthing caught her arm and gestured to the pond.

"Come, Miss Di Silva, there is a lovely outlook from the water."

She allowed Worthing to draw her closer to the edge of the pond, where he pointed out the small island in the centre. "Did you know there is a folly there, mostly tumbledown now, but it makes a lovely place for a picnic. Perhaps we should all go one afternoon?" He looked around at the others as they joined him and Elodie.

"Splendid idea," Thomas said, earning an approving nod from Luisa.

Countess Godwin made a noncommittal noise and cast a look at her brother. He in turn rose an eyebrow at Mistbourne, who stood back from the group. Elodie took a deep breath and looked at the duke's shoulder, before working her way up, noting his thick black hair curling against his black jacket. She knew it would be feather-soft to the touch. With her head swooping in dizzying waves, she prepared herself to look at his face, but she somehow knew it would be strong, with tanned skin and sharp cheekbones as if hewn from stone itself. She caught a glimpse of one piercing green eye, before the countess stepped in front of her, blocking her from catching a full look.

It was if the moon had been eclipsed, Elodie thought desolately. Countess Godwin moved but the Duke of Mistbourne was already walking towards his carriage without a backwards glance. His back ramrod straight.

"That went well, I thought," Angelina said helping herself to a glass of madeira.

"Well, as in, she didn't even look at me," Raphael growled. "Thanks to you."

"I panicked – I could not allow the risk. One glimpse was more than enough, this time," Angelina said.

"At least she didn't run screaming," Hunt observed with a wolfish grin. He sat, brandy glass in hand, booted feet up on the arm of the sofa.

"Do you mind, Hunt, that is an antique."

"So are you," Hunt replied, and ducked when Angelina tossed a tasselled cushion at his head.

"Throw another at him from me please, Lina," Raphael said and downed his brandy. He looked at the glass, then at Hunt. Better not, the cushion would do, he decided.

"Easy there, cousin." Hunt removed his feet and sat up, concern swimming in his eyes as Raphael poured another glass.

"Why? What does it matter if I drink myself into a stupor? It won't change anything. We are still no closer to ending this torment."

"Rafe," Angelina said and shot a helpless look at her brother. Hunt just shrugged.

"What, Lina?" Raphael set down the glass, pushed away from the sideboard and walked towards the door. "I'm going out."

"Let him go," Hunt said watching his cousin stalk out the door. "Better he take his frustrations out on some unsuspecting fool at Gentleman Jackson's than to drink us out of brandy."

Angelina threw her hands up. "Is that all you are worried about?" On a huff of frustration, she marched to the door, before whirling back, grabbing another cushion and launching it across the room. She gave a satisfied laugh, as it hit her brother's hand, splashing brandy all over his favourite cravat.

An exasperated, "Lina!" followed her out of the room.

She caught up with Raphael at the front door. "We will find a way out of this, I promise. She just has to get to know you. She will remember and she will stay. It *is* different this time, I feel it."

Raphael stopped, and fisted a hand against the door. "But it's like you said, can we really take that risk?"

With his mood dark, and his heart heavy, Raphael strode out into the grey afternoon, ready to fight his way into oblivion.

Twelve

"A gift from Lady Darlington." Hannah dropped the long wide box on Elodie's bed.

Elodie smiled. "She is too kind." With Hannah's help she lifted the lid off the box, and pushed back the protective tissue paper.

"Oh, Miss," Hannah breathed. Together they pulled out the dark silver brocade gown, and matching lace eye mask.

"I could never wear that," Elodie said, taking in the heart-shaped bust and full draping skirt. Its sleeves were long and ended in floaty silver and black lace cuffs.

"Oh, but it is a masquerade ball, Miss. Everyone will be wearing similar attire. Besides, no one will know it is you, your face will be half-covered, and we can powder your hair if it would make you feel more comfortable," Hannah explained earnestly.

Elodie relented. "Very well. It will probably be my one and only time when I am able to attend such a ball."

Understanding flared in Hannah's eyes, before she clapped her hands together in delight. "I shall be back after dinner to help you dress."

Elodie nodded distractedly, and followed the maid out of her room. She made her way to the dining room, and smiled in greeting at Lady Beaumont and Luella.

"I really do not know if I am entirely comfortable about you girls attending this ball tonight," Lady Beaumont started, and Luella rolled her eyes.

"Really, Mama. You said the same thing at dinner yesterday. We shall be well-chaperoned with Luisa and Thomas, and Countess Godwin is co-hosting. She is the height of decorum."

"But your brother..." A flash of concern crossed the older lady's face.

"Isn't here, Mama. Do not vex yourself. I will keep an eye on Elodie." Luella picked up her drink and took a sip as if the matter was closed.

As Lady Beaumont muttered under her breath, but proceeded to eat her dinner, and spoke no more about it, Luella gave Elodie a satisfied smile and raised her glass in her direction.

Elodie inclined her head, acknowledging the other young lady's victory, but one small part of her wished that Lady Beaumont had been firmer in voicing her concerns. Elodie had heard whispers of what went on at such balls... where under the mask on anonymity morals were forgotten and inhibitions abandoned. She vowed to stay close to Luisa at least, she could not trust Luella to stand by her word, not when handsome eligible bachelors would be dressed rakishly and perhaps behave more freer than at a standard Society ball.

Picking at her fish and vegetables, Elodie watched the clock. Were the hands moving faster than normal? she mused. Of course not, it was simply nerves pooling in her stomach making her awareness heightened.

"There, perfect." Angelina adjusted Raphael's mask, the one half was completely solid, while the right eye could be seen through. "The lights will be dim, with plenty of shadowy alcoves. The perfect setting for you and Elodie to converse without any fear of-"

"Fleeing, death, destruction," Hunt supplied helpfully.

Angelina gave a long-suffering sigh. She tossed a gold mask at her brother. "Here, put that on." She lowered her voice. "Preferably over your mouth."

Raphael regarded himself in the mirror. He wore a long many-buttoned black damask jacket. Black lace peeped out from the bottom of the sleeves, while tight black breeches were tucked into matte black knee-length boots.

"You do make a dashing pirate lord, cous," Hunt remarked, placing his own mask over his eyes and adjusting the gold and cream jacket he wore.

"Yes, yes, we all look splendid," Angelina said. She smoothed down her long full bronze gown.

"Why are you so on edge?" Hunt asked her as he

watched her begin to pace.

"Because, everything is so uncertain, and I hate the not knowing." She pressed a delicate slim-fingered hand to her stomach.

Hunt did not like seeing his sister so rattled. He pressed a glass of wine into her hands. "We have been through this multiple times before; you just have to have faith that this time it will be different."

Angelina gripped the wine glass. "Well, now that is the most sensible thing I have heard you say in... well... ever," she said and took a huge gulp of the red liquid.

"I am not just a handsome face," Hunt replied, and met Raphael's eyes in the mirror.

Raphael toasted him with his own glass. "Shall we go? Carriages are arriving."

"I hear the ballroom is simply divine," Luisa said, as she clasped Thomas' hand.

Elodie, who sat next to Luella and opposite Luisa, gave her a smile. The lace mask itched, and she was thankful she decided to forgo the powder in her hair, she could only imagine the torment her scalp would be going through at that moment.

Luella fanned herself with a white lace fan. "I really do not know why you could not gift me an exquisite gown too, Luisa. I am, after all, your sister."

Luisa's eyes twinkled. "It was a coming-out gift for Elodie. I knew you would already have plenty of gowns to choose from. You have spent more time at the modiste's since you have been back from Scotland, than I have in a month!"

"And you are there plenty, my dear," Thomas said, his lips twitching.

Luisa tapped him on the arm with her own fan. As their eyes caught and held, Elodie sighed. Love really was all that mattered.

She shook herself out of her melancholy and turned to the window to watch the duke's townhouse come into view. From what Luisa had told her, Lord Huntingford, the countess, and the Duke of Mistbourne all resided there while they were in town. It had imposing white marble pillars either side of the double-fronted black door. The front walkway was a-throng with members of the ton all dressed in their finery and elaborate masks, while the street filled with carriages.

Luella leant forward in excitement to peer over Elodie's shoulder. "Oh, it is going to be a crush." But she didn't sound disappointed.

"Ladies, stay close to me, until we get the lay of the land," Thomas warned. "Some gentlemen think this type of ball gives them leave to be less gentlemanly than they should."

Elodie felt Luella's eye roll, but her own stomach clenched. Her second ball would test her mettle for Society for certain.

"I am certain Hunt will not allow anything unseemly, Thomas. He is a most proper gentleman," Luisa said with a frown.

"It isn't him or Mistbourne I am worried about,"

Thomas said. "Oh, here we go, after me, ladies." The carriage stopped and the door opened.

Thomas stepped down and assisted Luisa out, before taking Elodie's hand. She gripped the voluminous skirts in her other hand and stepped onto the pavement. While Thomas helped Luella out, Elodie tilted her head up to the sky. The evening was clear with a few twinkling stars peppering the sky. The moon hung in a glowing crescent and Elodie smiled. It was a beautiful sight.

"Elodie, why are you gazing at the heavens, when we have so much diversion here?" Luella joked, slipping her arm through Elodie's.

Surprised at the other lady's warmness towards her, Elodie allowed her to draw her up the path behind Luisa and Thomas.

"Now, do not claim all the best bachelors for yourself, Elodie, dear, save some for the rest of us." Though Luella tittered, there was a desperate edge to it, and Elodie looked at her fully. Perhaps Luella's haughtiness was just a mask. Perhaps, she too looked for love, but upon not finding it was now resigned to settle. Elodie hoped she did not settle.

Patting the other lady's hand, Elodie smiled. "You will have no shortage of admirers, Luella. You look particularly beautiful tonight."

Luella startled, then gave a genuine smile. She looked down at her gold gown. "Thank you, as do you."

Feeling a small thaw between them, Elodie felt calmer as they entered the townhouse. They waited in

119

the marble-tiled entrance hall, while the squeeze of guests moved through to the ballroom. Finally, with Thomas guiding them, they were admitted into the low-lit ballroom.

Two massive chandeliers hung from the domed roof of the ballroom, while gauzy fabrics and bead-drop garlands were strung from the walls and ceiling. Lacy screens had been placed along the border of the ballroom, allowing for some secluded areas. A string quartet sat on a podium at the far end of the room next to the open double terrace doors. Fancily dressed masked guests clustered together conversing or laughing over cups of wine.

Luisa and Thomas ushered Luella and Elodie over to a set of tall-backed black velvet chairs. "I will go and get us some drinks," Thomas said with a bow.

Elodie, too on edge to sit, took out her fan and slowly wafted it over her heated skin. It was already warm, and if more guests arrived it would soon be stifling. While Luella and Luisa tried to guess which members of the ton they thought were beneath the masks, Elodie trailed her gaze over the crowd. She knew exactly who she was looking for, and every instinct told her that mask, or no mask, she would recognise him when she saw him.

Her nerve-endings thrummed as her eyes landed on a tall dark-haired man framed in the terrace doors. Even in the low light, she knew him. She *knew* him. Her cheeks flushed as he looked in her direction. Drawn to her, as she was him? Instinctively, she began to move towards him. A hand on her arm stopped her.

"Wine, Miss Di Silva?" Thomas offered her a small crystal cup.

She took it with a distracted smile. Raising the cool liquid to her lips, she turned back to the direction of the terrace doors, but the duke had gone. Her heart sank. Would she ever get a chance to speak with him, to look fully upon him?

Suddenly he was standing before her. "Miss Di Silva, may I have this dance?"

She rose her gaze, her breath stopping in her chest, as she took in his mostly covered face. Only one bright green eye gleamed through the black mask. He looked exactly as she had thought with tanned skin, and what she could see of sharp cheekbones and angular chin.

He held out a large, sun-kissed hand, and without thought or pause, she instantly settled her small, gloved hand into it. Immediately, her skin heated beneath the glove and something inside her said. *There*. There you are. Did his hand flex beneath hers?

She passed her glass to a wide-eyed Luisa, before the Duke of Mistbourne was leading her into the centre of the ballroom. As the string quartet started a slow haunting tune, other couples took to the floor around them. Elodie stepped and twirled, with hands brushing and gazes lingering, causing her to feel as if she were in a dream.

The duke stepped up close as others spun around them. "Are you enjoying yourself?" he asked in his husky deep voice.

"So much," she replied. And she was, truly she was. Now she had seen him properly everything felt right with the world. But she needed to know. "I saw you outside Madame La Coeur's and again outside the Darlingtons."

He tensed, but then nodded. "Yes. I wanted to speak with you, but as we had not been introduced, it would have been improper."

The smooth explanation made sense, but still somehow she thought there was more to it. So much more.

"But now we have," Elodie said simply, and Mistbourne smiled then, and Elodie's heart stuttered.

The music stopped and the duke bowed over her hand. Elodie felt desolate. She wanted the dance to never end. "I shall return you to your friends," he said. "But perhaps, a second dance?"

Elodie swallowed. *Two* dances? Was that permitted? "I would be honoured," she said.

He deposited her back with Luisa and Thomas. Luella, herself, was just being guided from the dance floor by Worthing if Elodie was not mistaking the copper hair.

"Ah, Mistbourne, fabulous ball. The countess has outdone herself," Thomas said enthusiastically.

"Darlington," the duke acknowledged. "Speaking of which, I must go and find her. Please excuse me."

With a final glance at Elodie, and a bow to them all, he melted away and was swallowed by the cluster of guests.

Thirteen

"It worked!" Angelina clapped her hands together, relief clear across her beautiful face. "Watching you two dance was like poetry. I could have wept."

Raphael downed his brandy with a shaking hand. "She is..."

"Yes?" Angelina prompted, a rapturous expression across her face. She clenched the door frame of the study.

Raphael could not form the words. How could he form the words? Because she was absolutely everything. And if she was everything, then he had so much to lose.

He looked up, and Angelina simply said, "Oh, Rafe. I understand. Take a few moments here to steady yourself. Then go be with her, get to know her again. Let her know *you*." She swept over to him to take his face in her hands. "Let her love you, for in loving you, you both have a chance at changing it this time."

Raphael took a shuddering breath. "Thank you,

Lina."

Angelina smiled with tears shimmering in her bright blue eyes. "Do not tarry too long, you have this night to be with her." She let go of him and left the room.

Raphael stared into the bottom of his glass, perhaps he hoped to see the future in there. But, although what awaited them was still so uncertain, he was determined to make this chance count.

He set the glass down and pushing down his churning emotions, he headed out into the hallway.

"Elodie, are you well? You appear quite flushed." Luisa pulled Elodie behind one of the lace privacy screens.

Elodie did not know what she felt. Elated and bereft all at once. "Oh, just heated slightly from the exertion of the dance," she said not meeting her friend's eyes.

"Hmm," was all Luisa said.

"Well, if it isn't Lu and Lo, what are you two up to hiding behind there?"

Luisa groaned and turned to meet the heavily rouged lady in an over-the-top black and red gown. Ribbons and bows covered every available surface, while her red lace mask did little to cover her face. Perhaps, she did not care about hiding her identity. "Mariska," Luisa acknowledged, and Elodie wondered how the other lady had figured out who they were so easily.

"No one has hair like yours, Miss Di Silva, so I knew instantly it was you. And wherever you are, little Luisa is not far behind," Mariska Murrow drawled.

Elodie saw the hurt in her friend's eyes, and overlooked the pointed insult at her own appearance. Black hair wasn't *de rigueur*, but Elodie loved her hair, so like her mother's. Luisa was indeed petite, but not overly so. "Miss Murrow," Elodie said not bothering to hide the curt tone.

"Tell me, that *was* the Duke of Mistbourne I saw you dancing with?" While her tone was light, Elodie saw the interest sparking in the taller lady's eyes. Her shiny brown ringleted hair bounced around her oval face as she tilted her head.

Elodie saw a chance for mischief of her own. She leaned in close. "I truly have no notion. It is scandalous, is it not, to not know with whom you are dancing with."

Luisa let out a snort, quickly turned into a cough.

Mariska narrowed her eyes. "Yes, Miss Di Silva, *most* scandalous. Perhaps you should have a care, after all you are yet new out. You cannot afford to be shunned for making an... indiscretion." Mariska waved her fan at them and turned to vanish into the crowd.

Luisa rolled her eyes. "I really dislike that creature. Imagine, she could have had her claws into dear Thomas, before I met him. But seriously, Elodie, perhaps it is not wise to provoke her. She is prone to spreading vicious rumours."

"Do not worry about me, Lu-"

"Who is spreading vicious rumours?" Luella asked, joining them. Breathlessly, she fanned herself. She looked between the two.

"No one of consequence, and anyway, no rumours have been spread yet. We were just speculating about Mariska Murrow and her penchant for gossip," Luisa said dismissively, no doubt wanting to shoo the other lady from her mind and the conversation.

"Oh, well, I heard..." Elodie filtered out Luella as she leaned in close to her sister. She walked out from behind the screen, hoping to find a spot where the air was cooler.

"Are you enjoying yourself, Miss Di Silva?" Thomas asked as he spotted her. He stood to one side with Worthing and two other masked gentlemen.

"Thank you, Lord Darlington, I am, although, a trifle overheated."

"Then allow me to escort you to one of the retiring rooms, a dash of water on one's wrists is just the thing," Thomas said with a bow. He disappeared around the screen, no doubt telling Luisa where he was going.

He reappeared, and held out his arm. Elodie took it with a smile. Luisa and Thomas were so lucky to have found each other. Their complimentary personalities made them perfect for one other. Elodie could clearly imagine the adorable cherubic children they would create together.

"Here we are," Thomas said, stopping outside a

polished black door.

"Thank you," Elodie said gratefully, and entered the room.

Thankfully, it was empty and Elodie could take her time, dabbing her wrists and the back of her neck with the rose-scented water in the bowls. She caught her reflection in the mirror; the lace mask shadowed her face, while her elaborate coiffure of tumbled black curls made her look like something from a renaissance portrait.

Feeling ready to re-join the ball – she did not want to miss her second dance with Duke Mistbourne after all – she exited the room, and stopped short when she saw the corridor before her stood empty. *Where had Lord Darlington gotten to*? Surely, he would not leave her unattended.

She hovered in the hallway, unsure of what to do next. Should she wait and see if he returned, or should she try and make her own way back? Which corridor had they even taken? She looked blankly at the two set before her. She could hear the strains of music in the distance and decided it was coming from the left-hand one.

She set off along the darkened hallway. Furtive sounds coming from further along in front of her had her pausing. A giggle, abruptly silenced, had her turning back. She did not want to stumble upon two lovers in the dark. Footsteps behind her, had her hastening her own.

"Wait, little beauty, I have plenty to share." The teasing, mocking voice had Elodie's heart hammering in her chest.

She rounded the corner and bumped into something, both hard and welcoming. A pair of strong arms righted her. She closed her eyes as she inhaled the scent, so familiar to the heady scent of the black feathers – was that why she was so drawn to *him*?

"Trenton. Terrorising my guests are we?" Mistbourne spoke with barely restrained anger.

"No harm intended. I simply thought the young lady was looking for a bit of sport-" Trenton's words were cut off abruptly as the duke let go of Elodie and shot out one hand, gripping him by his cravat.

"Time to leave, Trenton."

"I say, steady on my good man. I apologise. I was mistaken."

"Yes. You were. Now go." Mistbourne let him go with a shove.

Elodie kept her eyes lowered as the other man backed away and disappeared out of sight.

"Are you hurt?" the duke asked, his tone gentle.

"N-no, I'm fine. I just lost my way," Elodie said, her breath hitching in her throat, extremely well aware she stood alone in a darkened hallway with an exceptionally handsome man. But unlike the times with Lord Beaumont, she felt safer than she had ever felt. "Is there somewhere I can gather myself for a moment?"

"Come with me," Mistbourne said, and Elodie willingly followed him.

He opened a door further along the corridor and

allowed her to precede him in. She smiled as she saw she was in a large candlelit library; the floor to ceiling walnut shelves were filled with slim books and chunky tomes. "You will be comfortable in here," the duke said, hovering on the threshold. "Shall I get one of your friends for you?"

"Would you stay a moment?" Elodie was shocked as the bold plea slipped from her lips.

"As you wish," Mistbourne said, and entered the room leaving the door open slightly. Elodie thought his eye flared for one moment and the thought thrilled her.

"Is this yours?" Elodie asked sweeping a hand at the shelves.

"My cousin, Hunt, it is actually his house, but he opens it to Angelina and me when we are in town. I much prefer the country."

"Oh yes, as do I," Elodie said warmly. Without her even noticing he had moved closer to her, his eye roving over her face. "You hail from Cornwall?"

Something indistinguishable flickered over the duke's face in the candlelight, before he gave a slow nod. "I do."

"Then you have heard of Angelhaven?" Elodie enquired, longing to speak with someone of her beloved home.

Mistbourne's throat worked a few times. "I have indeed."

Elodie felt her spirits lift, before they plummeted when a pang of homesickness so painful almost stole her breath and doubled her over. "I miss it so much," she whispered, turning away to blink back tears.

"El – Miss Di Silva," the duke quickly covered his mistake. "How can I help you?" He gestured to a seat, and she sank into the plush armchair with a sigh.

"I know not," she said despondently. "There is nothing anyone can do really. Grief is as powerful as love." She bit her lip as the declaration crept out.

"Love... love is just *delayed* grief," Mistbourne said with feeling, pouring two glasses from a decanter on a side table. He turned and pain rippled across his visible features.

The air between them became electrified. Elodie stood to accept the glass as he towered over her. His fingers brushed hers, and as the tingle shot up her arm, she wondered who he had loved and lost to warrant such a statement. But she understood. To love, and love wholly, was to give yourself over to the possibility – nay, the certainty – that all things must come to an end, and there would always be someone left behind to grieve what was lost.

"But grief is the gift of that love," Elodie said, feeling as if she were in a dream. "To grieve is to remember, and if we remember, then those we love are never truly gone. They live on in here-" she pressed a gentle hand to his temple "-and in here." She settled her hand over his heart, feeling the thunderous beat beneath her gloved fingertips.

Mistbourne released a long sigh, and closed his eye. His free hand snaked up to rest over her hand, and Elodie's lashes lowered. They stood in that suspended moment for what felt like an eternity. A

131

delicious never-ending moment of eternity.

"Ah, cous, you had better return her, before some gossipmongering fool gets suspicious."

Lord Huntingford's voice had both Elodie's and the duke's eyes shooting open.

Elodie's lips parted. Mistbourne dropped his hand and stepped back, while Elodie's hand hovered in the air for a moment. "Forgive me," he said.

Elodie lowered her hand. Heat worked its way across her cheeks. She could not believe she had not been aware enough of what was happening around her. It was lucky it was the duke's cousin who had found them in such close quarters.

"Would you like me to escort her back?"

The duke looked up, and gaze on Elodie, said "No. I will make sure she is safe." He gestured to the door and Elodie set her glass down, and walked in front of him, wishing she could have had longer alone with him. But no matter how long they'd had, she had a feeling it would never be long enough.

As she passed Lord Huntingford, he gave her an unreadable look. She inclined her head and kept going.

Fourteen

Out in the hallway, Thomas came running up to Elodie. "Oh, Miss Di Silva – do forgive me! I have been out of my mind with worry. I only left for mere minutes - Miss Murrow almost fainted out in the hall, and I had to take her somewhere to recover. Luisa is most vexed with me for leaving you, but I couldn't very well leave Miss Murrow unattended in the hallway, not when there are opportunistic rakes about." As Thomas's rambling came to a stop, he saw who followed her out of the library. His eyes flicked from his friend to Elodie and back again. "Mistbourne." His tone took on one of stern concern. "Are you well, Miss Di Silva?"

"I am fine, thank you. The Duke of Mistbourne has been the perfect gentleman. I lost my way; he is just taking me back to the ball." Elodie injected reassurance into her tone. She knew her friend's husband would not have left her voluntarily. Being the epitome of propriety, he, of course, thought to help a lady in distress. Even if it *was* Mariska

Murrow. Elodie wondered what Luisa would think about that. No doubt her friend would tell her all about it.

"I will leave you in Darlington's hands," Mistbourne said, but his tone held a warning note. "Let us hope he will not abandon you again." With a curt bow, he turned and re-entered the library, this time completely closing the door.

"Oh dear, I seem to have earned the disrespect of Mistbourne. I do apologise, Miss Di Silva." Lord Darlington frowned at the door.

Elodie laid a hand on his sleeve. "I am sure it will blow over. He seems like a reasonable gentleman."

Hunt, on the other side of the door, gave a grimace. "Reasonable? Not where you are concerned, Miss Di Silva," he said, more to himself, moving away from the door and pouring himself a drink. "That Mariska Murrow is a sly chit," he directed at Raphael.

"Mmm?" Raphael said distractedly.

"I said the Murrow chit, she is a sly one. I wouldn't put it past her to have created that little diversion to leave Miss Di Silva unattended." Hunt tossed back his drink.

Raphael's green eye sharpened on his cousin. "She does not know what she is meddling in... if word gets back to Beaumont."

"Calm yourself, Rafe. No harm was done."

"This time," Raphael ground out. "I am going back to the ball. It appears I need to keep her in my sights."

Hunt did not need to ask which lady he meant.

134

The gleam in his cousin's eye said everything.

"Elodie! My word, Thomas, I am most vexed at you! This is only Elodie's second ball, and she has been left unchaperoned." Luisa swatted Thomas' arm, none to gently, with her fan.

"Luisa, my dear. She was perfectly safe. Mistbourne came to her aid."

Luisa and Luella both stared at Elodie's flushed cheeks.

"Is that so?" Luella asked, a shrewd look behind her mask.

"He was just about to escort me back to the ball when Lord Darlington arrived. I somehow got lost," Elodie said with a small laugh. She would not dare mention her near miss with Trenton. She would be whisked away from the ball faster than a waltzing miss. Thinking of waltzes, she hoped the duke would reappear and take her to the floor again, and with any luck it would be a waltz, this time. She longed to feel his fingers at her waist. She shook her head, her blush increasing. *Really, Elodie*, she chastised herself.

As if summoned, he appeared beside Luella. A silence fell over the group until Luella gave a pointed cough.

"Dance, my dear?" Lord Darlington asked his wife.

"Oh, but I couldn't possible leave Elodie," Luisa

replied.

"I am sure she will be in safe hands," Thomas said with a nod at the duke.

"And I?" Luella pouted.

Lord Huntingford joined Mistbourne. "May I have this dance?" he asked Luella.

Blushing prettily, Luella forgot her protests and took the blonde man's outstretched hand.

Luisa looked at Elodie staring at Mistbourne and gave a delicate shrug, took her husband's hand, and drifted onto the dancefloor.

"Shall we?" the duke asked and Elodie took his hand without hesitation. Just as she wished, the opening strains of the waltz began.

Everything faded around them, as the duke slipped a hand around Elodie's back, his fingers lightly resting above her waist. For one yearning moment, she wished he would trail his hand higher, the spot between her shoulder blades tingled, almost crying out to be caressed by his fingertips. Her breath stuttered as she took his hand and rested her other upon his broad shoulder.

They moved as one, completely in synchronisation, anticipating each other's moves, so they skimmed seamlessly over the floor as if flying. A sigh escaped Elodie's lips, and Duke Mistbourne's green gaze dropped to her lips.

"I do not know your name," Elodie blurted. Pain lanced through his visible eye. No, that wasn't right, she *did* know his name. She knew it as surely as she knew her own. "*Raphael*," she whispered, drawing it out slowly, testing it on her tongue, embracing it.

He pulled her tighter to him as if he could absorb her very soul, and a sigh of his own escaped his full lips. "Yes... Elodie." *Elodriel.* The longer name whispered into her mind, and she swayed unsteadily. That name felt truer than her own.

They turned together completely unaware of anyone else around them, too caught up in the world they had created, a world where they had an eternity stretched out before them. Their clasped hands above their heads lowered, and Elodie hated the mere seconds that blocked her view of his face. She could never get enough, she craved it. Her fingers itched to remove his mask, to look fully in his eyes. She *needed* to see them both.

As if hypnotised, she raised her hand, brushing her fingers against his mask. The duke stiffened.

"No!" he said, letting her go so suddenly she almost lost her balance.

In confusion, the spell broken, Elodie watched him swivel on his heel and stride from the dancefloor, leaving her among the sea of dancers. She hoped no one had seen.

The music changed and partners either left the dancefloor or changed hands.

Elodie quickly hurried from the dancefloor, not caring where she was going. Picking up her skirts, she stumbled around the edge until she felt a cool breeze on her cheeks. She aimed for the terrace doors, and did not care that she would be out there alone, she only wanted to cool the shame burning in her cheeks.

What had she been thinking? She had been about to take his mask off. He obviously wore a patch for a reason, she had no right to humiliate him that way.

Staggering out onto the terrace, Elodie clutched the wall running along it, overlooking the vast gardens. She sucked in breath after breath, but it was not enough.

"Here," a feminine voice said, and offered her a glass. "It is only lemonade," the lady continued when Elodie hesitated.

Elodie took the glass with a trembling hand and turned to look at her rescuer. The light filtering out from the ballroom, illuminated the lady's blond curls like a halo. "Countess Godwin."

"Angelina, *please*. Whenever anyone calls me Countess Godwin, all I can think of is my late husband's mother." She gave a delicate shudder, her eyes derisive behind her subtle copper lace mask.

"I am sorry for your loss," Elodie said and took a sip of the refreshing lemonade.

"Oh, don't be. He turned out to be an awful man."

Elodie paused. "Then I am sorry for that," she said simply.

Angelina smiled a tight smile at her. "Unfortunately, the ton is absolutely littered with awful men." Lord Beaumont's warning came back to haunt Elodie, when she had spoken of Worthing being harmless. Awful men, men who could be pushed to awful limits? "But sometimes, they are a means to an end..." the older lady trailed off, her tone musing.

"Surely there are some good men?" Elodie truly believed there were, she knew of some.

"Oh, my dear, pay the ramblings of a cynical widow, no mind. Of course, there are. My brother and cousin are the best of men," Angelina said.

At the mention of Angelina's cousin, Elodie winced.

Astutely, Angelina noticed. "What is the matter?"

Elodie swallowed, setting the glass down on the wall. While giggling voices filtered up to them from the gardens, Elodie lowered her eyes. "I am afraid I almost removed your cousin's mask... I – I do not even know why," she confessed.

At Angelina's intake of breath and muttered, "Silly girl," Elodie's eyes filled with tears. Had she completely ruined everything? She had finally found someone she felt comfortable around and now, now, perhaps he would not want to see her again.

"I am truly sorry," Elodie said.

Angelina's eyes softened behind her mask. "It is not your fault. None of this tragic occurrence is." She swept away from Elodie to pace up and down the terrace, her long bronze gown trailing along the floor. "I apologise for snapping at you."

"No, I deserved it and more," Elodie said.

Angelina stopped pacing, her expression earnest. "No, my dear, you deserve to be happy, and to be loved. As does Raphael."

Elodie's heart gave a sudden thump in her chest. Could they find both... *together*?

"Come along, I will see you safely back inside.

139

The gardens are a den of debauchery tonight," Angelina said, casting a disdainful look over Elodie's shoulder.

Elodie flushed, finally appreciating how reckless she had been, especially since she had almost found out earlier what really goes on in the shady alcoves of a masquerade ball.

Angelina linked arms with Elodie and walked her back to the doors. "Do not worry about Raphael, I will speak to him. He has a tendency to be over-emotional – with good reason you understand. No, of course you do not." Angelina shook her head, and patted Elodie's arm. "Never mind, I have a good feeling this time."

Slightly befuddled by Angelina's cryptic words, Elodie allowed her to walk her back to the Darlingtons. "Here she is. I am afraid, after her dance, I drew our lovely Miss Di Silva aside for a little tete-a-tete without thought to tell you." Angelina let out a tinkling laugh. "I simply wanted to get to know her better."

Luisa's face cleared, and Elodie hoped Thomas had not gotten the blame again. "Oh, that is quite all right, Lina. I long for you and Elodie to be as close friends as you and I are."

Angelina pressed her cheek to Luisa's. "Indeed. I long for that too." She inclined her head at Thomas and waved at Elodie before she moved away.

"Is she not the sweetest?" Luisa said, clutching Elodie's hand. "To be friends with *the* Countess Godwin is to have all the doors of Society opened to

140

you. But not just only that, she is lovely company to be around."

"I like her," Elodie agreed. "She is very pleasing."

"Capital, we shall make a lively group indeed. Hunt mentioned he and Angelina are amenable to joining us all on our picnic to the folly tomorrow," Thomas said. He cast a beseeching look at his wife.

Her eyes sparkled and she pressed close to his side. "Then I will look forward to it even more."

Thomas' grin of relief told Elodie he knew he had been forgiven for not keeping a better eye on her. She lowered her gaze, uncomfortable at the moon eyes they were now throwing at each other. She wondered if not for her, would they, too, be seeking a darkened alcove or a shady bush.

Scandalised by her thoughts, Elodie watched the dancing couples, hoping Angelina would indeed speak to Raphael and convince him to attend the picnic tomorrow. She must put things right between them, before Lord Beaumont returned and spoiled everything.

"Stop being so bull-headed, Rafe. The girl had no control over it any more than she does this whole travesty." Angelina stopped before Raphael, hands fisted on her hips.

"Then what is to stop her from trying again? What if she succeeds next time?" Raphael shot back.

Hunt, from his position reclining on the sofa, watched them lazily. "He does have a point, sis," he

141

said.

Without looking at him, Angelina snapped, "Get. Your. Feet. Off."

"You are no fun anymore. I much prefer you back home." Hunt sulked, but he did remove his booted feet from the arm of the sofa.

"You and me both, dear brother, you and me both." Angelina wilted, sinking into an armchair.

"You really think I should go tomorrow?"

Angelina said, "Yes," at the same times as Hunt's, "No."

Raphael looked from one sibling to the other. "You two are no help to me at all." He scowled.

"Rafe, please come. It will be fine. She will not try again; she was so upset. She will just think she was caught up in the moment. But due to her proper upbringing she will fight against any further urges, I am sure of it. The last thing she wants to do is hurt you," Angelina said, her eyes earnest.

"She may not *want* to hurt me, but there are things far beyond both of our control, and I fear we are being manoeuvred into place." Raphael turned from them both to gaze broodingly out of the study window. "Besides, ultimately, it is *she* who will be hurt."

Fifteen

Elodie could not concentrate. She fidgeted with the tassel on her reticule as the carriage pulled into the park.

"Elodie, please do stop that. I have the headache and your *swish-swish-swishing* with that tassel is making it worse," Luella groaned, one white-lace-gloved hand to her brow.

Elodie immediately stopped.

"Well, perhaps you should not have indulged last night, sister dear. I declare you did not sit down for more than five minutes all night," Luisa said with a twinkle in her eye.

Luella withdrew her hand and sat up straighter. "I was taking full advantage of my first masquerade ball; heaven knows if I will be permitted to attend another." She nibbled on her lower lip. "I do hope Lucan won't be too cross."

Elodie could not help the shiver that ran up her spine. She wished the same. It was pointless now to hope that he would not find out. People had recognised her and were prone to gossip. The truth of their attendance would certainly reach Lord Beaumont's ears. She had defied him. But it had been worth it, to get to know Duke Mistbourne. She prayed he would be at the picnic, that was why she was so on edge. She longed to see him and put right her faux pas from the night before.

"I will speak with your brother," Thomas spoke up. "You were all perfectly safe."

Elodie stared at her friend's pleasant husband. Did he really think he would be able to soothe Lord Beaumont's anger? To her, at least, it was terrifying. But perhaps, he would return home in a better mood.

Elodie put all thoughts of Lord Beaumont from her mind. She did not want his dark shadow to spoil the day, and it promised to be a lovely day for the picnic. The sun shone brightly, and a gentle breeze kept the air fresh.

The carriage stopped and Lord Darlington helped the three ladies out. The footman removed the straw picnic basket and blankets.

A barouche, and a cream-coloured carriage pulled up behind them, and Worthing hopped out of the barouche, followed by Lord Bamford... escorting Mariska Murrow, and her maid. Bamford had obviously decided to put aside his apathy of the duke for now and join the picnic party.

Luisa did not bother to hide her groan at seeing Mariska, but luckily the brown-haired lady was too far away to hear. "Why has he brought her? I thought he was pursuing you, Luella?"

"I do not know. At first I thought he was interested in Elodie." Luella shot Elodie a look. "Then he was so attentive to me, but at the ball, he only had eyes for Mariska," she finished in disgust, but her eyes lit up as the occupants of the second carriage emerged. "But do not worry about me, sister dear, I will have plenty of admirers today." She gave a satisfied smile as Lord Huntingford, Angelina... and Raphael walked towards them.

Elodie's heart faltered, before speeding up to a rapid staccato. The greetings of the others faded away as Elodie searched Raphael's face. His patch firmly over his left eye, his right eye clashed with her gaze. She tried to convey a thousand lifetimes of apologies in her gaze. She hoped he would forgive her. His lips lifted at the corners, and she relaxed.

"Miss Di Silva, you can ride in our boat." Angelina walked forward to link arms with Elodie. "It is four to a boat, is it not?"

"Oh, but-" Luella started.

"Miss Beaumont, you can ride with Bamford, Miss Murrow and I," Worthing interrupted her, a genial smile on his face.

Luella pouted, then brightening, said, "Oh, but what about Miss Murrow's maid?"

"Henriette can stay in the carriage, I will not need a chaperone now we have Countess Godwin and Lady Darlington present," Mariska said, with an airy wave of her hand.

"Well, that is all settled then," Thomas said. "My lovely wife and I will take the picnic basket and the other things over in our boat."

The group walked down to the small pier where a line of row boats were tied. The footman stowed the basket and blankets into the first boat before heading back to the carriage. The Darlingtons settled into the boat and, with a giggle from Luisa, Thomas set off rowing towards the island a short distance away.

Luella, with a frown marring her pretty ice-queen features, was helped into the second boat with Mariska. Worthing and Bamford sat opposite them and with an oar each, set off after the Darlingtons.

The breeze dropped, and Elodie felt suddenly out of her depth as she stood with the statuesque siblings and brooding duke.

Lord Huntingford, dressed in a blue jacket, beige breeches and shiny black boots, stepped nimbly into the boat and held a hand out for Angelina. With her free hand, she clutched her lemon-yellow gown to lift the hem, as she stepped after him. Settling her lace parasol over her shoulder, she took a seat.

Elodie waited as Raphael boarded the boat. Her anticipation rose as she knew in moments he would be helping her aboard too. "Miss Di Silva," he said, holding out one tanned hand.

She placed her rose-coloured-gloved hand in his, and let out a small intake of breath as he pulled her towards him. She almost forgot to step over the edge of the boat, but at the last moment, she remembered and lifted her black half-boot over. The boat shifted precariously beneath her feet, but Raphael steadied her, before helping her to sit beside the countess.

Sitting opposite, his long legs brushed the skirt of her pink sprigged dress, and an immediate awareness came over her. Goosebumps rose up along her arms and she was thankful for her rose-coloured velvet Spencer jacket.

The men set off rowing, and Angelina leaned into Elodie with a smile. "I do hope you enjoyed yourself at our ball last night. It was lovely to see you there, Elodie – you do not mind if I call you Elodie, do you? It is such a beautiful name."

Elodie could not help but return the smile. "I do not mind, and yes, I had a lovely time," she said with a blush. Though she spoke to Angelina, she wished it was the duke she was giving her permission to. She knew it was not the done thing, but to hear her name upon his lips... she trembled as Raphael shifted, and the warmth of his skin filtered through the fabric of their clothes melding into her leg.

They docked and disembarked at the little jetty on the island and while the others chatted and organised carrying the basket and blankets, Elodie held back. Raphael looked at her with one arched black brow.

"Before we follow the others, I just wanted to apologise for my behaviour last night. I have no excuses, I cannot explain what happened, I-"

"Please, Miss Di Silva, do not trouble yourself. I understand, and I should be the one to apologise. I should never have left you alone on the dancefloor," Raphael broke in, and Elodie let out a smile.

"Perhaps we should both forgive each other and

put it behind us. Friends?" she said simply.

His green eye flashed and he paused, before holding out a hand to accept the one she offered. "Friends," he agreed.

The air between them hummed and a sudden wind whipped through the small copse of trees where they stood.

"Rafe!" Lord Huntingford called, and Raphael let go of her hand.

Elodie sighed and looked around. She had been so lost in the moment that she had forgotten where she was.

Raphael moved past her before turning to face her again. "My friends call me Raphael – or Rafe." He smiled.

Elodie smiled back, she had already been referring to him as that in her mind already. "And my friends called me Elodie – or Lo."

The breeze skimmed back, but this time whispering a name... *Elodriel*. Elodie put a hand up to her brow.

"I–"

"Yes?" Raphael said. "What did you hear?"

Elodie looked at him with wide eyes. Had he heard the name too? She believed she was somehow hearing things, that she had been overwrought with grieving and the state of affairs with Lord Beaumont. But if Raphael was hearing it too, then that meant...

"I heard a name."

Raphael took a deep shuddering breath. "And did you recognise this name?" He watched her closely.

Yes. She wanted to tell him that she knew it, she knew it like she had known his name. But would he think her crazy?

"You two really are trying my patience," Lord Huntingford said, rounding a tree. "I have Angelina prodding me in the back and giving me pointed looks, while she tries to distract the others from noticing your absence."

"I am sorry, Lord Huntingford," Elodie said.

He let out a huff. "Hunt," he said shortly. "Seeing how close friends we are all becoming," the words had a sarcastic snap, but his bright-blue-eyed wink softened the barb and Elodie let out a laugh.

Hunt held out his arm, and Elodie took it. "This way, Elodie dear," he said with a mischievous look at Raphael, who growled at his cousin's back, and walked Elodie towards the tumbledown folly.

Hunt deposited Elodie next to Luisa, who looked up distractedly from setting out the blankets in the grassy clearing in the centre of the folly. "Ah, Elodie, would you be a dear and help me. Luella and Mariska are embroiled in a battle of cloaked insults." Luisa rolled her eyes.

Elodie looked over to see Luella and Mariska facing one another, their haughty faces schooled into masks of overt politeness. Elodie was surprised, seeing how alike the young ladies were in temperament, that they were not actually friends.

With a shake of her head at the complexities of Society, Elodie helped rearrange the blankets so they would accommodate everybody. The men were busy opening the basket and rifling around inside.

A pop of a champagne cork had Elodie jumping.

"Oh, capital," Worthing said, as Bamford filled flutes and passed them around.

Mariska swanned over to accept a glass and lowered herself delicately to the blankets. Over the rim of her glass, she watched Elodie. "Did you enjoy yourself last night, Miss Di Silva? My cousin, Lord Trenton said he saw you in the hallway. Did you get lost? I hate to think you missed out on all the *pleasures* available."

Elodie flushed as she looked around to see if anyone else had heard the other lady's words. Thankfully, mostly everyone else appeared to be busy settling themselves down and setting out the food.

Angelina pulled Elodie down to sit next to her and Raphael, who looked disgusted at Mariska's attempted at sullying Elodie's reputation. "I am sure you would know all about the pleasures to be found, Miss Murrow. Hunt's gardens are particularly fine at night, are they not?" The countess sipped her own champagne, her bright blue eyes innocent as she regarded Mariska.

Hunt let out a snort, and Elodie looked up to see his eyes dancing at the exchange.

Two spots of colour high on Mariska's cheeks showed Angelina's words had hit their mark. She raised her glass at Angelina, before she tried a different tactic. "Is your brother back yet, Luisa? Surely, you are most bereft at his absence." Her eyes never left Elodie's face as she spoke.

Elodie tuned out Luisa's murmured answer and looked away from Mariska's smug countenance. She was curious to notice Hunt, Angelina and Raphael exchange a dark look. Whatever had they fallen out with Lord Beaumont over? It was most curious. But she knew one thing; Lord Beaumont would surely be to blame.

Raphael reclined back, propping himself up on his elbows. His position allowed Elodie to turn her head slightly and catch his eye. She had to forcibly remind herself to stop. She did not want to give Mariska any more weapons to use against her.

They spent the next hour conversing and nibbling on the meat pies, and fruit tartlets. Elodie allowed the conversation to wash around her. She enjoyed observing, and noted the lingering touches between Luisa and Thomas as they passed each other food, or the watchful gaze Bamford settled upon Luella when he thought she was not looking. Was he using Mariska to make her jealous? Luella, in turn, giggled slightly too brightly over something Worthing said, all the while fluttering her eyelashes in Hunt's direction. Every now and then Luella flicked a curious look her way, and then at Raphael. Did she suspect how Elodie felt about him?

Elodie sat up straighter. How she *felt* about him? Raphael opened his eye and looked over at her. Had he heard her heart speed up? They had indeed formed a close friendship so quickly, one that scared and enthralled Elodie in equal measure.

Did he feel it too?

151

Her lips parted, and she took a hasty gulp of champagne, turning her face so no one would see her suddenly flushed cheeks.

Sixteen

"Top up?" Angelina waved the champagne bottle in front of Elodie's face.

"Oh, no, thank you. I have had quite enough," Elodie said decidedly, setting the glass down on a tray placed in the centre of the ring of blankets.

"Who is up for an exploration of the folly?" Worthing stood up. "I have spent a lot of time here, so I offer myself as guide."

"I am too full to move," Mariska groaned, patting her slender figure. "I would beg off this time, Lord Worthing. Perhaps Lord Bamford could keep me company?"

Bamford inclined his head. "I would be honoured."

"Thomas and I will stay also; we have explored the folly many times." A becoming flush stained Luisa's cheeks.

"Explored the folly's alcoves, you mean," Luella said waspishly, leaning in so only her sister, and Elodie who was close, heard. Luisa's mouth dropped open, but Luella had turned her attention to scowling at Bamford and Mariska. Perhaps because Hunt had not even returned a look in her quarter, Luella had given up her pursuit of him, and she had decided Lord Bamford was more likely prey.

"I will stay too; I am not clambering around some old folly. I have had my fill of those," Angelina said, and poured herself another glass of champagne.

"Miss Di Silva?" Raphael asked, and she mourned the lack of her first name on his lips, but understood in polite society, he would act appropriately for her sake. He helped her stand and tucking her hand through his arm, led her behind Worthing, Hunt, and Luella, who had decided to go with them despite Bamford staying behind.

Worthing led them around the stone walls, pointing out places of interest. "Careful, here, there are some stairs that lead up to a spectacular view. They are sound, but, ladies do have a care, I would not want any mishaps."

Luella clutched tightly at Worthing and Elodie felt sympathy for his poor arm as he led the other lady up. Hunt sprang lightly up the steps after them.

"Hold tightly to me, Elodie," Raphael whispered, as they traversed the wide stone stairs.

"I will," she whispered back, savouring the sound of his husky voice saying her name.

The sounds from the others moved away, and it was just the two of them in an enclosed stairway of stone. A musty smell rose from the damp bricks, and a soft breeze whistled through the gaps. A loose stone had Elodie missing her step and she stumbled. Raphael caught her. He loomed over her as she leant back against the wall, trying to still her startled heart, staring up at him with lips parted and breath rapid.

"Raphael," she said the name like a prayer, understanding with a stunning clarity that what she felt for him wasn't simply friendship. It never was. It was a knowing, a belonging and something she could not yet define. Because if she defined it, she would have to accept that what she thought she had wanted paled in comparison because, *this*, this far surpassed that and it terrified her. Because, what if he did not feel the same?

Please feel the same, she thought.

As if in slow motion, pulled by some invisible force, he dipped his head, his lips almost on hers.

She closed her eyes in acceptance. *Finally*, her soul whispered.

"Elodie, whatever *are* you doing?"

Elodie looked up to see Luella framed in the stone archway at the top of the stairs.

Raphael immediately moved away from her. "Miss Di Silva tripped, and I managed to catch her, I was just checking she did not bump her head on the wall," he said smoothly.

Elodie watched the warring thoughts clash on Luella's face. Finally, she gave a jerky nod. "Are you well, Elodie?" she asked.

"Yes, I am fine, thank you. Just startled." Without looking at Raphael, Elodie climbed the last few steps and joined Luella and the others.

Hunt glanced at her face, and an exasperated expression filled his eyes as he looked from her to Raphael as Raphael entered the open-roofed room behind her. Elodie was beginning to realise not much got by Raphael's cousin. Perhaps, he was prone to lingering moments in crumbling follies himself.

"Ah, Miss Di Silva, do come and observe this view. You will never see one to rival it, I am certain." Worthing drew Elodie over to the edge of the room, where the wall had mostly tumbled away to reveal the vast sky above and the pond beyond the canopy of trees. Reeds and wildflowers bordered the edge, and Elodie gave a sigh of contentment. Worthing was right, in that it was a view to behold, but nothing beat that of the misty moors at Angelhaven.

"It is pleasing," Hunt said, "but nothing compares to our views at home." He voiced exactly what Elodie wanted to say.

"Cornwall? It is tolerable, but I am not one for mist and rain," Worthing said with a teasing glint in his eye.

"*Tolerable*?" Hunt blustered, and Elodie felt his incredulity blasting off him in waves. "I wager if you stayed at Mistbourne's new country estate you would change your opinion of that."

"Is that an invitation?" Worthing said.

"Hunt," Raphael said in a low voice, but Hunt carried on, "Why not? Rafe was just saying he needed to return home for a spell, so why do we not all go along for a house party. I am sure we could entice some of the others to join us."

"Capital," Worthing enthused, and Elodie's heart fluttered. A visit back home to Cornwall - would that be permitted so early on in her first Season?

Raphael gave Hunt a black look, and threw up his hands. "Why not, indeed?"

Luella pulled Elodie aside. "I do not think this is wise. Attending balls and picnics is one thing, but I can only thumb my nose at my brother for so long. I know for certain that he would not approve of staying in Duke Mistbourne's *house*."

Elodie thought exactly the same, but a reckless feeling had come over her. She was prepared to take the risk to see her beloved Cornwall again... and spend time with Raphael. "Luella, we can say that my dear friend, Caroline, has extended us an invitation to visit. Your brother need never know."

Luella looked at her as if she had never seen her before. She blinked and a calculating look came into her eyes. "Now I understand clearly who you have set your cap at."

"Whatever do you mean?" Elodie stalled. "I am just eager for a chance to go back home."

"Mmm-hmm," Luella murmured, and with a swish of her bright blue gown, turned and joined Worthing.

"Will you come?" Raphael stepped up close behind her, his breath stirring the hairs on the back of her neck, beneath her bonnet.

To the ends of the earth, her inner voice said. "I would love to," Elodie replied and felt him relax behind her.

"There is something you should know," Raphael continued in a stilted voice and Elodie turned, wondering what he could possibly be about to tell her.

"Rafe." Now it was Hunt's turn to add a warning tone to his voice.

The cousins stared at one another for a moment before Raphael nodded. "Never mind, it can wait," he said. He gave her a bow before walking away.

Hunt smiled at her apologetically. "I regret interrupting your chat. But you shall have plenty of time to converse at the house party. I am quite looking forward to it."

"As am I," Elodie said with a smile. "Thank you for making it happen."

"Making things happen is what I am good at," Hunt said with a wink.

"Shall we go back down?" Worthing asked. At the sounds of assent from the others, they all carefully made their way down the steps, through the folly, and out into the clearing.

Elodie lifted her face and breathed in. *Rain is coming*, she thought with a contented sigh.

"I think perhaps we ought to pack up and get across the pond, rain is coming," Raphael said.

Elodie looked at him sharply, startled by how in tune they appeared to be.

"Oh, how tiresome," Luisa said with a pout. "I was enjoying myself."

158

Raphael watched the Darlingtons' carriage pull away, behind the barouche, before turning to Hunt. "Why did you not let me tell her?"

"Tell her what?" Angelina asked, pausing in the act of getting into the carriage.

"About the place we call home," Hunt said wryly.

"Ah," Angelina replied, understanding filling her eyes. "Rafe, it would be too overwhelming for her, considering what happened."

Raphael scowled up into the now cloudy sky, revelling in the first drops of rain that stung his cheeks. "I know, but perhaps a bit of advance warning would have been kinder."

"If you had told her, she would have wavered. This way is the best way. She needs to get to know you again, without all these distractions." Hunt gestured at the members of the promenading Society now hurrying for their own carriages to avoid the sudden downpour. "That is really why I suggested the house party, not some silly wager with Worthing."

"Thank goodness you decided not to extend an invite to that Murrow chit, she is not known for her discretion," Angelina said with a satisfied nod. She settled herself into the carriage, and as soon as Hunt and Raphael were seated, and Hunt tapped the roof, the carriage set off.

"Indeed," Hunt said. "I am not averse to forward young ladies, but that one is too much."

"Really, Hunt." Angelina swatted him in exasperation with her parasol, while Raphael turned to stare out of the window caught up in his own thoughts about whether Elodie coming to stay was the best idea.

"Luella, whatever is the matter?" Luisa asked as Luella once again let out a long-suffering sigh. "Is it because Lord Bamford will not be coming to Cornwall?"

"Do not laugh at me, sister. Unlike some-" she shot a look at Elodie "-I am running out of suitable options."

Elodie bit her lip. She understood Luella's plight, but did she have to resort to being so spiteful?

"What about Lord Chester – he was attentive towards you the other morning, when he came to call," Luisa said in gentler tones.

"He came to call on Elodie!" Luisa said, the words almost a wail. "And besides, have not you heard, he and Bedelia Castor are soon to announce their engagement – Mariska told me."

"Oh," Luisa said, and sat back. She exchanged a helpless look with her husband, who sat with a grimacing smile on his face. Elodie almost laughed at his tortured expression, but thought perhaps she should contain it and not risk furthering Luella's indifference towards her.

"Here we are," Thomas said in relief, as the carriage pulled up outside the Beaumonts' house.

Luella shoved off the seat and opened the door. "Thank you," she said in dignified tones, before she added brightly, "Oh, Lucan has returned!"

Elodie froze halfway off the seat, before sitting back down with a thud. She could not face him, she could not.

"Elodie?" Luisa said in concern. "You have gone frightfully pale."

"I feel suddenly light-headed," Elodie said.

"Then you shall come with us. I will look after you. Luella tell Mama, Elodie is coming home with us," Luisa decided.

"Oh, fine, leave me to face our brother alone," Luella snapped. She accepted the footman's hand and alighted without a backwards glance, and dashed through the April rain towards the house.

"Thank you," Elodie said. She knew she was only delaying the inevitable, but now she had a chance to prepare herself before facing him. She needed a moment to lock away what she felt for Raphael, so Lord Beaumont would not see it, because right at that moment, she sensed if he spoke of Raphael, all the denials in the world that slipped from her lips, would not convince him.

And she needed to convince him. She did not know why, but felt with a sickening clarity it would have disastrous consequences for both her, and Raphael, if Lord Beaumont perceived she had formed a tendre for his dark-haired rival.

The carriage pulled off, and the sound of rain hitting the windows did nothing to drown out the sound of Elodie's thundering heart or that of her tumultuous thoughts.

Seventeen

Elodie pushed her potatoes around her plate. Even her favourite asparagus and salmon could not tempt her to eat.

"I am so excited to get away from town for a bit, Thomas. When did Hunt say we are to join them?" Luisa turned her face to her husband.

"He, Rafe and Angelina are going on ahead tomorrow, and we will set off two days after," Thomas reminded her good-naturedly.

"Oh, yes, I forgot," Luisa laughed. She picked up her wine, went to take a sip, before setting it down, wrinkling her nose.

"Something wrong with the wine, dear? It is your favourite one." Thomas reached a hand across the table to clasp his wife's hand.

A frown marred Luisa's face and Elodie forgot about her own troubles for a moment as Luisa let out a confused laugh. "Perhaps I have gone off it."

"Take it away please," Thomas said, and a footman swooped in and removed Luisa's glass. "We shall have to find you a new favourite," he said with a smile.

"You do indulge me," Luisa replied, and Elodie hid a smile behind her napkin. If a husband could not dote on his wife, then who could?

"My lord." The Darlingtons' butler, Simpkins, appeared at the door. "I am sorry to disturb your dinner, but Lord Beaumont's carriage has arrived for Miss Di Silva. His note was most insistent she return home post haste."

Elodie's easy amusement vanished in an instant. In her mind she heard the clanging of a cage door as it slammed shut behind her.

Her time was up.

She must face Lord Beaumont.

"Would you like me to come with you, Lo?" Luisa asked. She, herself, looked pale, but Elodie did not think the reason for it was the same as Elodie's discomposure. Luisa had no reason to fear her brother, she had the protection of her husband, and a loving home to find refuge in if she ever needed it. No, sunny Luisa knew not of her brother's dark side, and Elodie did not want her friend to come with her and see it unleashed, because Elodie was under no illusions that he would unleash it, and unleash it on her.

"Thank you, Luisa, but it is time I went back." *Time I faced the inescapable.*

Elodie said her goodbyes and collected her jacket, bonnet and reticule as if in a dream. As the footman handed her up into the Beaumonts' plush carriage she took a deep breath. But it was Hannah who waited inside to chaperone her. Her eyes appeared enormous in her freckled face.

Elodie gave a start, but re-composed herself quickly. She had expected Lord Beaumont to be waiting inside, only too eager to begin the interrogation, but he was the master of mind games, and this would only draw it out and set Elodie's nerves on edge. He had no doubt designed it that way.

"Good evening, Hannah," Elodie said and settled herself opposite the girl.

"Miss," Hannah said and flicked her eyes away.

"Is everything all right?" Elodie asked and Hannah swallowed a few times before nodding her head.

"I have been ordered not to speak with you," she burst out in a small voice.

Anger rose up inside Elodie, not for herself, but for the young girl who had already been on the receiving end of Lord Beaumont's temper. She should have gone directly home, instead of trying to hide. Perhaps she could have saved Hannah from his curt demands.

Elodie fell silent until they reached the Beaumont house. "I am sorry, Hannah," she said quietly as they were handed from the carriage.

Hannah dropped her eyes and let Elodie precede her up the path. As before, the door opened before she had touched the doorknob. Wells peered down at her; his face impassive. Elodie entered, wondering if she would ever be permitted to leave again.

Hannah vanished down the hallway, while Wells collected Elodie's things. "Lord Beaumont has asked you be sent directly to him upon your return," he told her solemnly. Elodie nodded.

A sob rent the air, and Luella suddenly appeared from the direction of Lord Beaumont's study. Elodie's heart dropped as the girl ran towards her, tears streaming down her face and a fist pressed to her mouth. She pulled Elodie into the drawing room.

"I am so sorry, Elodie." Luella sobbed. "Lucan already knew about the masquerade ball, and demanded I tell him everything in minute detail. He was so harsh. He *shouted* at me!" She paused; shock written across her face. "The worst thing is he has banned me from going out – for a week!" She stormed up and down the drawing room floor.

Elodie watched Luella, her heart breaking at seeing the other young lady so distraught. She had seen her beloved brother in a new light, and now Elodie witnessed how appalling it was for her.

"But do not worry," Luella lowered her voice to a harsh whisper, "I did not tell him about the house party. I am so vexed with him. Instead, I mentioned your friend Caroline is unwell, and begging you to visit her. So, you must go; go and if need be elope with your duke! One of us should have a happy ending."

Elodie gripped the doorway, shock now rippling through her. "Luella!"

"Elodie, my brother frightened me this night. I

165

think he... is losing his mind, and I fear for you. When he spoke of you..." she trailed off, horror hovering behind her blue eyes as she shuddered.

Elodie caught Luella's eyes with her own, feeling a kinship growing between them. A kinship stemming from the shared understanding that, as women, they were powerless against the men that controlled their lives.

"I must face him." Elodie let go of the doorframe and flexed her stiff fingers. She hadn't realised how tightly she had been gripping the frame.

Luella nodded, then with a rush, hurried over to enfold her in her arms. "Be careful," she whispered and Elodie gave a shuddering breath.

"I will. Thank you for your discretion about Cornwall, and for telling me what happened."

Elodie left Luella sniffling into a lace handkerchief, and walked towards Lord Beaumont's study. With each step, she heard a knell clanging within her mind. A clanging signifying the death of her freedom? She knocked at the door, knowing she was about to find out.

"Come," the imperious voice called.

Elodie pushed open the door and took in her first look at Lord Beaumont since their last encounter. She steeled herself.

"Miss Di Silva." He turned from his position at the window, glass of brandy in hand. He looked at her dispassionately, and Elodie relaxed. He appeared perfectly composed; he was dressed immaculately in a dark grey jacket, black breeches and white shirt.

Perhaps the storm of his anger had passed.

"Lord Beaumont," she said giving a polite curtsey.

"Please sit, you look a trifle pale." Lord Beaumont set his glass down on his desk, and gestured to the chair opposite.

Perhaps this was the eye of the storm, Elodie thought as she walked the short distance across the room and lowered herself into the leather chair.

Lord Beaumont wasted no time in rounding his desk, and Elodie sat back with a surprised squeak as he leant over her, caging her in, his hands clenching the arms of the chair either side of her. His icy blue eyes swirled mesmerically.

"You-" he moistened his lips "-gave me your word," he said, his voice a low hiss.

"I did not know who you meant..."

"More lies," he ground out.

Elodie tried again. "You did not say who, just '*him*'. I was perfectly safe, everyone acted with the utmost propriety."

He pushed back off the chair and stared down at her. "Do not take me for a fool. I know exactly what goes on at these masquerade balls, Miss Di Silva. Do you want your reputation ruined?" He turned away, not waiting for her answer, only to whirl back. "Were you ever alone with him?"

"W-who?" Elodie asked, her mind desperately stalling.

His eyes flashed. "You *know* who. Miss Di Silva, my patience is about to evaporate. Answer the question, and do not lie, I know all there is to know."

"I danced with him," Elodie acknowledged. There was no way Luella would have known about her moment alone with Raphael in the library, and she was not going to reveal that bit of extra information to Lord Beaumont.

"That is not what I asked," he said tightly.

Elodie shook her head. "No," she said quickly, "I was not."

Before she could even anticipate his moves, he was upon her, grabbing her arms and pulling her up to look fiercely into her eyes. "I gave you a chance, to show I could be reasonable, but still, you lie to me."

How could he possibly know? *Trenton... Mariska's cousin,* she remembered with a sudden clarity of thought amongst the tumult of her terror. Perhaps Lord Beaumont had encountered one or the other upon his return to London. But still, she would not let gossipers ruin her chances at a visit to Cornwall.

With as much calmness as she could muster, she said coldly, "Whoever told you is nothing more than a gossip." She pulled at her arms, and he released her. She stepped away from him, taking a breath. "I do admit, I got caught up in the excitement of being out and perhaps did not pay heed to your warnings. But they were perfectly unfounded; everyone I have met has been very welcoming and gracious."

Lord Beaumont narrowed her eyes. "Is that so? In that case, I do apologise." He gave a mocking bow, and sat on the edge of his desk. "Well, it appears we are at an impasse. I have punished Luella of course. I left you in her care under strict instructions. She should have known better. You, however... I sense a flightiness in you, one that must be curtailed."

The calm mask left Elodie, and she waited in apprehension.

"Luella mentioned your ailing friend. To show you I can be a reasonable man, I will allow you one final visit to your beloved Cornwall. Perhaps you will exorcise the ghosts of your past-" Elodie held her breath, she could not believe what he was saying, what he was gifting her. Hope bloomed in her heart, but his next words had that hope shattering "-but upon your return, I will be announcing your marriage."

Marriage?

"But-" She searched his face with her eyes. Who had he possibly picked out for her? "-to whom?"

He smiled then, fully. "It is time I took myself a wife."

"No," Elodie breathed out. She'd had her suspicions, but she thought they were simply just that. She never thought he would actually follow through with his insinuations.

He pushed off the desk and walked close to her, taking both her hands, gently this time, in his. "Yes, my dear. You must have wondered why I am so affected by you, why I express myself so violently. I have *fallen* for you."

Elodie's vision dimmed to pinpricks as images of huge wings flapping and floundering in the star strewn sky filled her mind. The ground rushed up to meet them with a shuddering thud. *I cannot breathe*, she thought in desperation. His hands tightened on hers and she sucked in a monumental breath.

"This is my wedding gift to you... a final visit to your beloved moors. If you refuse my hand, then I am afraid you will have to stay in London and perhaps find a better suitor." His implication was clear. If she turned him down, she would not have this one last chance at seeing home... and, though Lord Beaumont did not know it, Raphael. But perhaps, this was just another one of his tricks, perhaps she *had* no choice. How did she know he would honour her refusal? He might still order their wedding to go ahead, even without her getting her visit home.

Her heart cracked. She felt herself nodding slowly in acceptance, knowing this was the only way she could get what she wanted most, one final time... it was time she said goodbye to both home and heart. Goodbye to dreams of what might have happened with Raphael, if they only had more time. The crack in her heart widened painfully as Lord Beaumont pressed a reverent kiss to her hand.

Triumph flared in his eyes.

Eighteen

Even if Elodie had not seen Lord Beaumont in person two nights before, she would have known he had returned. Her sleep had once again been filled with night terrors and impossible dreams.

She traced the rain on the window pane and waited to be summoned for dinner. Lord Beaumont had invited guests and wanted to give her a farewell dinner before she set off to Cornwall the next day.

A knock at the door had Elodie standing and smoothing down her violet silk dinner dress. "Come in," she called.

Luella appeared around the door. Dressed in a turquoise gown which complimented her eyes, she seemed in brighter spirits. "I thought we could go down together," she said.

Elodie smiled at her, grateful she seemed to have found an ally in Luella after all.

They linked arms and walked down the corridor. "I still cannot believe Lucan is allowing you to go, however did you convince him?" Luella asked.

Elodie swallowed down the truth. She refused to share what she had agreed to do. Luella might change her new opinion of her. Elodie had been plotting and planning all afternoon, and she had come to the understanding that she could never say goodbye to her beloved Cornwall, so she had vowed to go... and not return to London. She did not think, however, that eloping with Raphael would be an option. She was desperate, but not enough to prostrate herself upon a man whose feelings she was as yet unsure whether were reciprocated. Oh, she had debated it, to the point of tears, but she would not force a loveless marriage on Raphael, when such a marriage with Lord Beaumont would be so abhorrent to herself.

She let out a laugh. "Perhaps he realised he was being terribly overbearing, and tried to make amends," Elodie said lightly.

Luella scowled. "I wish he would make amends with me."

"I am sure he will make it up to you," Elodie soothed.

They entered the dining room and stopped short at the sight of two gentlemen stood with Lord Beaumont. They were unknown to Elodie and judging by the curious expression on Luella's face she had yet to make their acquaintance too.

"Ah, what a vision," Lord Beaumont said, coming forward to draw both ladies into the room. He appeared in a good mood. "These are my associates, Lord Nathaniel St. Clair and Earl Mikael Thorne." The two gentlemen bowed. The taller, St. Clair, had shiny brown hair smoothed back from his forehead, with solemn dark blue eyes. He was dressed in a foppish style with an elaborate brocade jacket and breeches revealing yellow stockings brightly matching his cravat. Earl Thorne had short russet coloured hair and his hazel eyes were strangely watchful. They lingered on Elodie, as Lord Beaumont introduced them. "My sister, Miss Beaumont, and family friend and my mother's ward, Miss Di Silva."

Elodie and Luella curtsied.

"A pleasure to make your acquaintance," Earl Thorne said. "You were right, Beaumont."

Elodie flicked a questioning glance at Lord Beaumont, but he merely gave her a vague smile and moved to the table to draw out a chair. "Miss Di Silva."

She moved away from Luella and took her seat, next to the head of the table, where Lord Beaumont took his seat. Earl Thorne sat the other side of Elodie, while Luella and Lord St Clair sat opposite.

"Where is Mama?" Luella asked.

"Her weekly dinner with the Braithwaites," Lord Beaumont said. "So, it will just be us. How cosy."

Elodie accepted a glass of wine, and with Thorne's gaze piercing the side of her face, took a hasty sip. She hoped it would settle her nerves and dull her senses enough that his perusal would not discomfort her so much. Had Lord Beaumont told his friends of his desire to wed her? She would not put it past him to go back on his word. As he had released her from his study, he had agreed to her request that they keep it a secret for now.

She wanted no one to know. She wanted to make good her escape without anyone ever knowing that she was almost his wife.

"I have not seen you in town before, Lord St. Clair, what brings you now?" Luella asked.

Was Elodie mistaken or had his eyes flicked from Lord Beaumont to Elodie and back again before he answered. "Nothing diverting, I am afraid, Miss Beaumont. I had to speak with my man of affairs. Dreadfully dull, is running an estate."

Elodie could not imagine the peacock of a man running anything but a ball but mayhap she was being a trifle unkind.

The thought that she might still yet be caught out from her lie of staying with Caroline weighed heavily upon her, and the butterflies that filled her stomach left little room for the venison being presented before them.

Luella and St. Clair conversed while Lord Beaumont watched Elodie with hooded eyes.

"Do you not enjoy venison, Miss Di Silva?" Thorne asked in a deep tone, and Elodie realised she had once again been pushing her food around her plate.

"I do," Elodie said with a smile, "but I am afraid I was distracted about my upcoming travels tomorrow. I am so looking forward to seeing my dear friend. She has been unwell, and longs for company during her convalescence." The lies tripped easily off her tongue, and though Luella shot her a quick look, she refrained from commenting, which Elodie was grateful for.

"I am sorry to hear that," Thorne said graciously. "To where do you travel?"

Elodie lowered her lashes. "The vicarage in the village of Upper Haven, it is near my old home, Angelhaven."

"Angelhaven," St. Clair said slowly. "Unusual name."

Elodie smiled a reminiscent smile. "It is said that fallen Angels once found refuge there, seeking a haven from their tragic past." She laughed lightly but noticed none of the three men joined in. Instead, Lord Beaumont gazed pensively into his glass while St Clair and Thorne exchanged a tense look. "It is nonsense, of course," Elodie continued, confused by their serious expressions.

"Of course, my dear," Lord Beaumont said, and the strange air cleared.

"I think it is a lovely tale," Luella said brightly. She gave a girlish giggle, and took a large sip of her wine. A look of impatience crossed Lord Beaumont's face.

St Clair smiled at the other young lady and Elodie was relieved that she had not created a huge faux pas, talking about such things. She had always loved listening to the tales her father had told her about their home on their long walks across the moor. He firmly believed it was steeped in some kind of divine essence, and Elodie had adoringly indulged him.

She hoped Raphael's new estate was close to her

old home. She wanted to hasten time so she could find out, and hopefully be permitted to walk across those same moors... but with a pang, she understood it would be alone and not with her beloved father. But perhaps, another man would consent to walk alongside her, and share otherworldly legends of bygone times.

Lost in her yearnings, she was unaware of the small smile that crossed her face.

"I am gladdened to see you so happy, my lady," Lord Beaumont said leaning in so only she could hear his words. *My lady*. She shivered at the bold title. She would never be his *anything*, she vowed.

To stall, and calm the anger that roared through her at his assumption, Elodie took a sip of wine. Feeling more settled and able to keep up the pretence, she rose her eyes and smiled. "It is a lovely dinner," she said.

Lord Beaumont merely watched her. Was he angry she purposely did not acknowledge his meaning. She did not care. For tomorrow she would be far, far away from him, and if her plan worked, she would never again have to gaze upon his cold countenance. She would of course miss Luisa and Thomas, and even Luella and kind Lady Beaumont, but she had to protect herself from a lifetime of torment. She couldn't fool herself that he would change after he was married to her. In fact, she believed he would be even more controlling. No, it was for the best.

The rest of the dinner passed by in a blur as

Elodie dreamt of the life she would make for herself. Perhaps the countess knew of someone who needed a governess or a companion. Feeling better, she manged to eat the rest of the meal.

After dinner, while the men disappeared off to Beaumont's study, Elodie pleaded tiredness, and so Luella waved her away to bed with a cheery goodnight, vowing to see her off in the morning.

Elodie leant against her closed bedroom door, a smile creeping across her face. Her trunk was packed, and Luisa and Thomas were to arrive in the morning to collect her. Luella had told Luisa of Lord Beaumont's anger, and they, after some persuading, had finally vowed to keep the secret, telling Lord Beaumont they would be dropping Elodie off at Caroline's home on their way to visit friends, and bring her home on their return.

That last part was the only part Elodie felt uncomfortable with – she would not be returning with them. She would leave early on the final morning, before anyone could stop her. She would, of course, leave a note so they wouldn't think she had come afoul of some dastardly accident.

It was for the best, she repeated to herself. She pushed away from the door and walked over to settle on her window seat, to stare out of the window and up at the moon. The same moon that hovered above the place of her heart. The place that soon she would set her feet upon. She wondered if Raphael, too, gazed up and thought of her.

"Rafe, stop worrying so. She will come. Things are being orchestrated into place; I can feel it. It is the same every time - no matter how we try to change things or even keep you from each other, there is a higher power in charge moving the pieces." Angelina spoke from her chair by the fire. She felt most contented. A book in one hand, a glass of wine in the other and the dogs at her feet.

Raphael turned away from the window, where he had been contemplating the moon. It glowed over the mist-soaked heather, casting an ethereal light. He couldn't think of a more appropriate setting for this next part. He knew Elodie felt something for him, he saw it on her face, felt it in her actions. This time around was the first time they'd been able to really get to know one another. Every other instance it had been sudden and immediate tragedy.

"I wish I knew how it will turn out," Raphael said. "Leaving her with Beaumont is such a risk. I am ready to pluck her up and keep her here for eternity."

"Nice, cous. I think Beaumont trying that was how we all got into this mess." Hunt rose his glass in a sarcastic toast. "Nobody must force her hand. She must choose for herself. Run to, or run away. That is the pattern, time after time."

"But she always flees away," Raphael said. "If only I could tell her everything."

"We do not know if that will change anything, Raphael, and besides, she would think you had escaped out of bedlam with such a tale," Hunt said.

"She is different this time. I fancy she would believe it. How could she not, spending her childhood in Angelhaven – myths and legends abound, she must have heard of them." Raphael stroked one of the wolfhounds' shaggy heads as he joined Angelina by the fire.

"I am inclined to agree with you, Rafe," Angelina said. "When she is here walk with her and tell her a tale. See how receptive she is to it. She might open to you in a way you have both never experienced before."

"Certainly, why not give it a try. Nothing says spend your eternal life with me than a tale of tragedy, death and destruction." Hunt tossed back the rest of his glass, before setting it down with a heavy hand and leaving the room.

Angelina looked after her brother. "Pay him no mind, Rafe. He is overwrought, and just shows it in a different way than you. He wants it to go right this time, just as much as you and I."

Raphael gave a nod. But he knew, ultimately, it was out of any of their hands. The fate of all of them rested in the hands of someone who had no idea who she truly was.

Nineteen

Elodie, dressed in her travelling clothes of a woollen heather-purple cloak and lavender gown, paced up and down the drawing room. It was not like Luisa to be late. Having already said her goodbyes to Luella and Lady Beaumont, she felt anxious to be on her way, before Lord Beaumont changed his mind.

A noise outside had her racing to the window. With a relieved heart, she saw the Darlingtons' carriage pull up outside. She wasted no time in making her way to the entrance hall where her trunk waited. The footman opened the front door, and she was just exiting the Beaumont house, resolving to not look back, when a voice behind her had her closing her eyes in despair. The painful pricking of the point between her shoulder blades warned her that she would not be flying free so easily.

"Miss Di Silva, a moment please." Lord Beaumont's words were not a request, she heard the steel beneath the innocent words.

Pausing on the threshold of freedom, she waited

long enough to maintain her dignity before turning and raising one eyebrow at him.

He descended the rest of the stairs before coming over to her. "It seems I will be seeing you sooner than expected."

What new game was this? "Oh, my lord?"

"Yes, I have been called to inspect a new business venture in Devon. I will be leaving shortly after yourselves by horseback. I have been over the route with Darlington, so tomorrow, after I have concluded my business, I will meet you all at the coaching inn you will be staying the night at. Mayhap, I will join your party for the rest of the journey."

Elodie had gone somewhere else as he spoke, the words sounding as if they were being shouted at her from the end of a very long tunnel. She only concentrated fully when he spoke the final damning sentence.

"I can see you are overcome, but my aim is to show you how accommodating a husband I will be, my dear." He smiled his tight smile, his eyes not showing even a flicker of warmth, just the usual knowing that came whenever he looked at her.

Lord Beaumont gestured for the footmen to take Elodie's trunk and together they carried it out to the waiting carriage. He turned back to her. "I will see you tomorrow evening," he promised, before he moved off down the hallway towards his study.

A wave of dizziness washed over Elodie, and she gripped the doorframe. She swallowed down the nausea. What was she to do now? She couldn't very well refuse to go; he would know something was amiss. No, she must follow through with the plan, but when tomorrow evening came Elodie would not be waiting at the coaching inn. She would make good her escape. Her only option now, was to find a way to truly visit Caroline, and see if she knew of anyone who needed a governess or companion. With her heart breaking fully, Elodie knew she couldn't even contemplate finding Raphael, not when Luisa would undoubtedly crack under the pressure of Elodie's disappearance and tell her brother the truth. Tell him where they had really been heading. To Lord Beaumont's nemesis, the Duke of Mistbourne.

Feeling as though she was being moved into place on a gameboard, one of which she did not know the rules of, she walked down the path and allowed the footman to help her up into the carriage.

"Miss Di Silva!" Worthing exclaimed from his seat opposite Thomas. Luisa sat beside her husband, nearest the door, looking a trifle green.

"Are you well, Luisa?" Elodie asked after smiling in greeting at Worthing and Thomas.

"Just a little out of sorts, but I am sure the country air will do wonders for me," Luisa replied, patting her hand.

As the carriage set off, and the two men struck up a conversation, Elodie leant forward. "Luisa, I need to speak with you."

Luisa whispered, "If it is about Lucan then I already know. He visited yesterday and sequestered himself in Thomas' study. It was most vexing. I came over all dizzy yesterday, and really wanted my husband. But my brother can be most persuasive."

Elodie did not like the sound of that, but her concern for her friend took precedence. "Oh, Luisa! Are you really sure this journey is the best notion?"

Luisa waved an airy hand. "I do indeed. Thomas promised me he did not ruin the secret, and to be perfectly honest, Lucan's behaviour has been too overbearing of late. Forbidding Luella to leave the house is one thing, but stealing my husband's attention away when I need him is another. No, it will do my brother good to see he is not in control of everyone's lives. We shall journey forth, meet him for dinner at the coaching inn, and then be on our way."

Elodie listened to Luisa's tirade, glad to see it injected some colour into her cheeks. But something gave her pause. Had Lord Beaumont not told his sister he may be continuing on the journey with them? Why not? Maybe... maybe he had made *that* particular decision just before Elodie left the house to get a reaction from her. If that was the case, had she revealed too much?

Elodie moistened her dry lips, her mind whirring. Elodie realised it did not matter whether Lord Beaumont truly intended to continue on with them, or if it was just another of his mind tricks... because *she* would not be there to find out.

Guilt washed over her as Luisa turned to reply to Worthing who had just asked her a question. She would be putting her friend in an awkward position, but had to pray that it would all work out for the best.

She clutched her reticule where pre-written letters and the rest of her saved pin money were hidden. She'd hoped she would have had time with Raphael, time to say her own mental goodbyes to him, say goodbye to what might have been, and so she had the letters ready – for him, and for Luisa – to have left for them both when she had made her final departure. But now, having modified her plan, she must entrust them both into Luisa's care the next evening, and rely on her friend's discretion despite her own devastation at what Elodie had done.

Elodie could not take the risk of Lord Beaumont following them to their destination, and uncovering the truth. If what she had seen of his temper so far had been a storm, then finding out she had lied to him again, and that truly she was going to spend time in Raphael's home, then that storm would be nothing. His temper at that perceived betrayal would be a raging tempest, one she might just get destroyed by. It was much too dangerous to wait and see. She would go as far as she could in the safety of the carriage, before setting out on her own.

It was the only way.

The fanciful notion that she had ever been free to find a love that would rival any found throughout history, was just that – fanciful and naïve. She was a product of her upbringing and of her tragic circumstances. She was simply a young woman who had wished for blessings and ended up cursed instead.

She turned her face to the window,

surreptitiously dashing away a tear. The tear hung on her gloved fingertip, crystalline and shimmering. It reflected a tiny Elodie, encased in its crystal cage.

As Thomas and Luisa laughed over a tale Worthing was telling, Elodie had never felt more alone in her life. She pressed her thumb and forefinger together, crushing the tear. She hoped freeing herself from her real-life cage would be as simple.

The rest of the day's travels passed quickly, although it was not without its adventures. Luisa, still not feeling her usual self, had refused luncheon and had taken to reclining on the carriage seat with a damp cloth on her brow.

"Luisa, my dear, shall we return home?" Thomas asked, as Luisa gave another groan as the carriage rumbled over a hole in the road.

"No, no, I would much rather have the country air, Thomas. It is so suffocating in London," she mumbled.

Elodie exchanged a worried look with Thomas.

"We are almost at the coaching inn where we will be spending our first night. Perhaps a good night's sleep will see you in better spirits, Lady Darlington," Worthing said, perusing the scenery outside the window.

"There, Thomas. That will be just the thing." Luisa sat up and removed the cloth, already looking improved.

Relief clear on Thomas' face, he patted his wife's hand. "Capital," he said.

At the small but clean coaching inn, they enjoyed a basic but well-cooked meal of meat pie and potatoes, some of which Luisa was able to eat, before retiring for the night.

Elodie was given a connecting room to the Darlingtons'. Thomas was most insistent she could call on them if she required any assistance at all. But with her main door having a secure lock, she felt perfectly safe.

She spent the evening and a few of the early morning hours sleeplessly sitting on the small chair near the window, gazing at the moon. She thought of the next day where towards the evening they would venture into Devon. Despite the dangers of her plan, she relished at being that much closer to her beloved Cornwall. Her home and the village she grew up in sat just the other side of the Devon/Cornwall border on the northern coastline. If she closed her eyes, she could almost hear the waves crashing against the rocks.

Soon, she told herself, soon.

She wrapped the comforting thought around herself, and finally settled herself down to sleep in the somewhat lumpy bed. Her dreams were filled with the sound of rolling waves and the beating of powerful wings, while she herself floundered under a tidal wave of suffocating moss, and deadly mist.

"Something does not feel right," Raphael said, ignoring his dinner and instead pouring another glass

186

of wine.

"You are just allowing your nerves to overset you," Angelina reassured him. She set down her knife and fork on her empty plate. "Elodie and the others would have all left this morning, bright and early and be well on their way. Darlington has the best carriage money can buy, and will change horses regularly so they will make good time. Perhaps we should have suggested Elodie ride with us – although it is a fair distance in the saddle." She smiled, but Raphael did not smile back.

"It is not that, I am certain they are on their way... but I feel every move *we* make, sees a counter-move made against us." Raphael tossed back the wine and would have reached for the bottle to pour another had Angelina not stayed his hand. She moved the bottle out of reach, and cast him a sympathetic smile.

"That has always been the way, cous. You cannot allow doubts to creep in now. We must have faith that once Elodie is here, once she gets to know you and remembers her true love for you, it will end differently," Hunt said. He leant forward to clasp Raphael's arm.

Raphael looked up at him, his eyepatch put aside for these few days before Elodie arrived. His piercing green eyes swirled like the sea thundering against the cliffs near the house. "I hope you are right, Hunt." He slowly pulled his arm away. "It has to end differently, it just has to," he added in a savage whisper before he pushed back his chair, stood, and strode from the room. Intent on walking the moors, he whistled for his dogs. He vanished into the mist, his cloak flapping like a pair of giant wings, his two wolfhounds at his heels.

Twenty

"Oh, I could eat two breakfasts this morning!" Luisa announced. She wore a sunny yellow dress which complemented her blonde curls, and her cheeks were rosier than they had been the day before.

"I am glad to see you so improved," Elodie told her friend as she sat opposite her at the breakfast table. She herself wore a dress of sage-green wool. Its cut was comfortable and warm. She had dressed with intent that morning, knowing that by the end of the day, she would be making a hasty getaway and would need to be dressed accordingly.

"I admit I felt a trifle wobbly upon first awakening, but Thomas suggested I was simply hungry as I did not eat a lot yesterday." Luisa picked up a piece of toast and nibbled delicately.

Elodie poured the tea and smiled. "I am sure Lord Darlington is right." She ate her own eggs and toast and enjoyed two cups of tea. She herself would need all her strength for what lay ahead.

With a pang, she looked at the food set before

her, knowing that this might well be the last day she enjoyed the liberty of choosing what, and how much, she ate. There was no telling how soon she would secure a position and in what kind of household. Feeling the food begin to curdle in her stomach, she pushed her plate away, resolving to make her last day with her friend count. In entertaining Luisa, she could hopefully lift her friend's spirits as well as her own.

"Are we ready, ladies?" Worthing appeared at their table. "Fresh horses are all hitched up, and the carriage is ready to go."

Luisa dropped her half-eaten piece of toast, her eyes clouding again. "Yes, let us go," she said in a determined manner.

Elodie followed Worthing and Luisa from the coaching inn. She hoped her friend would be back to her bright self soon.

They settled themselves once again in the carriage, and with the early morning sun lighting their way, set off out of Wiltshire into Somerset. Elodie was a mix of nervousness, heartbreak and anticipation. She would need to time it right and wait until they reached the final coaching inn of the day. She would slip away while everyone else would be distracted. She must leave all of her things behind and throw herself upon the kindness of Caroline. She hated putting both her and Luisa in such predicaments, but she was left with little choice.

Elodie sat next to Luisa, and they spent a pleasant day conversing, and alternately stretching their legs when they needed to change horses, but the longer the day went on, and with Luisa refusing luncheon again, Elodie could see her friend was struggling but stubbornly refusing to say so.

As they headed into Devon, Elodie listened attentively to Luisa's hopes for hosting her own ball. "I was thinking of creating an inside garden of sorts in the ballroom, it would be like something out of a fairy tale." Luisa's eyes sparkled in her pale face, but she suddenly gave a moan and put a gloved hand to her mouth.

"Are you well?" Elodie asked quickly. Luisa shook her head, tears filling her eyes. "We need to stop the carriage," Elodie announced, and without waiting for Thomas to take charge, stood and thumped the roof.

The carriage ground to a halt and Luisa staggered to the door, not waiting to be assisted down. Thomas hurried out after her.

"Oh, I say," Worthing said, as he and Elodie leaned out of the carriage and watched Luisa and Thomas head to the verge of the road.

"Oh, indeed," Elodie said with a wince, as retching noises and groans filtered back to them. Elodie and Worthing retreated into the carriage.

"Lovely day, Miss Di Silva," Worthing said with a look of panic in his eyes.

Elodie hid a smile at the poor man's discomfiture. "Lovely," she agreed.

Thomas appeared at the door supporting Luisa. "I think Luisa needs to see a physician. Thankfully, the next coaching inn is the one we are to spend the night at."

"My estate is not too far from here," Worthing, rallying admirably, said, "If need be we can divert there and send for my own physician."

Luisa, sniffling, shot a look at Elodie. "No, I am determined not to spoil our trip. Let us do as Thomas suggests and see if there is a physician available."

Thomas looked from Worthing to his wife, indecision written across his features. "If there is not, we will divert to Worthing's estate, Luisa. You would be much more comfortable there," he said firmly, and after a moment she gave a tremulous nod.

"I am at your disposal," Worthing said, and reached out to help Luisa up into the carriage.

Elodie nibbled her lip. Of course her friend's health came first, and she could make her escape from Worthing's estate instead if it came to it. At least there she would not run the risk of inadvertently meeting Lord Beaumont.

The carriage once again set off with Luisa reclining on one seat, the others sharing the one opposite. Elodie looked out of the window and watched the beautiful countryside pass by in the early evening light.

Luisa groaned every time they hit a rut, and Elodie leaned over to pat her friend's hand sympathetically.

It was a great relief for everybody once they reached the next coaching inn, and Luisa was helped from the carriage. Elodie hesitated, looking around the bustling courtyard. If she did not go now, Lord

Beaumont would be arriving soon, and she would be trapped.

"Elodie," Luisa groaned, "I need you."

Elodie shook her head, shoving away her own selfish thoughts. What was she thinking? Her friend needed her. Clutching her reticule to her, she hurried after Thomas and Luisa. Worthing was already speaking to one of the men in the yard and she saw coins pass hands. Hopefully, the man would soon bring back a physician.

Luisa was helped up to a room and, with cloak and bonnet removed, settled onto the bed. Still pale, her eyelids fluttered on her cheeks, and she held out a hand for Elodie. Elodie pulled up the chair and sat next to her, clutching her hand.

"What can I do?" Thomas asked. He raked a hand through his hair.

"A cold, damp cloth would be most refreshing and perhaps some weak tea," Elodie said softly.

Thomas gave a jerky nod. "Of course," he said and with a final look at his wife, strode from the room, pulling the door closed behind him.

"Let me remove your boots, dearest," Elodie said, hating to see her friend so still and quiet.

Luisa, with a sniffle, let go of Elodie's hand and Elodie moved to the end of the bed and untied her small black boots and set them under the bed.

Thomas came back into the room carrying a tray. "Here, my love." He set the tray down, before placing the damp cloth over Luisa's forehead. He threw a helpless look at Elodie, as he saw his wife now slumbered.

She patted him on the arm. "She will be fine," she assured him.

He sat heavily in the other chair. "What if she is not?"

Elodie recognised the fear in the man's eyes. She recognised it and knew it. She blinked her eyes and saw her parents' carriage flying over the edge of the cliff. Her breath caught in her chest.

"Have faith, Thomas," she said huskily. She needed him to be strong, because if she too thought about Luisa becoming deathly unwell, she would crumble. She could not bear it if another person she cared about died.

"You are right, Luisa needs me to be strong." He stood and looked out of the window at a clatter of hooves in the courtyard. "That might be the physician," he said, his voice steadier. He gave her a nod and left the room.

Elodie hoped he was right and that it was not Lord Beaumont. She resumed her position of holding Luisa's hand, her heart in her mouth.

Moments later Thomas returned with an older gentleman.

Twin spears of relief filled her and Elodie carefully let go of Luisa's hand and stepped back. "I will wait outside," she said.

"Thank you, Miss Di Silva. We have secured a private dinner room downstairs. Worthing is waiting for you." Thomas turned back to his wife, and Elodie slipped from the room.

Out in the hallway, she leant against the wall and for the first time in what seemed like hours took a full breath. She could not leave now, not until she knew Luisa would be well. At least, it seemed, Lord Beaumont was running late. If he had even planned to meet them at all.

Removing her bonnet, and loosening the ribbons on her cloak and taking it off, Elodie pushed away from the wall and made her way down the steps. A serving girl showed her to the private dining room.

"Miss Di Silva, I hope Lady Darlington was comfortable when you left her?" Worthing turned from the window, as she came in.

"As comfortable as we could make her," she said. "Thank you," she added as he pulled out a chair to the table.

Worry settled heavily on Elodie's shoulders, and she picked at her food. Worthing tried to coax her into conversation, but her noncommittal answers had him giving up and instead he settled by the fire, nursing his drink.

The door opened and Elodie immediately stood as Thomas stepped in. His face was a picture of shock, and Elodie rushed over to him.

"What is it?" she asked urgently, gripping his arm. Her heart began to thud sluggishly in her chest. Horses' neighs and screams filled her mind, threatening to consume her. *No, not Luisa, too.*

"Luisa is... with child," Thomas said slowly, and Elodie almost sagged to the floor. Only her grip on his arm kept her upright.

As Worthing said, "Capital, Darlington!" and moved to pour Thomas a drink, Elodie let go of his arm, a smile beginning to work its way across her face.

"That is just the most wonderful news," she said. "But there is something troubling you," she carried on as Thomas took a seat.

"She appears to be suffering a severe case of the morning sickness. The physician has ordered her to remain on bed rest for a few weeks." He looked at Worthing. "He has agreed that we can carefully move her to your estate, if that is agreeable with you?"

Worthing lifted his glass. "As I said before, I am at your disposal."

Elodie looked at the affable young lord. He really was a most kind gentleman. She hoped Luella would turn her eyes his way, he would be a great balance to her sometimes self-centred behaviour.

Now that she knew Luisa was going to be well, Elodie turned her thoughts to her own predicament. She did not know when to make her escape. She did not want to worry Luisa, but if she lingered much longer...

As if summoned by her trailing thoughts, a chill ran down Elodie's spine and she heard the clatter of hooves come into the courtyard.

He was there.

She stood and with panic motivating her, picked up her bonnet and cloak, and moved across the room and into the hallway, with Thomas calling after her, "Miss Di Silva!"

Putting on her cloak and bonnet, and with head down, she threaded her way through the patrons of the inn and stepped into an alcove as she heard Lord Beaumont's imperious voice carry through from the courtyard.

"I see my brother-in-law's carriage. Direct me to the Darlington party."

Elodie bit her lip, hoping he would not pass her by. She knew he would instinctively know she hid there. He seemed to have a preternatural instinct where she was concerned. She shivered as footsteps came her way. She pressed back into the shadows, as the serving girl walked past, her hands laden with a full tray.

She let out a breath, and poked her head out. Seeing the coast was clear, she moved along the flagstone hallway and outside. She arrowed for the stables, until an icy voice pinned her in place.

"And *just* where are you running off to?"

Twenty
One

Elodie turned slowly. "My lord," she said with a curtsey. Her heart hammered in her chest, like a frightened bird dashing against a crystal window. Able to see freedom, but unable to get to it ever again.

"I repeat, where are you running off to?" Lord Beaumont dressed in riding attire, his usually pristine black boots splattered with mud, stood before her. His eyes looked her up and down, as if absorbing her very being into himself.

Elodie clutched her reticule tight to her chest. She could not very well tell him she had been trying to find the carriage, to leave the notes there, and then flee. "I left something in the carriage," she said. "I was just going to fetch it."

"Is that so? Then please allow me to escort you. It is not safe for a young lady to wander around an establishment such as this, alone." Lord Beaumont gestured a hand and Elodie had no choice but to turn and walk towards the carriage.

She entered the carriage, and unseen by Lord

Beaumont, pulled her fan from her cloak pocket and swiftly tossed it onto the seat. He entered behind her, and she made a show of searching the seats.

"Is this, perchance, what you are looking for?" Elodie turned to see him holding the fan. She went to take it from him with a grateful smile, but he held it up, out of reach. "What a coincidence. More fans," he murmured, and Elodie flushed as she remembered using a fan as an excuse for falling at her ball.

"Indeed." She let out a nervous laugh. "Thank you, Lord Beaumont," she said and held out a hand, uncomfortably aware he blocked the exit of the carriage.

He held her eyes, and slowly lowered the fan into her outstretched hand. Instead of letting it go, he pulled her towards him. "I think we can dispense with the 'Lord Beaumont'. I am to be your husband soon. I wish you to call me Lucan."

Elodie moistened her suddenly dry lips. She could not... she *would* not be so intimate with him. With Raphael it was different, his name was like a song inked upon her heart. With Lord Beaumont, even the mere thought of uttering his given name, caused her lips to freeze.

"Beaumont! You have arrived."

Elodie closed her eyes briefly in relief at Worthing's shout. *Saved once again*, she thought.

Lord Beaumont smiled, the knowing look back in his eyes. "Come," he said and stepped from the carriage, before helping her down. The seconds he held her hand were like an eternity. One she had no care in repeating.

"Have you heard the news?" Worthing spoke to Lord Beaumont and while he was distracted, Elodie cast her eyes furtively around the courtyard, noting hiding places and escape routes.

The two men conversed as they all moved back into the inn, and Elodie belatedly noted the interested gleam that came into Lord Beaumont's eyes when Worthing revealed the new plan of diverting to his own estate.

In their private dining room, Elodie once again removed her outdoor things and sank into an armchair in the corner of the room. The men moved to the table and poured drinks. Conflicting thoughts battled in her mind; while Luisa and Thomas's future held joy, hers held only uncertainty and loneliness. She did not feel angry, she felt nothing but happiness for her friends, truly she did, and nothing was more important than Luisa's health but a small part of her selfishly railed at the injustice of her situation. How would she ever get away now?

She took a shuddering breath to stop the tears from falling. It was all over. Her bravery dissolved, as she clutched the arms of the chair.

"My dear, Miss Di Silva, whatever is the matter?"

Elodie jerked her head up. Her watery eyes cleared as she saw Lord Beaumont standing beside her, his face, disconcertingly, a picture of concern.

"I am just worried for Luisa," she said in a monotone voice. There was no good prolonging it. He had won and Elodie had no other avenues to explore.

Something – *victory* – flashed in his eyes. "I can see how upset you are at being unable to see your friend." He leaned over to help her stand. "I have the most diverting notion. I will escort you myself."

"Pardon?" Elodie asked. No, no, no, that could not happen He would find out she had lied about going to seeing Caroline. "Oh no, I could not expect you to put yourself out, Lord Beaumont."

He stepped up close, his voice lowering. "When we are married, I will be escorting you anywhere you desire, so why not begin now?"

Elodie was lost for words. How had everything become so turned around in mere days? If she refused, he would be suspicious, but if she agreed she would be found out. What was she to do?

"I will not take no for an answer, I am quite determined to show you how accommodating a husband I will be," he said quietly before striding from the room.

Nausea roiled through Elodie, and she sat back down to clutch at her stomach. The first stirrings of an outlandish plan worked its way through her mind. They still had the night at the inn. Before dawn, she would make good her escape. Her bravery and resolve returned in a rush. She still had this one final chance.

Elodie thanked her foresight in mentioning at that last dinner at the Beaumonts' house that she was headed to the vicarage in Upper Haven. There was *no* vicarage at Upper Haven. Caroline lived in the rectory in Port Haven instead. Elodie had inadvertently bought herself some time, and saved Caroline from an unwelcome visit from Lord Beaumont. Elodie was under no illusion that he would scour the ends of the earth for her, his arrogance would not allow her to humiliate him in such a manner. But she had to try.

It was the only way she would ever be free.

Feeling calmer, she straightened and walked over to the table and accepted a glass of wine from Worthing with a smile. She turned and faced the mirror above the fireplace. Her silver-grey eyes were enormous in her pale face, and she pinched her cheeks with her free hand to inject some colour into them. She had to make Lord Beaumont see that she was excited to see her friend. He could not suspect a thing.

Lord Beaumont re-entered the room with a satisfied smile. "There, that is all settled. I have spoken to Darlington. He and Luisa will spend some time with Worthing while my sister recovers enough to return home, and I will escort Miss Di Silva on to Cornwall."

Worthing flicked his eyes to Elodie. Had she made a sound of distress out loud? She forced a smile onto her face, and Worthing's features relaxed, although his eyes remained cautious. "Capital idea," he said. He knew where they had truly been going, and knew of Beaumont's and Raphael's apathy toward each other. She gave him an imperceptible nod, and he inclined his head, trusting her that she knew what she was doing.

The exchange was missed by Lord Beaumont,

who was busy taking his seat. A serving girl entered with a fresh plate of food for him, and he settled in to eat.

"I am going to retire," Elodie said, putting the wine down and picking up her things.

"Very well, my dear. Get the girl to see you to our room," Lord Beaumont said, pausing between mouthfuls.

"Our – *our* room?" Elodie said, her voice a surprised squeak.

Worthing downed his glass, his eyes wide as he looked askance between the pair.

"Oh, Worthing, did I not say – Miss Di Silva and I are betrothed. I hope her dear friend's father will marry us, and we will return to ton as man and wife." Lord Beaumont smiled a wide triumphant smile, while Elodie thought her heart would burst from her chest.

How could he? He promised to keep it a secret. Now, he would certainly not rest in finding her, not now he had announced her as his intended bride.

Elodie stumbled from the room, with Worthing's surprised, "Congratulations!" ringing in her ears.

She found the stairs and pulled herself up using the hand rail. There was no way she would be sharing a room with *him*. Now or ever.

"Lady Beaumont?" the serving girl darted up the stairs behind her. Elodie swallowed down the nausea at the use of the title. How dare he be so presumptuous. "This way." The girl showed her into a room, and with a frozen smile of thanks, Elodie wasted no time in closing the door, and turning the lock.

Throwing her cloak, bonnet and reticule onto the bed, she paced up and down. Why? Why, every time she took a step towards her freedom, did something happen to throw her off course? She felt like flinging open the windows and letting forth a scream up to the heavens themselves. A scream that would bounce back and echo across to Raphael.

Raphael. She had not allowed herself to throw her hope in his direction. But perhaps, she should not deny what she knew to be real and true. A hand pressed to her heart, she sat on the end of the bed, and finally let the tears come.

Raphael urged his black stallion, Bran, across the moors, his grey, and fawn wolfhounds, Solomon and Gideon, keeping pace. The moon hid its face, using the tattered clouds as its shroud.

He wanted to give into the urge of pushing Bran to his limits, but held back. The tumult inside him could, if released, court danger. And he had no wish to see harm come to his steed. He eased off as he neared the cliffside pass. With limited vision, it was not wise to carry on at the steady pace.

He patted Bran, and looked down to see Solomon and Gideon, slow down, tongues lolling. He pulled up the reins and, as Bran stopped, slid from the horse. He removed the water container and metal dishes from the saddlebag and poured water for the dogs, before lifting another dish to Bran. The horse drank his fill.

"Stay," he murmured, replacing Bran's dish.

He walked to the edge of the cliff, the breeze blowing through his loose black hair. He stood, legs braced, and stared out over the cliffside, across the inky sea. Pinpricks of light dotted through the clouds, and he took slow deep breaths, counting them, until his thundering heart resumed its normal tempo.

Tomorrow, *she* would arrive. Tomorrow, he had resolved to tell her what beat inside his heart. He understood Lina and Hunt's words of caution, but he sensed – no, he *knew* – time was running out. If he himself did not make a move, he feared, the moves would be made for him.

He closed his eyes, and brought her face to the forefront of his mind. Her wide-eyed gaze turned to one of desolation. Tears glimmered in her silvery-grey eyes, and soundlessly, she screamed his name, beating her small hands against a locked door. In the image, she stood in a gown that looked like a silver wedding gown. The vision shifted, and feathers surrounded her, but not grey or black feathers, these were white; a pristine, stark white, so blinding, it shielded her from his view. He knew whom she feared, why she called so desperately for him. Knew who held the keys to her cage.

It was always the same, always *him*. Since the dawn of time, plotting and selfishly planning, whispering seductive lies in her ears. Lies that had shaped the course of their past, present, and future.

But not this time, Raphael thought. This time, he would save her. He could not save her any of the other times, and that weighed so heavily upon his heart. A heart that balanced on a scale set against a feather so light, so ethereal, but one that hid so many secrets. The vision scattered and he thought perhaps, this time... they would save each other.

Twenty
Two

The door handle rattled, and Elodie held her breath. She sat in the chair, wrapped in her cloak, vowing to keep a nightlong vigil to protect herself.

"Open the door," Lord Beaumont demanded.

Could she feign sleep?

"I know you are awake," his icy voice came through the door, and Elodie shivered. "Do not be alarmed, my dear. I am a patient man... *extremely* patient, so your virtue is entirely safe." The words *for now* lingered in the air like a ghostly promise.

Knowing she could not stall him, she moved to the door. "Please, my lord-" she swallowed down her distaste, and corrected herself "-*Lucan*. I only wish for this one final night, if you would permit it."

She heard his intake of breath as she said his name. She hoped it would work in her favour.

"Very well. You honour me with your acceptance, so I will honour your request." Elodie slumped against the wall in relief. Her fingers brushed the wall, where on the other side, stood her jailer. But not for much longer, soon she would fly.

"Thank you," Elodie said. "I will see you at breakfast." She winced at yet another lie, but at his uttered, "I look forward to it," she pushed the guilt away.

She would have a long night ahead of her. She could not allow herself to sleep, planning to flee just before dawn. Using the cloak of darkness to shield her, she would make good her escape, while everyone else slumbered deeply. Her heart broke at not being there for Luisa, but she hoped, one day, her friend would understand.

Thankfully, Lord Beaumont had seen her luggage transferred into the room. She flipped open the trunk and rifled through her things. She chose a misty grey woollen dress, her riding boots and a charcoal-coloured cloak with full hood. She found a larger reticule and stowed another dress inside, along with a pair of plainer slippers. The dress had a demure cut, one that would give the appearance of a respectable governess or companion. She selected her most plain bonnet, a straw one with a grey velvet trim.

She used the water and bowl provided to freshen up, before dressing in her chosen clothes and boots. She stowed her smaller reticule inside the larger with the dress, remembering to pull out the letters she had pre-written.

She sat on the bed and stared at them. One entitled, Luisa, the other, Raphael. She debated internally for a moment before stuffing the one marked Raphael back in her bag. She owed it to him

– she owed it to herself – to say her goodbyes in person.

She added a scrawled addendum on the envelope of Luisa's letter to Thomas, pleading with him to implore Lord Beaumont to keep her departure from Luisa until she would be strong enough to deal with it.

She placed the goodbye letter on the pillow of the still-made bed, before settling down on the hard wooden chair by the window. She picked up a book of poetry from the top of her trunk and tried to concentrate, but Byron's words danced in front of her eyes. She wished there had been another way to free herself, because she hated herself at leaving Luisa, but she was no longer in control of her own destiny. Stay in comfort, with her friends, and marry Lord Beaumont, or vanish and live a hard, but free, life.

Unfortunately, she was now familiar with the realities of how hard life could be, but she was under no illusions that it was about to get a great deal harder.

With a sigh, she closed the book and instead turned to look out of the window, watching the night-time activity in the courtyard below.

Elodie jerked in the chair. She had dozed off, she realised with a swoop in her stomach. She stood abruptly and walked over to the dresser to splash water on her face. Feeling more awake, she studied the sky outside. There was a dusky navy tinge to it warning her dawn was fast approaching. It was time to go. Anticipation had her heart thumping. She walked over to the door, and with a deep breath, turned the key.

The muffled sound of someone sleeping had her carefully pulling the door open. She looked out into the corridor, horror curdling within her. Lord Beaumont sat propped on a chair; his head pillowed against the wall. She blinked, unbelieving. The proper Lord Beaumont was sat outside her room, forgoing the comforts of a bed in his desire to guard her. Did he suspect she would abscond?

She backed carefully into the room, quietly re-locking the door. She now had three choices; stay, creep past him and hope he would not awaken, or... her eyes trailed over to the window. Could she climb out?

Well, she certainly was not going to stay, and she did not want to take the risk of him waking and catching her. The window was looking more tempting by the second. With the sky lightening, Elodie pushed open the window, and looked out. Her room was above the pitched roof of the entrance porch. She closed her eyes at the thought of dropping onto it, but thanked her lucky stars of the positioning of her room. Anywhere else and she would not have been able to make it.

She pushed the chair close to the window, tightened the ribbons of her bonnet and cloak, before hefting her large reticule, and slinging the long handle across her chest. Gingerly, she climbed out of the window, and dangling her body out, lowered herself down. With a barely concealed squeak, she let go, and landed heavily on the thatched roof, thankful it cushioned her fall. She gripped the apex and wriggled down, until her feet found the chunky wooden trellis bordering the porch. Bracing her feet, she let go and shuffled backwards. She turned slightly to grip the trellis, and using it like a ladder, climbed down to the ground, thankful it supported her petite figure. A reminiscent pang of climbing trees, and the rigging of her father's ship with her father gave her comfort. Perhaps, he was guiding her. She wrapped that thought around her, and keeping to the edge of the inn, sidled around to the courtyard's exit.

Near the stables, she paused as jovial voices from within stopped her. It appeared the grooms made an early start.

She pulled up the hood of her cloak and swiftly moved past.

"Oy, miss, where are ye off to?" a voice called after her.

"Just an errand for my lady," Elodie replied over her shoulder, not slowing down.

She kept going, not looking back and not daring to breathe fully. Out on the road, she cast a quick look up at the sign post in the pre-dawn light. Getting her bearings, she set off along the road, moving into the cover of the trees that bordered it.

Only then, behind a wide oak, did she stop to catch her breath. She had made it.

She hugged her bag to her, needing something

physical to cling to and ground her. Her heart had suddenly grown wings and she felt as if it would float away, she was so deliriously happy.

After a moment of relishing in her triumph, Elodie peeped out from behind the tree, as the sun crested the horizon. She looked at the distant inn, and sudden tears welled. She murmured, "Goodbye and good luck," to Luisa. She locked her grief away, joining it with that for her parents.

Resolutely, she set off, keeping to just inside the treeline, but careful to still follow the road. She would have to make it on foot to a village or coaching inn and see if she could purchase passage to Cornwall. Her boots were already beginning to pinch, but it was a price she was willing to pay for her liberty.

The sun crept higher, spearing through the canopy of the trees, and Elodie lowered her hood as it warmed her face.

She rested when she needed to on moss-covered logs, and scooped rainwater from dimpled rocks, and ducked behind trees when carriages rumbled past. Wishing she'd had the forethought to stow away a few bread rolls, she tried to ignore the growling of her stomach. Unused to feeling true hunger, she thought she had perhaps taken on more than she had bargained with.

Pressing on, she noted the sun had peaked and was now creating a downwards arc. She had been missing for most of the day. She could only image the rage Lord Beaumont was experiencing. She sent up a silent prayer that he would never catch her. It would be worse for her than if she had never left, she knew that.

She took a look out onto the road and noticed a large building up ahead. Another coaching inn. Relief filled her, bright and fierce. She needed food; she was about ready to fall. She gathered her cloak around her, and walked with purpose into the courtyard. A stagecoach was unloading passengers, so Elodie blended in with them as they entered the inn.

Taking a quiet seat in the back of the room, she gave her order to a serving girl and fell upon the sparse soup and bread roll with gusto, feeling like it was the tastiest fare she had ever eaten.

She took the second roll and placed it into her bag for later. Retrieving a few coins, she stopped the girl, and paid for her meal. She added one extra coin, and leaned in close to the girl. "I need to get to Cornwall; do you know of a discreet way I could do so."

The girl looked her up and down, before pocketing the coin. "Farmer Crosse, just in the valley below, is off to market in Crackington Haven tomorrow. That any good to you?"

Elodie could not believe her luck. That larger village was close to her home. "That would be perfect. Do you think he would take me?"

"Well, you can but ask," the girl said with a shrug. She paused then added, "Perhaps the stagecoach would be safer than wandering about the valley."

Elodie knew the girl had taken her measure. Even in her plainest clothes, she could not hide the sheen of Society. "Thank you, but I cannot risk it."

Curiosity lit the girl's brown eyes, but she simply nodded. "As you wish." She proceeded to give Elodie directions. "He leaves early mind, so you won't want to tarry."

"Thank you," Elodie said, and reluctantly finished the last of her tea. She took out another coin. "If a man with golden-blonde hair comes asking after a young lady of my description, I would be grateful of your discretion." She offered the girl the coin.

Sympathy flashed across the girl's face. She closed Elodie's hand over the coin and pushed it back towards her without taking it for herself. "Of course," she said.

Elodie gave her a watery, grateful smile. The girl smiled back, and went on her way.

Elodie settled the hood of her cloak over her bonnet once again, and adjusted her reticule. It was time to move on. She did not want to linger in one place very long, just in case Lord Beaumont came upon her in his eternal search for her.

Dizzily, she swayed. *Eternal search* – what a fanciful notion. Shrugging it off, she ducked her head and moved through the hustle and bustle of the main room of the inn. Raucous laughter and the clink of cutlery and glassware filled her ears like the buzzing of angry bees. She craved the quiet stillness the woods had afforded her.

She entered the courtyard, pausing as a sudden downpour erupted from the sky. Ordinarily, she would have basked in the rain, but knowing she would be unsheltered for as long as it took to get to Crosse Farm, she did not relish in it. Squaring her shoulders she took a step, then froze as a horse galloped in, throwing up water with its hooves. She took one look at the rider, the extremely familiar rider, with his golden hair in disarray, and his jacket unbuttoned, and her heart did a flip.

A group passed in front of her, hurrying through the rain, and mobilised into action, Elodie fell into step with them, turning her face from Lord Beaumont's searching gaze. The spot between her shoulder blades burned painfully, and she resisted the urge to scratch at it. The group moved towards the stagecoach, and as Lord Beaumont's haughty voice called out to one of the grooms, Elodie ducked around the coach, thankful for her boots protecting her feet from the puddles. She waited until Lord Beaumont was deep in conversation with the groom before she slipped from the courtyard and made for a group of dense bushes. Slipping and sliding on the muddy ground, she pushed her way inside and crouched low, her mouth dry and her heart hammering.

She sucked in shuddering breaths, her eyes never leaving the inn. She must wait until he left before she could carry on with her escape.

Twenty
Three

Water dripped through the twigs of the bushes in a constant rhythm onto the brim of Elodie's bonnet. She pulled the hood of her cloak further down over the hat and shivered. Before long, she would be drenched.

She kept her eyes on the inn, waiting for Lord Beaumont to leave, but knew in reality he would tear the inn apart in his search for her. She had kept to herself and only spoken to the girl, and she was sure she would not give her away, but Lord Beaumont could be formidable and extremely persuasive when he wanted to be.

She debated what to do. Perhaps she should leave now. It was only a ten-minute walk to the farm, surely Lord Beaumont would want to be thorough in his pursuit of her. Biting her lip at her indecision, a sudden deluge had her gasping as a large leaf folded under the weight of the rain and dumped its contents down her front. She resolved to go, not wanting to stand in the constant dripping any longer. She wagered on Lord Beaumont speaking to everyone within the inn, and leaving no stone unturned, and so she would take the risk.

She forced her way out of the bushes and turned right down a narrow lane, as per the girl's instructions. She hurried down the slick cobblestones, careful to keep her footing. The wide path snaked around a densely shrubbed hedgerow, before descending into the valley. She paused, putting her hand up against the now drizzling rain and scanned around. Smoke furled up from a small farmhouse with barn attached below, and with a relieved sigh, Elodie kept going, her destination in sight.

Against the thundering of her heart, she barely heard the hoofbeats coming up behind her. Without thought, she slid down into a ditch beside the road and tucked up into a ball, thankful her dark cloak would blend in against the mud and stone. Her face pressed against the grassy verge, she listened as the hoofbeats came closer and closer until they were almost upon her. Her heart almost stopped – was the horse slowing? But it carried on, passing her by, and with a sob, she pushed herself up to watch the horse head towards the direction of the farm.

The drizzle stopped, but Elodie's spirits were already drowned. Had the serving girl given her away? Sobbing quietly, she crawled out of the ditch. Again, she realised how futile her situation was. Was she never going to get away from him. He seemed to have her in some kind of net, and slowly by slowly, inch by tiny inch, he was reeling her back in. Desolate, she sat on the sodden grass clutching her bag. How long she sat there, shivering, she had no idea.

A gentle hand on her shoulder had her jumping up in shock. "Don't be afraid," a feminine voice said.

Elodie looked up to see the serving girl from the inn. She offered a hand, and Elodie took it, allowing the girl to pull her to her feet.

"I am glad he did not catch you, a cold one is that. I sent him two farms past ours. You are safe for now," the girl said, and Elodie let out a quivering breath, hardly able to believe this fortuitous occurrence.

"Thank you," she said with feeling. "But just a moment, you said 'ours'?"

The girl nodded. "I'm Josie Crosse. My pa's the farmer. Come on, let's get you warmed up," she said simply.

Elodie blinked at the kind girl. "Thank you, Miss Crosse. I am Elodie Di Silva."

"I know," Josie said with feeling. "The man was very insistent the entire inn be searched for you. He wouldn't let the stagecoach leave either until he had checked everyone's trunks." She cast Elodie a sideways look as they made their way into the farm's cobbled courtyard. "Is he your husband?"

Elodie shuddered. "No... but he wanted to be."

"And you did not want that?" Josie asked gently.

Elodie simply looked at her, knowing the helplessness she felt would be displayed in her eyes.

218

Josie nodded sagely, and pushed open the wide farmhouse door. "Pa, we have a guest," she called out.

An older man, with a grey whiskery beard and a flat cap, emerged from a back room, a border collie at his heels. He whistled in shock, before pulling off his cap. "What happened to you?" he asked.

"Pa!" Josie snapped. "This lady lost her horse and needs a place to stay for the night. You'll take her with you to Crackington Haven tomorrow."

Josie's Pa scrubbed a hand over his face. "Right you are," he agreed, before setting an old black kettle on the fire.

"Thank you, Farmer Crosse," Elodie said, unsure whether he was angry or merely bemused.

"Don't mind Pa, he's a man of few words, but he's a good man," Josie said, throwing an affectionate look at the older man's back.

"My father was too," Elodie said quietly.

Josie helped her out of her sodden cloak. "Then you should accept nothing less either." She looked meaningfully at Elodie. Elodie tilted her head at this shrewd young lady. Perhaps, she strove for a better life too.

Josie took her into a small side room, housing a narrow bed, and a dresser – the top covered in drawings of gowns. "This is my room, but your need is greater tonight," she said.

"No, Miss Crosse, I cannot take your room," Elodie protested, aghast.

"I insist," Josie said, folding her arms. "I will fill the bath for you. You should wash and warm yourself. We do not want you catching a chill." She left Elodie staring after her, her heart full of gratitude.

Elodie removed her bonnet and allowed her black waves to tumble free. She stared at her mud-splattered reflection in the old mirror. Would Lord Beaumont even recognise her? She hoped he would not, because she was no longer the Elodie of old. This Elodie was determined to do whatever it took to ensure her freedom. Even if it meant travelling with the pigs to get to where she needed to be.

Josie returned to find Elodie sat in the chair by the window admiring the skill in the designs of the sketches she had found on top of the dresser. "Did you create these?" Elodie asked.

Josie flushed but nodded. "I have a dream of one day opening up my own dressmaker's shop in Exeter. I work at the inn and Pa helps me save any spare pennies."

"You have an exquisite eye," Elodie told her, replacing the designs. "I look forward to visiting Exeter one day and buying one of your gowns." If fortune smiled on Elodie and helped her secure a position and earn money herself, that was.

"It would be an honour to create a gown for you," Josie said sincerely. "Your bath is ready. Pa has gone to feed the pigs."

Elodie followed her out into the larger room, where a small tin bath sat near the fire.

"It's not what you are used to but..." Josie trailed off as she saw the tears running down Elodie's cheeks. "I'm sorry, it's all we have," she continued in a gruff voice.

"Oh, it isn't that at all. I am just so thankful for you, for your kindness." Elodie sniffled through her tears.

Josie blushed. "Oh, well, I'm happy to help you." Ducking her head, she pulled an old screen around the bath, shielding Elodie.

Elodie wasted no time in removing her mud-encrusted boots and gown, and her undergarments, before slipping into the warm water. She bent her legs and slid her head under the water completely soaking her hair. She used the bar of plain soap to lather up her hair and body. She felt as though she were scrubbing away all vestiges of her old life. The sheen of Society would be thrown out with the bath water, leaving just a young lady who would fade into the background, but be happy there.

"Here," Josie said, coming around the screen with a large towelling cloth. She averted her eyes respectfully as Elodie stood, wrung out her hair and wrapped herself in the cloth before getting out of the bath to dry by the fire. "I have cleaned your boots and your cloak should be dry by morning."

"I cannot thank you enough," Elodie said.

Josie inclined her head. "I have left a clean nightgown and shawl on the bed for you. I will awake you early, so you don't miss Pa setting off. But first, come and have some stew."

Elodie, moved to wordlessness, went into the small room and donned the nightgown, before braiding her hair into a thick waist-length side plait. She settled the soft creamy-coloured woollen shawl around her shoulders and joined Josie at the long kitchen table. She scooped up the meat and potato stew, and thought it far superior to the soup she'd had earlier at the inn. She would never again take food for granted.

An almost hysterical laugh bubbled up inside her at the thought of Lord Beaumont seeing her now, dressed in a pig farmer's daughter's nightgown and about to sleep on a straw-filled mattress, after washing in a tin bath in front of a fire in the living area of a pig farm. He would look disdainfully down upon them, seeing only their class, not seeing what kindness and goodness lingered beneath the surface. No, he would not even accept their offer of help, thinking it would demean him. There were so many good people in the world, but he was too proud and blinkered to see that. He only saw *his* societal class, thinking the fortitude of their birth made them better people to associate with. But Elodie was learning that class did not equate goodness. No, *that* was innately inside you, no matter where, or to whom, you were born.

Her eyelids drooped and Josie put a kind hand on her arm. "Time for bed, Miss," she said, putting an arm around her waist and helping her to stand.

With a yawn, Elodie murmured another, "Thank you," and made her way into the bedroom, closing the wooden door behind her. She was asleep as soon as her head hit the downy pillow.

As slumber took her deep under its gossamer wing, the moon guarded her overhead, while another searched for her, his anger building to rival that of his insanity.

"Why have they not arrived?" Raphael asked for the third time.

Angelina, dressed in a gown of dark-red silk, moved away from the fireplace. "I know not, Rafe, perhaps the journey was taking longer so they stopped off for the night. I am sure they will arrive tomorrow," she reassured him, yet again.

Hunt potted his billiard ball, and looked over the top of his cue at his cousin. "Stop worrying so, you know how these ton members like their comfort. They probably drove sedately through the countryside, and got their timings wrong."

Raphael heard the sensible answers, but shook his head. "What if they have had an accident."

Angelina pursed her lips, her eyes sympathetic. "We would *know*, Rafe. We would know if something deadly had happened to her," she said meaningfully.

Raphael met her eyes, his own tumultuous, swimming with the haunting memories of a tragic past. "I appreciate that, but she could still be lying in a ditch somewhere, alone and frightened."

"Oh, Rafe," Angelina said softly. "If they have not arrived by mid-morning, then yes, go and search. But I am sure they will be here." She moved across to him to draw him in her arms, squeezing tightly. "She will be here."

After a moment, Raphael embraced her back, before letting her go. He picked up his own cue. "I will give them until mid-morning," he agreed. He struck his cue and watched with satisfaction as it hit his ball into the pocket.

Hunt pulled a face, before toasting Raphael with his brandy glass. "Well played," he said.

Raphael moved towards the window, and looked up at the moon, hoping against hope that the next night he and Elodie would be looking up at it together.

Twenty Four

"Thank you, Miss Crosse. I will remember your kindness always." Elodie looked down from the cart to where Josie stood dressed in a cloak and bonnet.

Josie smiled. "May you find what you are looking for," she replied. "I must be off; Cook is a fierce one if any of us are late." She clasped Elodie's gloved hand. "Good luck, Miss Di Silva."

"Elodie, please." Elodie squeezed the girls' hand before letting go. "I hope we will meet again one day when you have a thriving dress shop." Elodie hoped the girl would not be insulted at the handful of coins she had left on top of the dresser next to the sketches with a hastily scribbled note... *To help you with your dreams, as you helped me... E x*

"As do I," Josie said, her brown eyes sparkling. She rose her hand in a wave. "See you tomorrow, Pa."

"I'll be back by supper time," Farmer Crosse promised, and with a nod, Josie turned and started the walk up the cobbled lane that led back up to the coaching inn.

Elodie watched her go, inspired by the young lady's confidence and independence. It lifted Elodie's spirits. If Josie could do it, then there was hope for her too.

Farmer Crosse set the two horses walking down the wider lane leading towards a distant village. "We will join the main road after the village there. Best if we avoid the coaching inn, eh?" It was the most the man had said to Elodie, but for all his lack of conversation, he was obviously very perceptive.

"How long will it take to get there?" Elodie asked. They were leaving before dawn, and Elodie hoped it would be but a few hours until she was back in her treasured Cornwall.

"We're not far out, just over the border. Few hours at most," Farmer Crosse said, and Elodie gave a sigh of contentment.

They travelled at a good pace, but the farmer had resumed his quiet way, and Elodie took to looking about the countryside. She kept her hood up, and pulled it over her face as they passed carriages or riders. She had no knowing if Lord Beaumont had paid people to keep a lookout for her. She hoped she was not putting Famer Crosse or Josie in danger.

But the further they got towards the border, the safer Elodie began to feel. She had not experienced the itching in her shoulder blades since she saw Lord Beaumont the day before so took it as a good sign that he was not in the vicinity.

"Ah, 'ere we are." Farmer Crosse's voice startled Elodie out of her thoughts and she looked up at the signpost he gestured to. *Crackington Haven, 10 miles.*

"I hadn't even realised we had entered Cornwall." How could she have missed that?

"Oh, aye. We'll be passing Port Haven in a few miles." Elodie's heart gave a twist as she thought of Caroline. She would be seeing her friend soon, but she thought of someone else she needed to find first.

"You are familiar with the estates in this area?" Elodie asked.

Farmer Crosse gave a nod.

"Do you know the Duke of Mistbourne?" she asked quietly.

"Fine man. Aye, I know 'im. As a matter of fact, 'is new estate is not far from Port 'aven." He looked over at Elodie as she stared at him, her mind whirring. She knew of all the estates in the area. How had she never known Raphael had lived so close to her?

The first stirrings of unease tickled the base of her neck, as they fell into silence. They travelled onwards until they came to a fork in the road. A fork Elodie now recognised. She should, it led to her old home, Angelhaven.

Something pulled at Elodie, hard. An undeniable tug. A longing and a grief so visceral she thought it would grow wings and drag her physically towards the place she grew up.

"There's your duke's estate," Farmer Crosse said, pointing down the road cut through the heather covered moorland.

Elodie thought she had misheard. "Pardon?"

"Mistbourne, 'e lives down there now."

"You mean to tell me; Duke Mistbourne's home is... is *Angelhaven*?" Elodie started shaking. That could not be true.

"Aye, miss. 'E inherited it recently. Are ye well?" The farmer took a good look at her.

Elodie could not make sense of any of it, but she was about to. "I will get off here, Farmer Crosse. The duke and I are – well – friends," she said.

"Are ye sure, miss?"

She had never been so certain about anything ever. She was going to find out why Raphael now lived in her old home... and why he never *told* her. She felt the betrayal like a hit to the stomach, but her confusion fuelled her determination. "I am," she told the farmer.

"Then I wish ye well, miss."

"Thank you, Farmer Crosse – for everything." Elodie patted the man's arm and with a smile hopped down from the cart. She waved him goodbye and watched as he trundled on, before turning to face the road across the moors.

Restless, and bored of pacing the manor waiting for the Darlington party to arrive, Raphael had decided to head to Port Haven and pass the time there.

He chatted to a few local merchants and when he saw dark clouds creeping across the sun, decided to make his way back before being caught in a downpour. On his way out of the village, he passed a cart, and the driver hailed him.

"Duke Mistbourne! What an unexpected coincidence."

Raphael pulled up Bran, and said, "How so, my good man?"

"I just dropped off a very lovely young lady near the entrance to your new estate," the farmer said.

Awareness came over Raphael, and he did not need to ask anything more, but still the words slipped huskily out, "A lady with a mass of dark hair and silvery eyes?"

"The very same. My daughter told me she'd lost 'er horse, but a lady like that doesn't travel alone. No, if ye ask me, she was running from something."

Raphael sucked in a breath. *Or someone.* There was only one person Elodie could be running from in her current predicament.

"Ye will offer 'er protection, I hope, sir. She's a pure soul, is she," The farmer spoke with concern similar to that of a father.

"You have no notion," Raphael muttered under his breath. When it came to souls, there were none purer than hers. "You have my word, sir, I will protect her. Good day!" he nudged Bran into a trot around the cart, before setting off at a gallop.

Elodie stopped halfway down the road and veered off into the heather. She waded through the mounds before sitting on a familiar rock and taking in deep breaths of the fragrant air. Calmness settled in her bones, as the comforting sensations of being back in her homeland filled her. She closed her eyes, not noticing the dark clouds converging overhead, until one drop of rain fell onto her upturned face.

She opened her eyes and smiled sadly as mist snaked around her feet, and rain drizzled from the sky. *Now* she was truly home. With a sigh, she stood, knowing she could not prolong finding out the truth. If things had gone differently, she would be arriving in a carriage with Luisa, and she would have made the discovery of the truth about Raphael's home then. What would her reaction have been? The same as this dull feeling of betrayal?

Through the gentle rain, she set off across the moor, instinctively knowing the way to go. She had walked this route countless times. She clambered over a rocky outcrop and looked down through the mist at the ghostly outline of Angelhaven. *Oh, Mama, Papa*, she thought, tears mixing with the soft rain to course down her face.

She stumbled back onto the road and towards the large gates with two wrought iron wing shapes emblazoned on them. She reached out to push them open, and her blood turned to ice as the sound of hooves behind her had her sliding bonelessly to the floor, thinking Lord Beaumont had found her after all.

Strong arms caught her just before she hit the ground. "Elodie! Elodie, can you hear me?"

A warm hand pushed tendrils of sodden hair

from her cheeks, and she looked up into the one-eyed green gaze of Raphael.

"Why did you not tell me?"

"I wanted to – I tried to at the folly... but would you have come?" Raphael asked tenderly, cradling her into him.

"This is – *was* – my home, Raphael. I have so many happy memories here, but I left under a cover of grief. I... I would have come, but some warning would have made it bearable." Elodie looked up at him. She did not worry about the closeness of their positioning because it felt *right*.

"Then let me bring you inside and explain," Raphael said, standing, lifting her easily. "Bran, come." The horse walked after them as Raphael pushed open the gates with one hand, securely holding Elodie with the other.

Another soaking two days in a row had Elodie shivering, and fatigue from her arduous journey had her eyelids fluttering as she fought against the sleepiness. "You carried me once before," she murmured as memories, or perhaps the vestiges of a dream, filled her mind.

Raphael looked down at her in shock. Was she *remembering*? "I would carry you to the ends of the earth," he whispered.

A smile played about her lips, and she let out a sigh, as exhaustion claimed her.

A groom hurried out from around the house, he cast a curious glance at Elodie, but Raphael merely said, "Take care of Bran, please."

"Of course, Your Grace." The groom took Bran's reins and led him towards the stables.

Raphael climbed the rounded steps up to the house and as soon as his butler had opened the glossy black double doors, he carried on up the wide marble staircase and made his way along the plushly-carpeted hallway into a bedchamber with wide arched windows and gossamer thin drapes.

He loosened Elodie's cloak, before removing it and her boots, and laying her on the canopied bed. He stared down at her for a moment hardly believing she was actually there, at Angelhaven. With him. But, how was she there without the Darlingtons – what had happened to *them*?

He understood there would be a lot of explanations from both sides, but right now, he needed to make sure she was well, nothing else mattered right at that moment. Raking a hand through his thick damp hair, he turned and strode from the room, his long legs making short work of the hallway.

At the bottom of the staircase, he roared for Angelina. She came flying out of the drawing room, slowly followed by Hunt.

"Whatever is wrong, Rafe?" Angelina asked, a hand pressed to the chest of her golden-yellow gown.

"She is here," he said without preamble. "Alone. I found her outside, she might have caught a chill – I do not know." He slumped into a chair in the entrance hall, his head in his hands, missing the shocked looked Angelina shared with Hunt.

"Then we shall find out the mystery of her arrival as soon as she is well," Angelina said, clapping her hands together. "Hunt, get Maggie to bring some warm water and cloths, and if need be we will call for our physician. But first I will go and make her comfortable."

Raphael stood and looked at each of his cousins in turn. "She is *here*," he said, shock swirling in his one-eyed stare.

Hunt clasped a hand to Raphael's arm. "I know, cous. It will be different this time, I can feel it."

Angelina gripped his other arm. "Courage and faith, Rafe, dear," she said earnestly.

Raphael took a shuddering breath. They released him and he watched them hurry off, before gazing up the staircase. Right at that moment, courage and faith had deserted him, as instead happiness and terror vied for dominance.

She was there.

Twenty
Five

Elodie walked along a white-stoned path in a beautiful garden full of shimmering trees. The gentle sound of a stream filled her ears as the water flowed over the edge of the mist-strewn ground.

Joy and excitement swirled inside her as she made her way towards him. A hand stopped her... *Elodriel*. She turned, the smile falling from her face. *No, not again...* she pulled herself free and ran but it wasn't fast enough.

It was never fast enough.

The scream tore from Elodie's lips as she sat up in bed, the damp cloth on her brow falling off. A pair of gentle hands stilled her, and she looked up into eyes of soft hazel.

"*Maggie*?" Elodie said, taking in the round face of the younger girl. Her light brown hair was scraped back from her forehead into a neat bun.

"Oh, Miss Elodie, I could hardly believe it when

234

the countess told me we had a guest and I came in and saw *you* lying here so pale," Maggie said, tears sparkling in her eyes.

Elodie clutched at a familiar and beloved piece of her past, drawing Maggie into her arms. Together they wept, until Elodie let her former maid go, to ask, "But how are you here? I thought the staff were all let go when I left."

"We were," Maggie said, then smiled through her tears, "but as soon as His Grace arrived, he re-hired everyone. He is such a good and kind employer."

Elodie's mind reeled. "I still do not understand how the duke came in possession of Angelhaven."

"Well, Miss Elodie, as to that perhaps you had better ask him. It is not my place." Maggie ducked her head, and Elodie understood and respected Maggie's loyalty. It spoke volumes to how well-liked Raphael was by his staff.

"I will," Elodie agreed. "How long have I been here?" she noted the watery sunshine filtering in through the gossamer drapes. *Gossamer drapes*? She took a better look around the room she was in.

Maggie noted the comprehension dawning in her eyes. "You have been here two days... and yes, this is your old chamber," she said gently.

"Oh," Elodie said, suddenly overcome. She dropped her head into her hands, and that was how Raphael found her when he stepped inside the room, moments later.

Maggie jumped up from her seat on the side of the bed, where she had been trying to comfort Elodie.

235

"Your Grace." She bobbed a curtsey.

"Perhaps Miss Di Silva would welcome some tea and a light breakfast," Raphael said, and Maggie gave another bob before leaving the room.

Elodie slowly lifted her head. "I feel like I am in another one of my dreams," she murmured, her eyes latching onto his face. She was safe in her old home, with a servant who had also been a friend... and Raphael was there too. How was any of it real?

Raphael kept his distance, but his one-eyed green gaze was intense on Elodie. "I owe you answers, so many answers, but I will start with the easiest first."

Elodie sat back against the headboard and waited.

"Angelhaven has been a stronghold on this coast for many centuries, I am sure you know the stories-" at Elodie's nod, he continued "-originally, it belonged to my family – the Blackmores, but after a wager a few generations ago, it came into your family with the caveat that it would revert back to the Blackmore's if there was not a son to inherit."

"So, we have a shared history," Elodie murmured.

Raphael's eye gleamed. "Longer than you imagine," he said more to himself. Relieved Elodie had taken the revelation of why he now lived at her former home so well, he took a seat on the window seat and leaned forward. "How are you feeling?" He hoped he hid how terrified he had been the past two days that she would never wake up, that all this had been for nought after all.

"Truthfully?" Elodie let out a long sigh. "Like my whole body has been torn in two, and stitched back together, but in the seams, I sense a light slipping in. Perhaps, I could slowly heal given time." The words came from a place deep within her soul. She let out a surprised laugh. "I am sorry, I do not know why I phrased it so."

"I think you phrased it perfectly," Raphael said. "But do you feel well enough to speak of why you ran from the Darlingtons? We received a note just this morning telling us of Lady Darlington's situation and their decision to divert to Worthing's Estate, and that you... you had left. The news has, of course, been kept from Lady Darlington in her condition." Raphael raked a hand through his hair. Blame settled heavily on his heart at Elodie's plight.

While Elodie felt relief that she had not added to Luisa's worries, Lord Beaumont loomed front and centre in her mind and she clenched her hands on the dove-grey lace coverlet. She cast a terrified glance at Raphael, and he stood, ready to scoop her up into his arms, but she spoke quietly and slowly in measured tones, "If I had stayed, I would have had to marry him, and I cannot, I cannot..." she trailed off into gasping sobs.

Raphael did not hesitate, he strode over to the bed and wrapped his arms around her, and held her while she wept herself dry.

"He terrifies me," she whispered against his heart, and Raphael closed his eye at the pain in her voice. Anger, bright and fierce, shot through him. He and Beaumont were long, so long, overdue a confrontation. But he knew that was not the way. If he was to protect Elodie, then Lucan Beaumont must never know where she was.

"I promise you are safe here," Raphael said.

Elodie gently pushed out of his arms. "But I cannot stay here forever. This is *your* home now."

Emotion rippled across Raphael's face, his heart breaking for her – the young lady who thought she was all alone in the world. "It can be your home too." Questions sprang into Elodie's eyes, and he hastily added, "With no requirements. I simply want you to feel safe and comfortable. Angelina is here and Hunt too, and all of your old servants. You can be free to heal here. We can talk of the future when you are ready."

"But why, why would you do this for me? We did not know of each other's existence a few weeks ago." But even as Elodie said it, she knew it to be a lie. She knew him, had always known him... hadn't she? She shook her head as a dizzy rush had her gasping.

"Do not overset yourself, *amica mea*. There will be time to explain everything else soon. Please, eat and rest, and if you feel improved later you can come downstairs and see the others." Raphael stood, leaving Elodie confused at the tenderly whispered phrase she could not decipher, but still somehow seemed familiar. He stepped back as Maggie returned with a tray. "I will leave you two together, I am sure you have much to catch up on."

With a smile and a bow, Raphael left the room,

his footsteps lengthening until he was almost jogging down the hallway. He pulled open a wooden door at the end of the hallway and ran up the spiral staircase until he pushed out onto the top of the tower, gasping in the fresh sea air buffeted on the lusty breeze.

A roar, to rival the clap of thunder in the heavens above, ripped from him, carried away on the wind. If only it could be swept away to Beaumont, for him to feel the power behind it, the promise in it, that now Raphael had her beneath his protective wings, he would never let Beaumont harm her ever again.

The rain came and he let it soak him, washing away the anger, until he felt steady enough to return inside and speak to Angelina and Hunt. They needed to know Beaumont had made his move, and now that he had, Elodie would need supervision and protection. Whatever she thought about her future, she would have to come to terms with the truth that Beaumont would never give her up. But as long as she resided beneath Angelhaven's roof, she would be hidden. Raphael just needed to find a way to convince her to stay.

"Oh, my dear, it is so lovely to see you up on your feet and with a becoming colour in your cheeks too." Angelina swept across the drawing room floor towards Elodie. Dressed in a sapphire blue gown that complimented her piercing eyes, she clasped Elodie's hands and pressed a kiss to her cheek.

Elodie smiled. "Thank you for letting me borrow

one of your gowns." She gestured down at the blossom-pink silk gown, adorned with tiers of lace at the bottom of the skirt.

"Maggie is a wonder with needle and thread. I knew it would be perfect on you, just a little adjustment and voilà." Angelina slipped her arm through Elodie's and drew her over to the sideboard. "Wine?"

Elodie accepted the glass and sipped it.

"The men will be along shortly," Angelina said. "But, come, sit. I thought we could have a few minutes to talk."

Elodie followed Angelina over to the sofa and they settled onto the plush green velvet. Angelina placed a hand onto Elodie's. "My dearest Elodie, I want to start off by saying, I am here to listen to anything you want to talk about, but also if you are uncomfortable with anything just say. We all want nothing but the best for you."

Elodie lowered her lashes. She'd had all day to come to terms with the past few days, but guilt still weighed heavily upon her. "Thank you, Angelina. I am grateful for your counsel and discretion. I fear I behaved rashly. I abandoned Luisa. I hope she will one day find it in her heart to understand and forgive me, but I was not thinking clearly. My only concern was running as far away as I could." She did not have to add *from him,* it was clear by the outrage in Angelina's eyes that she knew.

"You did what you thought best under awful circumstances. Luisa cares for you, she will understand one day," Angelina said. Elodie remembered Angelina herself had been stuck in a loveless marriage – perhaps the other lady was impressed by her decision to flee instead of succumbing. "In running away, you found your way here. I believe it is a sign. A sign that you knew you would find refuge and rescue. This is a haven after all."

Elodie pondered on that. Had she known, deep down in her soul, that she would end up wherever Raphael was? She had been drawn to him ever since she knew of him, that was true, but was it another choice being taken from her? Had she run from one man to only end up relying on another. But Raphael was not merely a man, he was... her heart gave a sudden pump of awareness as he walked in. Their gazes met, locked, and everything else faded away. He was *the one*. The only one.

Elodie blinked, and everything rushed back in, and she flushed as she caught Hunt's amused smile.

He crossed over to her and gave a bow. "Miss Di Silva, a pleasure to see you again. I hope you are not too cross at us for keeping the secret of Angelhaven from you. You can blame me, I wrongly thought keeping it from you until your arrival was in your best interests." His handsome face showed sincerity.

"I am sufficiently recovered from the shock," Elodie said with a small smile, letting him know there were no hard feelings. But still, every step she took through the house, every smell permeating from rooms or every billow of a curtain at a window brought back memories of her parents and of a life she held crystallised in her heart. She *was* recovered from the shock Raphael and the others had kept about their home, but would she ever be recovered from the shock at losing her parents? She predicted that was one wound she would wear like a battle scar, a scar to honour their memories. One she would be proud to wear.

"Then may I escort you into dinner?" Hunt threw a dazzling smile her way, and Elodie stood to accept his arm, with a smile of her own. She was beginning to like the mischievous lord very much.

They passed Raphael, and his presence had her wavering, her heart urging her to clasp his arm instead. But hanging onto her dignity, she inclined her head at Raphael and allowed Hunt to lead her out of the drawing room.

Behind them, Angelina gripped Raphael's arm. "Patience, cousin," she whispered.

Raphael frowned. Oh, he could be patient. He'd had no choice but to be eternally patient.

Twenty
Six

Elodie stared around the dining room. It was so familiar, yet so different. The furniture had been replaced, but the forest green wallpaper and drapes were the same as Elodie remembered.

Upon entering the room, a wave of nostalgia had washed over her, stealing her breath, but Hunt had placed a hand over her arm, and immediately she felt soothed. So much so, she was able to eat and converse with ease.

Elodie was interested to note the table was circular, which was most unconventional by Society standards. She sat in-between Raphael and Hunt, and opposite Angelina.

Angelina noticed her look and said, "We have a more traditional table, of course, but being just us four we swapped it out for our cosy family table. There is nothing more tiresome than only conversing with the person beside you. This is much more agreeable."

"I like it," Elodie replied. "I think more houses

should adopt the idea."

Hunt laughed. "I shudder to hear the outrage from households all around the ton at such a notion."

"Perhaps you are right," Elodie conceded, raising her glass.

"But here, as you see, we are a much more unconventional family," Raphael said. He hoped she could see there would be a place among them for her as long as she wished it. And he hoped she would wish it for always.

She smiled. "I like that too."

He smiled back; an unrelieved, carefree smile. The first of its kind that Elodie had seen from him, and a fragment of a memory slotted into place. "I saw you in the garden, you smiled at me, but as I ran to you, your smile was replaced by horror. You caught me... and then it all goes black." In shock, at the force of the vision, she jerked backwards, knocking over her wine glass. The red liquid pooled darkly over the white tablecloth, and she pushed to her feet at the sight. "So much blood," she murmured, her hand reaching behind her back to grasp at something that was no longer there. Hadn't been there for so long. Too long.

"*Elodie.*" Raphael enfolded her into his arms, his voice breaking with hope and grief.

"Bring her over to the doors, she needs air," Angelina urged, and Hunt went ahead of them to throw open the tall glass double doors.

On the terrace, Elodie blinked and looked about her as the fresh, salty air washed over her cheeks.

"What happened?"

"You do not remember?" Raphael asked cautiously. Angelina and Hunt backed away into the room, allowing them privacy.

"I-" she broke off, her eyes clouding, and Raphael felt disappointment surge through him. For one shining moment he thought it was all coming back to her, that their continued proximity was unlocking something within her. Unlike all the times before, where the revelation had been swift and violent and had always led to tragedy. He had thought, this time, the differences in the circumstances would set them on a path of liberty.

"I am sorry. Perhaps, I am still a trifle weary." Elodie placed a delicate white hand to her brow and looked out into the gardens beyond the terrace. "Oh, look at the maze." Her blank moment forgotten in the face of her astonishment; she stared out at the tall hedges bordering the maze that had begun to grow in her early years.

"Does it please you that we kept it?" Raphael asked, standing close beside her.

She looked at him, her eyes swimming with happiness, her hands gripping the terrace wall tightly. "You have no idea how much. It was a venture my father and I planned as a surprise for Mama. She had always wanted a maze and I think I was but five when we conceived the design. It is in the shape of concentric hearts," she added in a whisper. "Hearts for Mama to show her how much we loved her."

Raphael slid a hand over hers as one tear slid

down her cheek. "I am sure she knew how much you loved her. I see it in you, that you never wasted a moment to let her know. You are the product of their love, and you are all that is goodness and light and love."

"How do you know exactly the right words to say?" Elodie said, looking up at him. If she was the product of an epic love, how could she ever settle for anything less?

She moved closer, her eyes asking him an aeons-old question. One he answered with his lips, slanting over hers. Gently he kissed her, but she wanted more, she wanted everything the kiss promised, and so much more. She leaned into him, and with a sound of acceptance, Raphael deepened the kiss, his knees almost buckling when she opened to him. It was a kiss he had been waiting lifetimes for, one he dreamed of and craved. The shared breath was like his lifeblood and now he had tasted it, he would never be the same again. For he felt the soul connection, that click, but did she? On some level he knew she must feel it too, despite the buried memories. His hope returned with a vengeance.

He would not give up. This time they had a chance.

They broke apart, and chest heaving, Raphael dropped his forehead to Elodie's. She took a shuddering breath. What had just happened? Never in her wildest dreams had she believed a kiss would be like that. It had lit her up from the inside, causing a burning – a *yearning* – in her very soul. Had

Raphael felt it too?

"I did not mean to take advantage-" he began, but Elodie placed one slim finger to his heated lips. She could not bear it if he apologised.

"I wanted you to kiss me," she said, with only a hint of a blush. "Would you walk with me in the gardens?"

"It would be an honour," Raphael said, and held out an arm.

They stepped down into the lower gardens and two large shadows melted into step behind them. Elodie let out a startled squeak, but relaxed when she saw they were dogs.

"This is Solomon and Gideon, the best and most loyal friends a man could ask for," Raphael said, and Elodie looked at the friendly faces of the wolfhounds with their lolling tongues and saw he spoke the truth. Solomon nosed into Elodie's hand, and she rested it on his back as they walked. He gazed up at her with adoring chocolate brown eyes, and she was instantly besotted.

Raphael cast the dog a look of chagrin, but how could he be jealous of the dog, when he felt exactly the same. Elodie had a way about her, an ingrained innocence that could either be taken advantage of or cherished. He intended her to be cherished for the rest of her existence.

Together, they walked the gravel paths beneath the moonlight, amongst hedges and statuary, some familiar to Elodie and some new. She enjoyed stitching together in her mind what was and what could be. Oh, and what possibilities there were, if only she was free to explore them.

Raphael stopped at the entrance to the maze. "Tomorrow, in the daylight, I will take you inside, if that would be agreeable to you?"

"That would be agreeable indeed." Elodie reached out a hand to brush her fingertips over the hedge. If only her father could see it now, he would be so proud. Love swelled in her heart at the gift she had been given, because if it were anyone else who had moved into Angelhaven, she would not have been able to stand there right at that moment, with the house at her back, the roar of the sea in the distance, and memories filling her heart. She had been blessed, and she could see that now. "Thank you," she whispered - to whom she knew not, but she, in that moment, was eternally grateful.

"Shall we retire inside?" Raphael asked and Elodie nodded. He clicked his fingers at the dogs, but they both stared into the depths of the maze, their hackles raised, low growls emanating from their throats.

Raphael stepped in front of Elodie, his eyes scanning the shadows. "Go inside the house," he told her.

"I will not leave you," Elodie said. *Not now, not ever*. Raphael looked over his shoulder at her.

"Then we will go back into the house together." He would see her safely inside before returning with Hunt to investigate. "Sol, Gid, come," he ordered, and the dogs immediately fell into heel, both keeping close to Elodie as they walked back up to the house.

Elodie's shoulder blades prickled, and if her steps hastened, she was not ashamed of it. She knew it couldn't conceivably mean *he* was there, but the spectre of his presence haunted her, and she wanted both her and Raphael to take refuge in the haven they both had been fortunate to call home.

Inside the dining room, Angelina looked up from her pacing. Hunt reclined in his chair with his feet on the now cleared table, a brandy glass in hand.

"What is it?" Hunt asked, sliding his feet from the table and standing.

"Something spooked the dogs in the maze," Raphael replied with a meaningful look. Angelina immediately took Elodie's arm and drew her further into the room.

Hunt set his glass down, his eyes lighting with an interested gleam. "Let us have a look, shall we?"

"But-" Elodie began, a feeling of dread curdling deep in her stomach. She could not bear it if something happened to Raphael. Not now, not when they had just discovered each other.

"Fear not, I will keep Rafe safe," Hunt said with a smile, clapping a hand to his cousin's shoulders.

Raphael shot Hunt a long-suffering look, before turning to reassure Elodie. "We will be perfectly safe. Solomon, stay. Gideon, come." The dogs did as they were ordered.

Raphael gave Elodie one long look, his eye patch adding to the shadowy mystery of his face, before leaving with Hunt and Gideon, and pulling the doors closed behind them.

The two men and dog kept to the shadows and headed back to the maze. Stealthily, they crept inside, both knowing the way through hours spent inside. Gideon appeared at ease, loping beside them as if going on an adventure. Taking his cues from the dog, Raphael finally came to the assumption that whatever had alarmed them had gone.

"Probably just another animal," Hunt said as they exited the maze and moved back to the house. "We should not jump to conclusions, not so soon anyhow. He will more than likely keep his search to the area Elodie was last seen at. He might even believe she returned to London."

Raphael did not need to ask who 'he' was. It was always *him*, that would never change. But what would change would be Raphael. No more taking chances. "Agreed. But still, we should keep her close until if she..." he trailed off.

"Not if, cous, *when*. She will remember, we must give her time." Hunt took the terrace steps two at a time.

But how much time did they have? Raphael thought. He could feel an icy breath skimming down the back of his neck.

Back inside the house, he realised it did not matter, all that mattered was Elodie and that she *would* eventually remember. She always did. But it had never turned out the way they hoped. He had to believe that this time would be different.

"I could have taken him right then," Earl Mikael Thorne said as he mounted his bay horse.

"Patience, old friend," Lord Beaumont said. "This was just merely a scouting mission. I needed to ensure she was there."

"Oh, she was there all right," Lord Nathaniel St. Clair said with a raised eyebrow. "It certainly did not take her long to ensconce herself back into his life."

Lord Beaumont moved so fast he was a blur. He gripped St. Clair by his peacock blue cravat and yanked him away from the horses. "Careful what you say. I always was stronger than you."

"S-sorry, old chap. Just an observation," St. Clair blustered, his eyes rolling.

"Then might I strongly suggest you keep your *observations* to yourself," Lord Beaumont said icily, before shoving him away. "I have taken us rooms in the inn at the nearby village. Let us return there and plan."

The two men mounted their horses, and with one final look at the house where *she* waited, Lord Beaumont followed his associates across the moor.

Now he knew where she was, a frosty calmness had slicked over the banked anger. But with one crack it would be unleashed, and there would be hell to pay for any who stood in his way of getting her back.

Twenty
Seven

Claws clicked across the tiled floor, rousing Raphael from his slumber. The episode in the maze earlier had unnerved him, delaying him retiring to bed, so he had taken refuge in the library. As Gideon rose his head at Raphael's feet, an immediate awareness came over Raphael. He looked around the arm of the chair to see Elodie walking across the library towards the bookcase ladder, Solomon at her heels. She wore a frothy pale grey nightgown, and in the candlelight she cast an ethereal glow. Her long black hair was bound in a single braid that sat over her left shoulder.

She reached the ladder and was just placing a slippered foot on the bottom rung when Solomon gave a warning rumble deep in his barrel chest. She looked at the dog. "I will be perfectly fine," she whispered, stroking a delicate hand over his massive head.

Raphael had to hide a grin as the dog gave the impression of being torn in his duty of protecting her and of lovingly giving in to her whims. Raphael could understand the sentiments entirely.

The love won out and Solomon allowed Elodie to climb up the ladder, but as she climbed with purpose to the top, her eyes scanning the shelves, Raphael's heart missed a beat. She really was up so high. *What if she fell?* Memories slammed into his mind, and without thought, he stood and made his way over to the ladder, but she had selected a book and was already on her way back down.

Raphael was just about to announce his presence when the light from the candles illuminated two angry red marks on Elodie's upper back. Her nightgown was cut low on the back revealing her shoulder blades. He let out a hiss, and startled, Elodie missed her footing.

With a squeak of surprise, and a bark of alert from Solomon, Elodie tumbled into Raphael's arms.

"Oh," she said breathlessly, clutching the book, and looking up into his shocked one-eyed gaze. "This is becoming a habit." She smiled.

"What is?" Raphael asked, mesmerised by her.

Elodie blinked, and confusion dulled her silvery eyes. "I thought I remembered you catching me when I fell... before."

Tenderness – and hope – engulfed Raphael and he clutched her to him as he carried her over to the sofa. "I would catch you a thousand times over," he vowed, reminding her of something similar he had said when he had found her at the gates of Angelhaven.

Elodie looked up at him, her eyes enormous, but

this time she had a reply ready. "And I would let you," she whispered back, before a flush stained her cheeks. She ducked her head as he lay her on the plump red cushions, her back exposed above the arm. He moved behind her.

"Does it hurt?" he asked, his fingers brushing the back of her neck and she shivered. She knew he referred to the marks she had been born with.

"Sometimes they burn and itch," she told him. *But mostly when Lord Beaumont is near*, she thought, barely suppressing a shudder. "Maggie found one of my old nightgowns, they are cut this way to allow some relief at night. The cool air soothes them."

"May I?" Raphael asked, and she turned her head questioningly. Not knowing exactly what he was asking, she nodded her head, instinctively trusting him.

He knelt behind the low arm of the sofa, where she sat. He traced one gentle finger around each large almond-shaped mark, and ripples of awareness shot through Elodie. The marks had only ever caused her discomfort, but this – *this* was something else entirely. As the sensations subsided, she gave a gasp as Raphael pressed a gentle kiss reverently to each mark. His soft lips soothed the skin like a healing balm.

"I am so sorry," he whispered against her skin, and Elodie turned then.

"Whatever do you have to be sorry for?" she asked. "I was born with them."

Raphael met her gaze. "I am sorry for your discomfort," he said in a stilted voice. He straightened before dropping onto the sofa next to her.

Elodie frowned, then reached out a hand to lay it on the sleeve of his loose white shirt. "Thank you," she said. Confusion at his reaction, and still feeling the effects of his touch caused her mind to whirl but she revelled in just simply being near him.

She took in his thick black hair tied back at the nape of his neck revealing his strong face. His shirt was open at the neck, and the candlelight played with the angles and planes of his tanned skin. She longed to reach out her hand and delve beneath the fabric, yearning to repeat their earlier kiss on the terrace.

Startled by her own thoughts, her lips parted as she looked up. Raphael watched her with one hooded eye, his other concealed, as always, by the black leather patch. To cover her sudden shyness, she broke the gaze, and her attention was caught by a book on a table next to the sofa... but it was the opal emblazoned on the front that called to her.

Elodie reached out to trail her hand over the stone and it seemed to glow beneath her touch. "Oh, it is so beautiful... but there is a kind of sadness to it too." For some strange reason a hot rush of shameful grief welled up inside her, and she turned away from it, from the pain it caused, as if she, herself, had wept the hard shard of opal.

Raphael saw the grief clouding her eyes and winced in a reflection of that grief. He knew what the opal was, how could he not? He had viscerally known its divine source as soon as he had discovered it in one of the rooms of Angelhaven, glimmering between two floorboards. But *how* it had come to be at Angelhaven he had no notion, for its story was seeded in a time, millennia ago, in a distant place from where he and his kin had finally made their haven. He wished Elodie could see it for what it was – a symbol of hope that whatever they desired within their hearts was possible. The reason he had discovered it in this cycle had to mean something. It just had to. But he knew she was not ready for the truth. Not yet.

"I-" Elodie said, breaking off, her eyes clearing of the last vestiges of bewildered sorrow.

"Yes?" Raphael asked, his attention now firmly on her in the here and now. He turned his body, his knees trapping her on the sofa. His gaze dropped to the small leather-bound book she had selected from the library shelves. "Byron."

"Oh, yes! I hope you don't mind me borrowing this? I could not sleep," Elodie said in a rush, relieved at having something to fill the charged air with.

Raphael covered her hand holding the book with one of his own. "Everything at Angelhaven is at your disposal," he told her. The gap between them lessened.

Even you? Elodie could not believe her bold thoughts. What was happening to her? This man had suddenly filled a void she did not know she'd even had. But now it stood gaping before her, and if she did not fill it with him, with his touch, she did not know if she would ever feel whole again.

"I-" she began for the second time.

"*Yes*," Raphael said, but this time it was not a question, it was the answer, the answer to her unspoken plea.

With one long breath of acceptance Raphael closed the gap even further until their breath mingled. Elodie leaned up and his lips brushed hers, the merest of whispers. She closed her eyes, willingly succumbing and suddenly his mouth was on hers. Like before, it was the kiss she had been waiting for what felt like an eternity, it branded her lips and then her very soul. Instinctively she angled her head, knowing it would shape their mouths to a better fit, pulling them both even deeper.

She had come home.

Flashes of images filtered into her mind. Raphael ranged over her, his chest bare, his hair longer... and his eyes, *both* his eyes slowly raising, about to meet hers. The kiss finished and Elodie blinked in bereft confusion, the images dissipating.

But Raphael had only stopped to press fervent feather-light kisses down her neck, dipping lower and lower until they met the heated skin of her collarbone. He pulled the ribbons of her nightgown and the fabric fluttered open revealing her pale skin.

He glanced up at her, and she told him everything with one longing look. This was what she wanted. *He* was what she wanted. The book fell to the floor as Elodie pulled Raphael to her, her hands plunging into his hair. The leather tie sprang loose, releasing his hair to frame his face and brush against her neck. His lips found hers once again as his hand pushed up the hem of her gown, igniting a flaming trail on her skin where he touched.

He reached her thigh before he jerked backwards, pushing himself off her to stumble away. Suddenly cold, Elodie felt the distance was more like a chasm than the few feet it actually was.

"I cannot knowingly do this, when you are... *unknowing*." Raphael raked a hand through his hair with a trembling hand. "You should go," he said, not looking at her. Solomon and Gideon stood up from where they had ranged themselves by the fire and watched their master uncertainly.

"But if you teach me, I would know. I would know what it is to be lov..." her voice small, Elodie trailed off, clasping the top of her nightgown closed.

Finally, Raphael looked at her. "That is not what I meant-" he broke off, aghast. He dropped to the floor and retrieved the book. On his knees, he offered it to her. With a shaking hand, Elodie took it. Both still holding the book, Raphael drew it towards him, and pressed a kiss to the back of her hand. "This is your haven too; you should be safe here. Safe until you know the truth."

"What truth?" Elodie asked, searching his face. What secrets was he concealing? Why could he not confide in her. She thought he too felt as she did. She would lay all of her secrets bare for him, but was she fooling herself even now?

Raphael released her and stood. "I have said too much," he said. "I will bid you goodnight, Elodie." His gaze shuttered, and Elodie, gathering the remnants of her strength, rose.

"Goodnight, Your Grace," she said formally, and with as much dignity as she could muster, left.

Solomon gave Raphael a disapproving whine before trotting after her, and Raphael resisted the urge to do the same. Gideon tilted his head and Raphael said, "Not you too." The dog thumped his tail against the fireplace, and Raphael relented and patted his head.

"You did the right thing in letting her go," Angelina said, coming in through the library door. She held up a hand at his shocked expression. "I only heard the last few words and saw her go."

Raphael let out a huff of breath. "Do you know how hard it was to let her go, do you know how completely she fits in my arms, how perfectly her lips shape to mine?" He paced up and down in frustration, before continuing almost to himself, "I almost didn't let her go, I almost gave in. What kind of monster am I?"

Angelina rushed over to him. "But you didn't. You released her. *You* are not the monster." She did not need to add who she thought was the real monster, but Raphael voiced what they were both thinking.

"But *he* would not let her go so easily. He would take what he wanted without thought or consequence." Raphael walked to the fireplace and stared down into the flickering flames. Gideon nosed his way into his hand, and Raphael ran a hand over his wiry back. "When will this be over?" His voice broke.

A rustle of a dress across the floor told him Angelina had joined him. She said quietly, "When she remembers in her own time; gently and gradually. We must be patient and adhere to the plan. Only then will she be free. Will we all be free."

Raphael clenched a fist against the stone of the fireplace, but gave a jerky nod. He knew his cousin spoke the truth, but it still did not make it any easier to bear. "Lina... she has marks on her back, beside her shoulder blades," he said softly, turning to face her.

Angelina's eyes widened. "Oh, Rafe," she said, subsiding into the armchair next to the fireplace. She dropped her head into her hands and wept.

Raphael understood the reaction, understood it but could not react in the same way. No, the effect at seeing Elodie's fair skin marred so, and knowing what the marks represented, gave free rein to something far more violent within him. His emotions required a supreme amount of willpower to contain them.

For something to do he walked over to the drink's cabinet and poured a glass of brandy and stepped to Angelina's side. "Here, drink this, it will help."

She looked up. "No, cousin, I will not find solace in the bottom of a brandy glass – I will leave that to Hunt." She smiled a small watery smile through her tears.

After a moment, Raphael smiled back. "It is late, you should go to bed."

Angelina stood, and clasped a comforting hand to his shoulder. "That is excellent advice. Perhaps you should take it." She squeezed his shoulder pointedly then let go. "Goodnight," she murmured and glided from the room.

Raphael stared unseeing after her for a moment, then turned back to the drink's cabinet. No, Lina would not find solace, but he sure as hell would. He snatched up the decanter, and carrying the full glass, strode from the room, Gideon at his heels.

Elodie tossed the book onto her bed. How did Raphael expect her to sleep now. Her blood still thrummed from his touch and from the confusion she felt at being spurned so suddenly. His capricious nature was beginning to trouble her. She had been fully prepared to give all of herself to him. Her cheeks burned with shame.

She sat on her bed, the emotion draining from her. All she wanted was to find someone to share her life with, someone who saw *her,* who accepted her and *wanted* her. She had believed she had found that in Raphael. Perhaps she had been wrong.

One tear tracked its way down her cheek, and she lay back, curling into a ball as Solomon let out a whine and jumped up onto the bed. He lay beside her, his back pressed comfortingly against hers. With the dog's steady breaths lulling her, she closed her eyes...

"He cannot give you what you desire. You deserve to be treasured, to be worshipped." Steel-like arms enveloped Elodie and cold breath leached the warmth from her cheek.

Opening her eyes, she saw mist surrounding her as she stood in a faded garden. It looked familiar, but somehow *wrong*.

Lord Beaumont held her, and she reluctantly met his eyes. "You are mistaken. *He* is what I desire."

His eyes darkened angrily, and he released her, one hand flying up. He stilled it millimetres from her cheek, but she refused to flinch. "He will be the death of you," he hissed.

Elodie faltered. Was there truth behind the words? "No, I refuse to believe it," she said, but this time her voice shook, and Lord Beaumont smiled his knowing smile.

"I only want the best for you, my dear," he said, his voice gentling. "I could give you the world, if only you would just willingly give in to me." His hand, just moments ago a near-weapon, instead now lovingly caressed Elodie's face while his eyes captured hers. Feeling as though she were falling and simultaneously held by some kind of insidious seductive thrall, she leaned towards him.

Triumph flared in his icy depths as he hovered over her, but with a sudden strength, one Elodie did not know she possessed, she wrenched herself away and ran. Ran through the misty gardens, with Lord

Beaumont's roar of rage following her.

Elodie awoke with Solomon standing over her, teeth bared, a growl rumbling deep in his chest.

With shaking arms, she leaned up and wrapped them around the dog's neck, comforting both herself and him. "Shh, it is all right. It was just a dream," she soothed.

She looked past Solomon at the curtains billowing out from the open windows. She shivered; certain she had closed them when she had returned to her room.

It *was* just a dream, wasn't it?

Elodie got up and closed the windows firmly. She froze as a lone white feather on the windowsill mocked her. Tentatively, she picked it up; it was ice cold. Dropping it, she stumbled backwards and pulled the blanket from the bed. Wrapping herself in it, she sat in the chair next to the fire. Solomon jumped off the bed to stand sentry next to her.

Sleep would be scarce for the rest of the long night.

Twenty Eight

"Angelina said I would find you in here." Elodie stepped into the stables, Solomon at her side. Whether Raphael had instructed the dog or not, he was now Elodie's protective shadow, and she found she did not mind at all. He was a comforting presence, and had kept her feet warm, and licked her hand when she had finally fitfully slept. But thankfully, the nightmares had stayed at bay.

Raphael stopped brushing the huge black stallion, and looked over at her. "What are you doing out of the house?" It came out sharper than he intended and Elodie paused. "I am sorry, I just meant, you should not be out alone."

Elodie tilted her head. Raphael's shoulders appeared tense. "Would you like me to go?" A flush worked its way across her cheeks. Was he still indifferent towards her? She hoped the new day would bring some clarity.

Raphael shook his head. "No, of course not, I am just out of sorts this morning. Come and meet my

264

other friends." He gestured a hand at the stables, and the black stallion tossed its head as if in greeting. Raphael leaned over and took Elodie's hand to place it on the stallion's neck. "This is Bran."

Elodie rubbed the velvety skin. "Hello, Bran, you are a most handsome gentleman." Bran let out a soft snort, and Raphael could not help the grin that slid onto his face. Yet another conquest made.

They moved onto the next stable which housed a creamy-white mare. "This is Luna, Angelina rides her when she is here, and this spirited fellow is Comet – Hunt's horse." Rafe patted the neck of a large chestnut stallion in the next stable. "And finally, this precious soul is Grace."

Elodie let out a gasp at the name. She looked into the gentle eyes of the small grey mare. "Grace was my mother's name," she whispered.

Raphael closed his eye briefly. Had he somehow known that? Was that why the name had floated into his mind when he had been offered the mare. He hadn't needed another horse, but knew he must take her, and now he knew why. "Then Grace shall be yours."

"Mine?" Elodie asked. "I could not accept such a gift." Though it pained her to turn it down, she knew she must. It would not be proper.

"Then for as long as you are here," Raphael said, and Elodie cast a wistful glance at the mare, before nodding.

"Thank you," she said. She knew she must broach her future plans, but she did not want to. She did not want to spoil what she had found with Raphael, and the others too. She let out a sigh.

"Something troubles you?" Raphael asked, his green eye keen on her face. He offered her a carrot which she took to hold out for Grace to nibble on.

So many things, Elodie thought, but instead she said, "Just a restless night's sleep." She dare not tell him the whole of it. Would he, perhaps, worry for her sanity? She could not tell him of being haunted by feathers, of being plagued with perplexing and terrifying dreams, ones that felt so very real.

Raphael nodded at that. "Would you like to see the maze? It might tire you enough so you can have a nap this afternoon." He felt confident that whatever had troubled the dogs the night before had long gone.

Elodie smiled. "I would enjoy that."

Raphael held out his arm and Elodie felt relief that their awkward parting the night before appeared to have not left a lingering tension. Together they walked from the stables, Solomon walking beside Elodie.

Inside the maze, Elodie ran her hand along the hedges. She and her father had chosen a robust shrub that would withstand the mist and salt air, while growing tall enough to make the maze a hidden mystery for guests and the family to enjoy.

Raphael let Elodie take the lead, knowing she needed this as part of her healing process. She went on ahead with Solomon. Raphael watched the mist swirl in and surround her. He blinked. Memories of another time took over and he saw her as she was –

266

as she should be. Anger and grief warred within him. She should be whole, not living a half-life destined to run, but in running, would she ever discover the truth, or just the truth of someone else's lies?

He shook his head, dispelling the thoughts. He walked around the curve of one of the concentric hearts, but she had seemingly vanished. His heart thudded once, twice, before he mobilised into action. "Elodie!"

His voice echoed back to him, and he started to run. The mist thickened and a scream filled the air, followed by a series of deep guttural barks.

"Solomon! Lead me to her!" Raphael shouted, and the dog barked again.

Raphael followed the direction of the sound and, to his relief, saw Elodie sat on the ground in the centre of the maze in the small heart-shaped courtyard. But *what* was it she sat upon? He stepped towards her, then hesitated as she turned a pale face up to his. *Feathers*. It was mounds of pristine white feathers.

"He has found me," she said, then her eyes rolled back in her head. He caught her before she slumped to the ground.

Holding Elodie, while Solomon let out a whine, Raphael cast a furtive look around, pressing a hand to the feathers with his free hand. The feathers were ice cold, but not damp. They had not been long there in the mist, and certainly not overnight. Whoever had placed them – and he was now under no illusions as to *who* that was – had been back recently, perhaps they were still even there in the maze.

He had to get Elodie back to the house as quickly as possible. "Solomon, come," he said but he needn't have uttered the words as the dog immediately trotted forward, sniffing his way from the maze, as soon as Raphael picked up Elodie and moved away from the centre.

At the edge of the maze, a sudden swirl of mist cut off Raphael's sight of Solomon. He took another step, ready to call the dog when a sharp pain on the back of his head had him stumbling. His vision greyed and he fought with everything he had to stay upright, clutching Elodie to his chest. If he let her go, she would fall. He could not let her fall. Another pain exploded at the back of his head, and he dropped to his knees, Elodie rolling out of his arms. The last thought that filled his mind as he collapsed was, *too late*.

A mournful howl brought Elodie out of the dark loop she had been re-living in her unconsciousness. She found herself lying on the gravel path leading into the maze, with Solomon sat beside her, howling.

Footsteps ran towards her. "Elodie, whatever has happened?" Hunt helped her to stand, and she shivered uncontrollably.

"We were in the maze," she remembered slowly. "Raphael and I – where is Raphael?" she spun in a circle, dread pinpricking between her shoulder blades. She clutched at Hunt. "He has him! I know it… there were feathers, always white feathers," she murmured almost incoherently.

"Who has who?" Angelina asked breathlessly, joining them.

"Lord Beaumont – he has Raphael." Elodie clutched her head with her hands. "Oh, this is all my fault. I should never have come here." She would give herself over to Lord Beaumont, who was she fooling to ever think she had any choice? It was always going to end this way. And now Raphael was in danger because she had been short-sighted, and selfish.

"No – Elodie, it is not your fault, it never was-" Angelina broke off with a frustrated look at Hunt as he said warningly, "*Lina*."

"I know, Hunt," she continued. "I know exactly what you are going to say, but our plan has not worked. She hasn't remembered on her own. We failed."

Elodie looked at the siblings. "What are you talking about. What plan?"

"Elodie-" Hunt cast his sister a frustrated look of his own before raking a hand through his blonde hair "-there are things you do not know about us, and you, and the rivalry between Lord Beaumont and Rafe. It began so long ago."

Elodie's blood began to thrum. Visions swirled in her mind, and her shoulder blades burned. "Does it have anything to do with a garden and feathers and… and…" she trailed off, her mind blocking out anything else past that point.

Angelina took her hand, while Solomon whined

again. She looked deep into her eyes; piercing blue to silvery-grey. "We cannot tell you the whole of it, we have no knowing of what it might do. You must remember yourself, you *must* try, and you must embrace the truth this time and try-" she swallowed back tears "-try not to run from him."

"Run from who – Lord Beaumont?" Elodie asked in confusion. She had already done that, and now Raphael was suffering because of it.

"No, not *him*... Raphael."

"But why would I run *from* Raphael? My soul longs to run *to* him." Elodie clapped a hand to her mouth as the words burst out. As the truth burst out.

Angelina's eyes swam with tears. "I know it does, it is doing what it is supposed to do. It is always the same. Time after time, like chess pieces being moved into position, we are all drawn to the same place until we reach check, and then it always ends in check mate, and not in our favour."

"I do not understand," Elodie said.

Hunt snorted. "Lina, no one would understand that cryptic metaphor. Either we tell her all, or we go and rescue Rafe."

"Raphael expressly forbid us to tell her. Weren't we the ones who told him to have faith and patience?"

"Yes, well I think we have run out of both," Hunt snapped back. He looked around. "Where did she go?"

Elodie had slipped away into the mist.

Hunt let out a groan. "She isn't going to do what I

think she's going to do, is she?"

"If you mean give herself over to Beaumont in exchange for Raphael, then yes, I think that is *exactly* what she is going to do," Angelina stated.

"Rafe is going to kill us," Hunt muttered.

A clattering of hooves had him looking up and he saw a grey shape streak through the mist. "She's on Grace, and without a saddle I might add."

"Really Hunt, the girl grew up here, she probably knows the land better than anyone. If anyone can ride saddle-less over the moors it is her. But come on, she has the right of it. They cannot have gone far."

Without waiting for her brother, she hurried over to the stables, where Solomon paced anxiously.

Elodie urged Grace on, the mist snaked around the mare's feet but thankfully visibility across the flat moorland was good. In the far distance, a group of horses galloped away from her towards the cliff edge. While her heart stuttered, her desire to get to Raphael before it was too late, grew stronger. She could feel him; with every hoofbeat, she could sense she closed the distance between her soul and his.

She could not think about Angelina's puzzling explanations, there was no time to decipher them. Not now. Not when Lord Beaumont had finally done the unthinkable and kidnapped Raphael. But why had he not taken *her*? She had been there, unconscious. Lord Beaumont could have incapacitated Raphael, and taken her. It was mystifying.

She rounded a rock on the ground and galloped on, nearly pulling Grace up when she saw the old carriage path snaking through the moors in front of her. The one that had not been used since... *since the accident*, she thought with a stab to the heart.

She looked up, recognising where she was. *No.* The rumbling sound of a labouring carriage filled her mind, and she saw it buckling under the strain of its lost wheel. In her vision, she reached out as if she could pull the carriage back from the brink with sheer force of will. But, of course, it was not to be. The carriage did what it always did as the horses broke free, it fell over the edge, leaving behind it only the screams of her terrified parents.

Why had Lord Beaumont taken Raphael to the exact place of her parents' tragic end. What mind trickery was this?

Elodie pushed Grace on, hoping she was strong enough – brave enough – to find out.

Twenty
Nine

Elodie got as close as she could without alerting Lord Beaumont to her presence, stopping behind an outcrop of rocks. In the misty light, she listened to Lord Beaumont's tirade as Raphael slumped weakly on his knees, flanked by two other men. Elodie recognised them as Thorne and St. Clair.

"I will not kill you, simply because I do not know what effect that will have on her soul, but I will take you so close to that edge. Over and over. I will keep you close, so you will know of our life together. Because I happen to like *this* life. I have money, power, privilege... and *her*."

Elodie knew she had to act fast, before Lord Beaumont hurt Raphael. She did not believe for one moment he was not capable of killing. She had seen the monster that lurked beneath his cool, handsome features. She dismounted Grace and, with the moss muffling her footsteps, approached, and hid behind a large rock.

Lord Beaumont ripped Raphael's eye patch off

and turned his face to his, leaning in close to spit, "Ah, that's right. I want you to look me in the eyes and see the truth I speak. She will come, she will want to save you, and then her choice will be... *me*."

"If she comes, then that means she did choose. But it is not because she wants *you*, it is because my soul calls to hers. From the dawn of time to this moment, right now. You know you cannot stop it; all you can do is delay it - but every time she runs from me... She. Still. Does. Not. Choose. You!" Raphael finished on a roar, and with the cry of anguish, huge black glossy wings erupted from his back.

Elodie blinked in shock, but horrified fascination kept her rooted to the spot as Lord Beaumont pulled back his fist and thrust it into Raphael's jaw. The cold lord's face showed more emotion than Elodie had ever seen from him before. She threw a hand up to her mouth, stifling the scream that wanted to tear from her.

As Raphael's head snapped back, two blinding white wings extended from Lord Beaumont's back. Lord Beaumont's associates acted fast gripping Raphael's wings firmly, preventing him from getting up and fighting back.

Elodie craved answers, answers that had eluded her for her whole life. *Lives*? She wondered dizzily, not knowing where that thought came from.

"Lord Beaumont... what are you doing?" she asked slowly, hardly believing what she was seeing, but perhaps it was all beginning to make sense. Piece by tiny piece tried to slot into place, but still something stopped the puzzle from completing.

Lord Beaumont turned in shocked silence, chest heaving from exertion, with Raphael's eyepatch in his hand. His position partially hid Raphael from Elodie's view. "How are you here? I did not hear you arrive... but no matter, you are here now," he continued in gentle tones.

At Raphael's groan of, "Elodie, no," Lord Beaumont's wings vanished, and he was once again the image of a man. Elodie blinked in confusion. Was she having some sort of mental breakdown?

Lord Beaumont ignored Raphael and said, "You have come to me. I knew you would see sense. It was so tempting to have taken you instead, but I know ultimately it must be your choice, and now you are here. Willingly give yourself over to me, and I will allow him to live."

Elodie swallowed down the bile that burned her throat. That was not a *choice*.

"Elodie do not listen to him, he will not kill me, he cannot risk our soul connection," Raphael ground out from behind Lord Beaumont. "Do not give yourself to him to save me."

"*Quiet,*" Lord Beaumont said through clenched teeth, whirling around, and in doing so inadvertently revealed Raphael to Elodie. Her gaze slowly tracked from one man to the other. "No, you must not look into his eyes – you must not see!" Lord Beaumont pleaded.

Raphael tried to tear his gaze away, but it was too late. Silver-grey eyes met the full bright green gaze and held.

Millenia fell away.

"Here we go again," Hunt said grimly as he and Angelina cantered up behind them and dismounted. "... *And* she's going to run," he added under his breath, but without any trace of his usual humour.

The ground beneath Elodie's feet shifted as thunder rumbled overhead. Her heart gave one painful thump. "No, it cannot be." Everything came rushing back. First the love, the epic all-encompassing love between her and Raphael, wings extended above a garden so green and verdant, flying together through the heavens, their soul forging a connection that would last for eternity.

A sob of recollection, of knowing, escaped her lips as she watched Raphael's face crumple as he saw she remembered. But she remembered because she looked into his full cursed gaze, not because it had come back to her gradually - naturally. Elodie remembered the bright, shining love and basked in it, letting it fill her up until she believed the love might overflow and pour from every strand of hair, from every fingertip. Her hands reached out to Raphael, the love seeking to seal the connection with him.

But it was not to last. It never did.

The other players in the scene watched it unfold, as they had countless times before, watched as the shutter came down on Elodie's face, her terrified mind repulsing the horror of what occurred after the love. The violence, the shame... *everything*, all she knew to be true, was rejected and hidden to protect itself. Raphael's eyes – the window to the soul – had revealed everything... and then taken it all away with one cursed look.

"Fight it, Elodie, *please*," Raphael begged, as Lord Beaumont's face froze in a mask of panic.

But Elodie had already been hollowed out, an empty vessel devoid of thought or feeling. She froze, staring blankly at Raphael. She did not know him; she did not know any of them. Why was she there? One sensation filtered through the desolation... panic. She turned, picked up her skirts and ran. Ran away from them all, ran away from the dark-haired man, and the strange shame prickling between her shoulder blades.

"Elodriel!" She knew not who shouted the strange name, she only knew she had to get away. Somewhere, anywhere where she would be safe. *Safe from what*? She staggered to the grey horse before her, that at least held some recollection for her. Had she been riding and fell and bumped her head?

She was caught before she attempted to clamber onto the mare.

"Elodie, wait." The tall blonde woman had followed her. "You must fight it. You must not run; you will die if you do. It is the same every time."

"How do you know my name? Why am I here?" Elodie clung to the horse's side and let out a sob as she took in *exactly* where she was. This was where the carriage fell. Where her parents died. Why was the woman talking of death, did she not understand what this place represented? Was Elodie, too, to die here?

She looked past the woman to stare at the two men, no not men, the dark-haired one had *wings*, while the golden-haired man stood still as a statue; appearing to be suffering from shock.

Her heart stuttered, taking in the bewildering scene, before a memory from *this* life, from Elodie Di Silva's life, slotted into place. She released the horse and walked forward. "It was *you*. You two battled in the skies above the carriage." She choked back another sob as anger seeped into her blood. "Did you cause my parents' death?"

"*No*, Elodie. I tried to stop it, to save them. I only followed Luc because I discovered he might have found you, but we weren't sure it *was* actually you – not then, but it was too late; Luc had already spooked the horses, I couldn't stop it." The dark-haired man spoke and his warm, husky voice stirred something deep within Elodie, despite his confusing explanation. "His plan was to orphan you, to ensure you would be deposited into his family's care, and ultimately into his hands so he could further discern if you were the one."

The one what? Elodie thought vaguely.

"Well, it worked out well for you, Raphael, did you not inherit her estate because of my actions?" the golden-haired man spat.

Elodie backed up, horrified at this revelation, as the dark-haired man gave her a pleading look. "No, I kept it in safe-keeping for you for when... when you would *remember*." His voice cracked and Elodie, through her uncertainty, heard the truth in his words.

The golden-haired man made a noise of derision. "I merely sought to speed things up. But you were in no danger, my dear. I would have flown you to safety, but providence was on your side. You were flung away before I could get to you, and then *he* prevented me from claiming you." He tossed away the eye patch and held out a hand to Elodie. "But come away with me now, I will take you to safety."

"You... you are mad. All of you. Why would I go with *you*, you killed my parents." Elodie shook her head, while her heart beat sluggishly in her chest. Why did she feel so weak? She staggered a few steps; she had to get away from them all.

"There is nowhere you can take her now, you fool. There is nowhere safe for her. It has been set in motion; all we can do is wait." The tall man, who looked as if he could be the woman's brother, cast a dark look at the one called Luc.

"You are wrong. If I keep him locked up within close distance to us, she will never run far enough away from him for the death curse to take her." Luc let out a mad, triumphant smile. He looked fully poised to leap forward and grab Elodie, despite her protestations.

"She should know the *truth*. You owe her that much, Luc, after what you have done," the woman said sadly. She stepped towards Elodie, and Elodie saw in her, at least, compassion. "Elodie, wait and hear the truth, then go if you must. It was never your fault, but you blamed yourself and had always run before we could try and convince you to try and remember what *truly* happened."

Elodie paused, although the urge to flee was still upon her, pressing on her, suffocating her, causing her heart to labour so she could not catch her breath. It felt like when her parents had died, but worse, like her heart truly was breaking into two, cleaving the very soul from her.

"You – we – but especially you, are cursed. Once you see Raphael's face and look deep into his eyes, the curse enacts. You remember how you were created for each other-" Luc let out a hiss, but the woman continued "-and then, in your belief that you are to blame for everything that happened, you forget... everything, who we are, who you were, *everything*, and so in terror and your perceived guilt you run, but the further you run, the weaker you get. Because you and Raphael are meant to be *together*, but you blame yourself for what happened. You believe it is your fault for Raphael falling, so you flee in shame. But in doing so you deny that love. Your soul connection stretches and stretches with the distance and the absence until eventually it snaps, breaking your heart and you... *die*. It happens every time." One tear rolled down the woman's cheek. "You must release your self-blame, and you will be free. We all will be free."

Elodie heard the words, and a light started to chink through the shutter. "How long?"

"I'm sorry?"

"How long has this been happening?" Elodie had

thought she would entertain them for now, until she could escape, but something niggled at the back of her mind. Something that told her perhaps she *did* know them in this life, that she had always known them. But how could that be? She fought against believing the woman's tale, but with a sudden stunning clarity she knew the answer to her question before the other woman even responded.

"How long have we re-lived this?" The lady let out a harsh laugh through her tears. "Since the dawn of creation."

Thirty

Elodie looked around at them all, until she landed on the black-haired man, on the man the others had called Raphael. She stared at him fully meeting his gaze. As a strange sense of guilt stabbed painfully at her heart, she battled against the impulse to tear her gaze from his, and flee. She had wronged him for thousands of years, hadn't she?

"Fight it, _amica mea_, remember how much I love you. How much you love me. _You are not to blame_," Raphael said and held her eyes with a look so powerful and loving that something shifted within her, releasing one memory; a kiss, a kiss so powerful and connecting that Elodie gasped at the ferocity of the sensation. Her lips tingled as if they had just been branded. As the ground moved once again beneath her feet, the something shifted again and _clicked_ and suddenly, the shutter swung wide open, letting in memory after memory, like the rifling of pages in a book. A very old and long book. Until it got to page one...

Elodie flew through the garden, laughing a tinkling laugh as she was caught by a pair of strong arms and wrapped in glossy black wings. She looked up at him, at his green eyes – green as the foliage around them – and felt the click, the original click, as her soul connected to his, and his lips lowered to hers. This was love of a higher power, one that should never be denied, one that would strengthen the edict that not only did love conquer all... but that *amor alas dat*... that *love bestows wings*.

She blinked. "*Raphael*?" It was a drawn-out heart song of recognition, one that spanned eternity.

Raphael's eyes widened in shock... and hope. He looked directly at her again, testing. He *could* look directly at her, but saw she had no inclination to run this time.

On a cry, Elodie started towards him, but Luc stepped in her way, a knife pressed to Raphael's throat.

"You were created for me, for *me*! I was the perfect angel; I was supposed to be rewarded! But when you locked eyes with *him*, it was all over. Your soul connection fused for eternity."

Elodie blinked and a vision – no, another memory – slammed into her mind leaving her gasping as the truth began to be revealed...

She sat with Luc in the garden, a platter of fruit between them. They laughed over something Elodie said. Her eyes trailed away and landed on a dark-haired angel. Her blood thrummed at the sight of him.

"*Oh*, who is that?" she asked.

Luc chose a grape and popped it into his mouth. "Hmm?" He followed her gaze, and said dismissively, "Raphael Blackfeather is his name. Kin to the Goldwings, I believe. He is new to this sector."

"But I know him," Elodie said slowly.

Luc laughed. "How could you possibly *know* him. He is newly arrived to this area." The laughter stopped abruptly as he studied Elodie's face.

Raphael looked in their direction, and in the vision Elodie saw the slow fear spread across Luc's face, as green eyes locked with silver.

"He knows me too, Luc. Look," Elodie murmured.

Luc clutched at her arm. "No, El. You are mi-"

Elodie broke the gaze to regard Luc. "Do not worry so, Luc, I am simply going to introduce myself." She patted her friend's hand with a smile, and pulled away gently.

Back then, she didn't see Luc's face change, but she saw it now, saw it change from one of handsome geniality, to something far darker. Perhaps, he too had heard the promise of a click, felt it, and, now she could see from his perspective, knew it spelled the end of everything he coveted.

Raphael and Elodie met and clasped hands in greeting, and in her mind's eye Elodie saw Luc's whole world fall away. Raphael leaned down to say something and with a nod, she had moved away to walk with him through the gardens, chattering happily...

"I am sorry, Luc. I never knew you felt more for me," Elodie said carefully, pulled back to the present. "You never told me."

"Would that have changed anything?" Luc asked desperately. Her silence told him everything. "No, of course it would not. Do you know what it was like? Every angel expected me to be happy for you both. Happy! A new soul connection had been forged. What joy. But how could I feel joy, when my own heart was crumbling inside me until what I felt for you grew teeth and claw."

"But Luc, I cherished our friendship. That would never have changed. Raphael accepted you would be a big part of my life. He accepted it because he loved me. And no, perhaps it wouldn't be the relationship you wanted, but we would have still been in each other's existences. I believe now, given time, you would have softened your feelings for me, until you too could have found true happiness elsewhere."

"There would be no other for me, Elodriel! I love *you*."

"That isn't *love*, Luc. It is obsession. You wanted to own her, control her. That is not our way. That is not love," Raphael said, Luc's knife so close to his skin. "If we'd known we could have been more understanding, but your abhorrent actions are no excuse for your perceived slight. You deceived me, luring me to The Fall. Did you not spare a moment to think she would follow! No, you never considered her feelings, but simply your own, and when she did not act as you thought she would you *ripped* the wings

285

from her back! How is that love?"

Horror worked its way across Luc's face. "I simply meant to hold her back, so she would not fall when you did, but of course she tried to save you. I did not mean to tear her wings. The fury inside me only wanted to stop her from making a grave mistake."

"A mistake you instigated," Raphael said. "If she had fallen and hit the mortal plain with no wings, she would have ceased to be, entirely. Did you understand that?"

"No, no, no," Luc groaned, clutching at his head with his free hand. "I only wanted to remove *you* from the equation, so I had Nathaniel tell you she wanted to meet you at The Fall-" Luc gestured at the taller man who held Raphael "-I knew you would go to meet her despite it being a dangerous place. You would go anywhere she desired, especially if you thought she had put herself in danger. But when I confronted you, told you of my feelings for her, my rage took over and that's why I pushed you to The Fall's edge."

"Yes, I would go anywhere for her... but she would for me too. We are drawn to each other despite this damned curse. And so, she followed me, rushing in to stop me falling. You underestimated her, Luc. Underestimated the power of our connection."

"I remember, I remember now," Elodie whispered, a hand fluttering up to press against her trembling lips, thinking of the narrow tunnel-like exit called The Fall. It was the greatest sin an angel could commit to choose to leave the place of their creation, and none would do so willingly. The cost of the eternal curse, the separation from their creator, was too great a warning. Elodie had known this, she had known what would happen if Raphael fell. She could feel the frozen terror of that moment, even now. "I saw that Raphael was losing his footing. Back then, I had no idea *you* had pushed him, Luc," she recalled slowly. "I pulled him back, holding onto him but in the tight space he could not stretch his wings to right himself. You held onto me by my wings-" she looked at Luc, comprehension slowly dawning "-I believed you were *helping*, Luc." Tears filled her eyes at the betrayal. "You were my friend. I thought you were trying to hold onto me so I could pull Raphael back in. But you weren't... were you?" The realisation came hard and fast, a painful punch to the heart. She was not to blame for what occurred. Luc was.

"I only wanted to stop you from damning yourself, Elodriel. If he fell, you would have fallen too. I couldn't allow that. But your combined weight and my pulling back on your wings caused them to tear away in my hands, and suddenly I was holding them, your shimmering blood was pouring out and the two of you were falling." With a trembling hand, Luc pushed the knife closer against Raphael's neck. "I had no choice but to fall after you, El. I tried to save you!"

Raphael gritted his teeth and spoke harshly, "I had to hold onto her with all I had. The fall *burned*; do you remember? It burned but I held onto her, because that is love. And when we landed, with the last of my angelic powers I had to call the very lightning down from the sky to sear her bleeding wounds closed. Do you know how her screams inscribed themselves on my soul. Do you! So do not talk to me about love and suffering, Luc. You know nothing of it."

Fragments of falling came back to Elodie, as the scene played out in her mind. She felt everything burn around her. They were a shooting star ripped from the womb of the cosmos. Wrapped in Raphael's wings, she could do nothing but stare into his eyes, until the moment the connection to their creator burned away. She felt it like a pain behind her heart carving away everything she knew; carving away the home she loved, and everyone within it.

The curse for falling manifested; it slanted across Raphael's eyes, sliced through Elodie and up to surround the falling Luc behind them. The force of the curse on three falling angels at once rebounded up to four watching angels above. It blasted into them, causing them to plummet after the three, helpless to do nothing but fall.

Raphael, his wings tucked protectively around Elodie, crashed to the ground and skidded across heat-seared sand, turning the grains into shards of glass. Pain tore through him, but he thought nothing of his own pain only that of the angel within his arms. He unwrapped his shredded, scorched wings and saw the blood pouring from her back, two large gaping welts where her beautiful wings should have been.

Luc crashed moments after them, and Raphael's roar of grief echoed across the desert. Luc took one look at what his betrayal had wrought and backed away, taking refuge in an oasis of trees, his head clutched in his hands, moaning. The lightning Raphael called forth with his last angelic power shot down in two prongs and seared the wounds on Elodie's back closed. Her scream reverberated up to the heavens and back, branding itself on Raphael's soul.

The four other angels hit the ground seconds later and for one still, silent moment, the earth held its breath.

Elodie gasped as she remembered this next part, remembered how Raphael had cradled her, frantically running a bloodied and burned hand across her face, desperately trying to rouse her. She wished she'd never awoke, because when she did, oh when she did, the curse enacted for the first time. His green eyes, so beloved to her, now carried the tools of her destruction. She gazed into them, not quite comprehending the magnitude of all that had just occurred. But then it all came rushing back in violent fragments.

She'd skittered away from him, pushing out of his arms. "It's my fault, it's all my fault," she moaned, heart labouring and breath hitching. She took in the tortured, injured faces and bodies of Angelina, Nicolas, Nathaniel and Mikael, and then finally Raphael, and knew if it weren't for her they would never have been damned. She took the blame for Luc's covetous sins. She took it and it imprinted itself onto her immortal soul. It *combined* with the curse created by falling until it was a burden too heavy to bear. With Raphael frantically shouting and stumbling weakly to his feet, Elodie had run like heaven's fury was after her, until her heart and soul could take no more.

In a lushly verdant earthly garden nestled within a desert oasis, the last of her angelic power fell in one potent opalescent tear, dropping heavily to the ground. As it solidified into a large shimmering stone, her heart broke for the first time, and she died.

She and the rest of them were entrapped in the cursed eternal cycle. Causing them to re-live it over and over, until it – or *if* it – could be broken, and redemption found.

"But this time was different. For the first time, *I* found you first." Luc, exultant, his eyes reeling wildly, broke through the combined memories and pushed the knife closer against Raphael's neck.

That was not *all* that was different, Elodie thought, feeling stronger than ever, feeling almost complete for the first time, in what she now knew to be, forever. *I am not running this time; I have no desire to run anymore. I accept the truth that I was not to blame... I am not to blame.* But still, if Raphael died now, it would all be for nothing.

Thinking hastily, she said, "You are right, you found me first, that must count for something, Luc." Pity for the friend she once knew warred with disgust of the man he had become.

"Elodie, what are you doing?" Raphael asked,

sweat beading his brow.

"Let Raphael go, and I will come with you, willingly."

"*Elodriel*, no," Raphael said, using her real name. It rolled off his tongue like a song. She spared him one loving and longing look. She had to save him. She had to save *him* this time. She had to put it right.

"You lie. I can see it in your eyes, I always could," Luc spat. "I tried so hard this past year. I sought to be your friend, but I could not merely be *just* that, simply being close to you unleashed so much feeling inside me, I had to fight to hide it but sometimes it pushed through in moments of madness. I had hope you would somehow recall what we had once meant to each other, and you would grow to care for me. But I see, I see now that it's too late, it is all over," he carried on, muttering incoherently.

"Luc, what are you going to do?" Elodie said slowly, her heart shooting into her mouth as she saw cold clarity come into his eyes.

Luc nodded at Nathaniel and Mikael, who released Raphael's wings. "What I tried to do in the beginning." He used the hilt of the knife to strike Raphael's temple.

Raphael crumpled, and unconscious, silently fell over the cliff edge.

Thirty One

"*Raphael!*" Elodie screamed and ran to the edge, stopping when panic clawed at her throat and the image of her earth parents' carriage plunging over the same precipice filled her mind. She pushed it away with the entire strength of her terror at losing Raphael too. With her heart screaming and her mind pleading, she dived after him thinking that she had to fall to save *him* this time. Luc barely missed grabbing onto her; his howl of rage followed her down like a harbinger of doom.

Wind rushed past her, but everything else slowed down as her eyes tracked the falling shape below.

A voice entered her mind. *Elodriel, you are forgiven. The curse is lifted. Your acceptance, sacrifice and love vanquished it. This is your reward.*

Two sharp tugs at her shoulder blades had her screaming in pain, but then release came and suddenly she felt whole as two enormous silver-feathered wings erupted from her back. Instinctively

292

– or remembering – she knew how to use them. She soared down and used all the strength of her powerful new wings to grab onto the unconscious Raphael before he crashed onto the jagged rocks.

Two more shapes flanked her. "*Help me*," she said through gritted teeth, and together with Nicolas and Angelina, they flew Raphael back up and further along the coast.

They landed on the ground and Elodie cradled Raphael's head in her lap. She laid a finger on his neck and relief filled her as the strong, steady pulse thrummed beneath her touch.

Nicolas and Angelina exchanged a thankful smile, before an awed look came over Nicolas's face. "Did you hear that? We can go home."

Angelina gave a sob, as she clasped her hands together. Elodie smiled at their joy. She had heard the redeeming voice too.

A thud behind Elodie, as something landed on the mossy ground, had the smile slipping and her eyes closing briefly. Gently, she removed Raphael's head from her lap and pillowed it on the grass. She stood and stretched out her silver wings. "Leave him to me," she told Nicolas and Angelina.

She turned to face Luc, every last vestige of pity gone, erased by the aeons of deceit. "You betrayed me, Luc."

"You broke my heart."

"I never knew it was mine to be careful with," Elodie said, allowing a final touch of compassion to colour her tone, before hardening it. "*You* killed my parents. *You* were the reason Raphael and I fell. *You* are the reason we were all cursed."

"But Elodriel, I only did all those things because I love you. None of that matters now, the curse is finally broken, *please* let us go back to how things were. You were created for me, I know you were," Luc said as if saying it repeatedly would make it true. He stretched out his pure white wings in supplication.

Elodie smiled grimly. "But *you* were not created for *me*. I choose him as we chose each other in the garden that first time. Even if you were the last angel in all of creation I still would never choose you. My soul is not for you." She could not even feel any sympathy for him now, his sins were too vast. Too abhorrent.

On a cry of fury, she launched herself at Luc, dragging him up into the sky with her. Memories of frightened Elodie Di Silva and the quiet strength of Elodriel of the Silver Wings clashed, *combined*, until she would *never* be fearful of him; Lord Lucan Beaumont or Luc White Wing, ever again.

He beat his wings, but she had the advantage of newly-returned wings and her newly-found soul connection to complete her. Her anger and anguish at his deception gave her the edge, and for one bleak, dark moment she found his ice-cold wings in her hands. She wanted nothing more than to do to him what he had done to her. To make him pay for her parents' deaths and almost killing Raphael in this life. To make him pay for the countless times she had been cursed to die in all the other lives, taking them all with her, re-setting the eternal loop.

Elodriel, hear me, that is not our way. You know we do not seek to harm each other. Luc will be punished sufficiently for his sins in harming you and Raphael, but he must return home to face it.

The voice had her letting go of Luc's wings in shame. *What was she doing?* That would make her no better than him. Had she been about to make a sinful error so soon? Horror clawing at her throat, she flew away from him, putting as much distance between them as she could. She spoke in a low voice. "Your sins are not mine to punish, Luc, no more than your blame is mine to bear."

A beam of light illuminated Luc from within. His eyes widened as the realisation of what was happening dawned on him. "No... *Elodriel*," he breathed, one hand reaching out to her, as he blinked out of earthly existence – and memory.

Two more blinks of light further along the coast flickered and extinguished, as Nathaniel and Mikael were taken in the same manner. Elodie understood their presence would be erased from the memories of the mortals who had known them, and the holes in the earth's fabric where they had existed, would be reabsorbed and adjusted.

Elodie dropped down to the ground and turned slowly. She took in the faces of her old friends, of Angelina and Nicolas, and their similar muted-gold wings. She rushed forward to embrace them both.

"How did I not know, how did I ever not know?" she rambled, pulling away to take in their beloved faces.

"You fell without your wings, the one physical thing that made you an angel, and so you forgot your angelic origins. You have no idea how it pained us." Angelina ran a hand over Elodie's newly restored wings, tears in her eyes. "In each life we were reborn, usually within the same family group or societal circle, and the memories would return to us little by little until there was no denying it. Our wings would reveal themselves to us in moments of extreme emotion. Raphael's dreams would get more vivid – more real, and we knew you were drawing closer, but we did not know when or who you would be, until you and he would meet as you always do, so drawn to each other as you are."

"And you would see, remember, forget and flee... every single time," Nicolas added. His bright blue eyes lit with a curious gleam. "But not this time. Luc's plan backfired. In his thrill and arrogance at finding you first this cycle, perhaps he thought the time with you would cause you to grow to love him. But instead it allowed you time to remember deep down what he did to you, causing that intrinsic fear of him."

Elodie nodded, looking down at Raphael and his peaceful face. "Back then, I refused to believe Luc could be responsible for something so appalling, so I blamed myself... for not saving Raphael, for believing Luc had fallen too because he'd been *helping* me. I blamed myself, because I couldn't bear the alternative – that Luc, my oldest friend, had betrayed me. But I see now, deep-down my soul knew the truth, so an ingrained fear of him seeded, and grew with every life cycle until in this one, I was openly terrified of him. But I accept now, that I was not to blame, I was never to blame." She gave a tremulous smile of acceptance.

"Luc bringing me into his family – his world – inadvertently allowed me to reconnect with you all gradually. Fragments started filtering in, and if we'd had more time, I think it would have all returned. Perhaps that what was different this time. It was a rash, violent decision on Luc's part that started it all, and he made another this time, with my parents' accident. He was, it appears, the instrument of his own undoing." Elodie thought of her beloved innocent earth parents, who had meant so very, very much to her. She would ensure their memory lived on and honour their epic love with an epic eternal love of her own.

Nicolas gave a humourless smile. "Pride goeth before a fall," he murmured. He knelt beside Raphael, whose eyes flickered, and clasped a hand to his arm, while Angelina gracefully did the same.

"We are free, cousin," Angelina said softly, before light shimmered from within her and within Nicolas. They let go of Raphael's arms and stood, anticipation in their gazes. "We are ready to go home," she said.

"Before you go - whose notion was the eye patch?" Elodie asked, and Nicolas gave a very Hunt-like grin.

"As if you need to ask," Angelina replied with a raised eyebrow. She held her free hand out to Elodie, who gripped it tenderly before letting go.

"I will see you soon, and we will have forever to catch up," Elodie promised.

With twin smiles on their faces, Angelina and Nicolas vanished in a glitter of ethereal light.

Elodie stared at the space where they had been before dropping beside Raphael.

"Wake up, *amica mea*, my love, it is time to go home." She brushed her lips over his and watched his eyelids flutter again.

The welcome redeeming voice spoke inside her mind one more time and had her smiling and nodding. "That is very generous of you. I will speak with Raphael and let you know our decision," she told it.

"You are carrying me?"

"I would carry you to the ends of the earth," Elodie said, looking down tenderly at Raphael as he leant against her chest. She had her wings wrapped around him like a protective cloak as they sat astride the largest of the horses Luc had used to spirit Raphael away. The other horses, and Angelina's Luna and Nicolas' Comet, and her own patient Grace, walked along behind them.

"Is that where we are going?" Raphael asked.

"Well as to that, I am taking you home-" she gestured to Angelhaven looming out of the mist before them "-if that is what you desire? You see, we have been given a gift, we can live out the rest of our earthly bodies' lives here together, before returning back to our forever home." She pointed upwards.

Raphael's green eyes gleamed with interest. "And what, my love, do you desire?"

Elodie let out her musical laugh, before her silvery-grey eyes enflamed with love. "You, my Raphael, only you. *You* are my heart's desire forever."

"Then let us find solace and healing and love in *our* haven." He looked at the house before them, and smiled.

Elodie leaned down to capture his mouth with hers. As they trotted through the mist, and through the angel wing gates, a small herd of horses behind them, Elodie knew she had finally found the epic all-consuming love she had eternally searched the ends of the earth for.

Epilogue

Raphael rose over Elodie, his black hair shielding his eyes. She tenderly pushed the hair away. She never wanted him to hide his eyes from her again. She wrapped her long slim legs around him as he completed her. *This.* This was what love was, not only a merging of the flesh but a merging of the soul too.

They moved together, instinctively finding a rhythm that built inside them both, until they felt release at the exact same moment. A moment that caused the candles to flicker and gutter, and the wind to gust through the open windows and billow out the gossamer drapes.

"I would spend an eternity wrapped up with you like this," Raphael said, dropping his sweat-sheened forehead to hers, "but I believe we are supposed to experience all that our mortal lives have to offer."

"I would have that too, but I believe you are right. What do you propose?" Elodie asked, feeling supine and limber, and so deliriously happy. Her eyes widened as he fell silent, and pressed a finger to her lips.

Naked, he walked away from the bed, retracting his wings, and Elodie already missed them. He returned to kneel beside the bed, and Elodie straightened up slowly.

He held out a ring of two twisted metal feathers – one silver and one coloured black combined into a delicate band. "I *propose* that we take every advantage of what is on offer. Marry me, Elodriel of the Silver Wings. Marry me, Elodie Di Silva. Wear a gown of molten silver in front of our earthly friends and bind yourself to me, as I bind myself to you."

One happy tear tracked down Elodie's face; she had never felt more complete. She thought of standing with Raphael before their friends and she prayed she and Luisa would be able to re-kindle their friendship, but with Luc erased from both their lives, she anticipated it would be an easy wound to heal. Elodie's thoughts turned to a more recent friend. "I accept – on one condition-" her eyes twinkled "-that my gown be made by a very special young lady who saved me when she did not have to. She has a gift; one I think Madame La Coeur might be interested in."

"Ah, Madame La Coeur," Raphael said. "There is something I need to explain about her."

"Oh yes, I remember her acting so strangely when Luc saw my debutante gown – it had *wings*," Elodie recalled.

Raphael grinned. "There are some mortals who are innately drawn to our light, our divinity. She was one. She knew not why, of course, but she was only too eager to help me with a little favour. She brought a pin to me, one that held a drop of your blood – your celestial blood. Only one of *us* could see what it really was, but I needed to know for sure."

"So that was why I saw you outside the modiste's. Why I sensed you so many times."

"Yes, *amica mea*, my love, I had to know it was *you*. I felt it, and I know Luc believed it to be you too considering his underhanded manipulations, but I had to *know* for sure, and as soon as I knew, I had to think of a way to free you from his cage. Hence the little nudge with the winged gown. But you, my clever darling soulmate, took your future into your own hands."

"And now, I take it once again into my hands." She held out her left hand, and watched as he slipped the ring onto her third finger. "Into our hands." She threaded her fingers through his, and pulled him towards her.

"For eternity," she breathed against his lips.

"For eternity," he repeated, enfolding her in his wings, before showing her all the delightful new ways an angel could fall.

About the Author

Estelle Tudor is an award-winning multi-genre author from the true land of myth and legend... Wales, where she lives with her husband, four children and crazy dog.

She is the author of the *Through the Fairy Door* middle grade fantasy series – writing under Estelle Grace Tudor, and the fantasy romance *Fated Partners Trilogy* for upper young adults, writing as E. G. Tudor.

You can keep up with her book releases on her Twitter @E_G_Tudor and Instagram:
@through_the_fairy_door_books
@from_the_shelf_of_e_g_tudor
@from_the_garret_of_e_g_tudor

If you enjoyed this book, please consider leaving a review!

Thank you for reading, and don't forget to always follow your heart's desire...

E x

Regency meets Fantasy

If you enjoyed this story, you may be interested to know that four more stories from this world are soon to be released. First up is the story of Elodie's mortal parents in...

The Legend of Angelhaven